Jennifer Brown's Journey

Enjoy my journey!
Best Wishes
Angie hangley

Jennifer Brown's Journey

Angie Langley

Published by Angie Langley
Copyright © 2018 Angie Langley

Jennifer Brown's Journey paperback edition
ISBN: 978-0-9955927-8-0

Also available as Kindle edition
ISBN: 978-0-9955927-1-1

For permission requests, write to the publisher, addressed
"Attention: Permissions Coordinator," at
angielangley64@icloud.com

https://jenniferbrownsjourney.co.uk

Designed, typeset and printed by Riverside Publishing Solutions Ltd

I dedicate this book to Brian, whose love and continuous support has given me the confidence to believe in myself.

Contents

Aknowledgments

Writing Jennifer Brown's Journey has been a labour of love for me and at times I couldn't have done it without the support of several people.

I'd like to thank my dear friends Jennie Pinch and Lynn Kimber for their friendship and support.

Ally Smith and Tish Tindall for reading and re-reading the manuscript offering their sound advice.

I would also like to thank Maurice Stevens for his inspired front cover illustrations.

Most of all I'd like to thank my freelance editor Howard Sargeant for his hard work helping me hold on to the wheel at times when I felt it slipping through my fingers.

"We cling to life by a system of delicate threads held together by others. When those threads suddenly frayed and snapped a few years ago, it was the love and support of my dear friends who threw a rope around me and held on tight"

Part One

The Office

1

How Dirty Is Your Rota?

'Jennifer. Can I have a word?'

Bugger. 'Sure.'

'Did you read this through? Before you sent it out?'

He swivelled his monitor round.

'Oh Jonathan. Sorry.'

'Not great, is it? I mean, for the department's image.'

No. And it's not great for your chances of promotion, either.

'Sorry. Won't happen again.'

But we both knew it would. It always did.

Like last week. Email to the Head of Finance. *This policy is at the core of our business.* What had I typed? A line emphasising that at the core of our business we had a *tits policy*.

Cue a bollocking. From Imogen, Secretary to the Head of Finance. If I wished to promote my size 36 double Fs, would I kindly do so in my own time.

Cow.

Jealous cow with tits the size of Christmas cookies.

And this latest gaffe? The duty rota for out-of-hours cover. Type it up and email it out. That was the brief. But fingers had not obeyed brain. Again. With the result that all fifty-six members of the staff of Intext Software Ltd now had, sitting in their inbox, a typo-littered missive carrying the subject line *Monthly Dirty Rota*.

Cue a flood of waggish replies (from men – shocker): just how dirty is the rota? will there be a demonstration? will I be allowed to join in?

'It just looks a bit ... unprofessional.'

'I know.'

I did try. I really did. But professional just wasn't my thing. At least, not here. Not in this office, with its flow charts and its Swiss cheese plants and its inoffensive magnolia walls. My heart wasn't in it. It just wasn't me.

Problem was, I didn't know what *was* me.

'I'll retype it and send it out again.'

Of course, this latest *dirty rota* gaffe had also played right into the hands of Hilary, Rose and Trisha (the HRTs). The three old crones huddled together in a far corner of the office like witches round a cauldron, pouncing on visitors, unsuspecting newcomers and anyone else within singeing distance of their collective hot flush. Trisha was the queen of venom. All tweed skirt and bloomers, the crusty old cow had had it in for me since the day I'd set foot in Jonathan's department twelve years ago. She couldn't be in the same room without giving me that look – the slow, top-to-toe scrutiny that says 'blonde tart'.

Now *dirty rota* had given the old bag even more ammunition. I wasn't fit to be secretary to her precious Jonathan Dashwood-Silk. That was the job *she* coveted. That was *her* job. Any opportunity to stick it to me and she'd pop a couple of newts in the pot and starts plotting.

She was an expert on every bloody thing under the sun and was forever banging on about her *gîte de caractère* – her bolthole in Normandy. She delighted in rolling French words round her fat lips. If ever I pronounced anything vaguely French, she'd be in like Flint with a correction.

I used to have a *pain au chocolat* with my mid-morning coffee – now I just have a waffle.

I tapped lightly on Jonathan's office door.

'I've retyped that memo. Would you like to check it?' A schoolgirl submitting a rewrite of a failed essay.

He looked up and smiled.

'No, I'm sure it's fine.'

He couldn't stay mad at me. Not Jennifer Brown, the friendliest face in the place. Five feet one and full of fizz. A fun-sized bottle of cheap champagne. My hemlines were on the short side for a woman in her late thirties. Together with my curves and my highlights, the short skirts dropped me into a neat pigeonhole: bimbo. I was dim. Good for a laugh. Not to be taken seriously.

It didn't help that the friendly face and the curves and the hair belonged to the worst typist on the planet. Annual appraisals always mentioned my can-do attitude. Then my can't-do typing. Like they were written by the author of my old school reports: *Jennifer won't achieve anything in life unless she stops her silly daydreaming.*

Nothing much had changed in thirty years. In the middle of boardroom minutes, I'd find myself on a beach in Paros, the sun on my back, sand between my toes, a cool retsina at my elbow.

Then Jonathan would nudge me and I'd be back in Portsmouth, rain lashing, staring at a mug of Co-op Instant.

Jonathan Dashwood-Silk was very fond of me. I was a tryer, and he liked that. I was also fiercely loyal and impeccably discreet. He rewarded those qualities by affording me the protection of his seniority. Nobody messed with me because they knew they'd have to answer to him.

And, as befitted a man with that impressive handle, he was indeed rather dashing. Intense blue eyes, a mane of silver hair, an unruffleable manner. As my old mum might have said, he charmed the very birds from the trees. No surprise then that he turned up to every work do with a different leggy beauty on his arm.

Add to these natural assets a string of cashmere suits cut to perfection and a nice line in Italian shoes and he was the sex magnet of choice for the HRTs.

When Jonathan arrived (8.47 am, barring leaves on the line at Haslemere), they'd drop the Macbeth routine and wet their knickers as he strode across the floor like Mufasa surveying his kingdom.

'Morning, ladies.'

'Oh, good morning, Jonathan.'

'Yes, good morning, Jonathan. How was your journey?'

'Fine. Thank you.'

He was well aware of the effect his striding had. His weakness was his ego, and it enjoyed a good massage. Even one delivered in tweeds.

How nice to be adored. Even by a gaggle of hormonal hags.

I'd been adored once. Pete had been the most attentive companion in the early years. God, that first night! He was so … gorgeous. A mop of black hair bouncing on his collar. Eyebrows upturned, all Jack Nicholson devilish.

Within a couple of weeks, I'd moved into his cute little flint cottage at the far end of Ditchfield village. We spent glorious summer evenings in his west-facing garden, watching the sun go down over the South Downs, then, with the log burner blazing to take the chill off, cuddling up on the couch, Pete's dark, frank, unflinching eyes looking right into me and liking what they saw.

Not so much these days. I was a little thicker round the middle – well, when you hit your late thirties, gravity takes the wheel – but I was still an attractive woman. Still getting plenty of (unwanted) attention from men in the office.

Just not from Pete.

He was still in great shape. Bit of a gym bunny, in fact. And wont to admire the results in the bedroom mirror. And the sleeker he looked, the worse it looked for me. Remarks about my weight, my hair, my clothes, my habits.

'They're doing a deal on membership at the gym.'

'Oh, I don't know, Pete. It's not really my thing.'

'No. It isn't. I know.'

Friends had started saying things. Was I alright? How was Pete? *Where* was Pete? Truth is, I often wasn't sure. Lots of hands on shoulders, which was unsettling. Other friends weren't so subtle. There'd been a lot of *He's not good enough for you* stuff of late.

But I wasn't listening. All relationships have their ups and downs. We were just a bit … bored with each other. Well, *he* was a bit bored with *me*. *I* was running around putting a smiley gloss on it, thinking everything would be alright, pandering to him. Kidding myself.

My mate Will had come round for a glass of wine. Okay, a bottle.

'Don't worry. I'm fine.'

'You're not. You're hurting. And it's because you're soft.'

'Bugger off.'

'Pete takes advantage. You need to stand up for yourself.'

'We're okay. It's okay.'

'It's *not* okay. If you're not happy, you're allowed to say.'

'It's fine. It's just the way men are. Sometimes.'

'Not all men.'

'Well, not *you*.'

'Right. Not me. Not a man. Gay, so not a real man.'

'I don't mean *that*.'

'He doesn't get to be a total bastard. You're too good for that.'

He was a smart guy, my mate.

Will worked in Finance, just across the corridor. I'd seen him around the office a lot before I'd spoken to him. I'd been in meetings where he'd brought people down a peg or two with a well-chosen word, and others where he'd flagrantly taken the piss. He had a fearless, caustic sense of humour at odds with his boyish looks and neat, scoutmaster haircut.

I'd first spoken to him face to face not at work but in the Oxfam shop. He'd lifted a red silk kimono and was looking at it intently when I walked up to him.

'Not your colour.'

He didn't miss a beat.

'Don't you think? I think it'd be gorgeous on me.'

I must have looked shocked. He'd decided to play me.

'You're so lucky, you women. Getting to wear these fabulous fabrics. In public.'

'I suppose.'

'Of course, in private, I can wear anything I like.'

He stroked the kimono.

'So sensual.'

He leered at me. I stepped back. Then he burst out laughing and put his arms round me.

We'd been best pals ever since. He looked after me. He was always in my corner. I could think of no one better. Or tougher.

I'd just sent an apology to the Head of Finance – Will's boss – for the *dirty rota* business.

Richard Hands (Handy Dick) could never look at me for more than five seconds without his beady eyes wandering down to my cleavage. *Tits policy* must have prompted an extended bathroom break.

I was nipping to the canteen for a coffee and a cake. I heard a voice behind me.

'Good morning, Jennifer. Loved the memo.'

And there he was. Handy Dick. Legs akimbo, hands in pockets, eyes on tits.

'Oh, hello, Richard,' I answered, upping my pace to a trot. He followed.

'Just a slip of the hand,' I smiled sweetly. 'Sorry.'

Jonathan and Richard were fighting over a directorship, a major kick upstairs and a major hike in salary. So each loved nothing more than seeing the other's department with egg on its face – a failure to hit monthly targets, a rumbling of departmental discontent, or, better still, some cock-up of the kind I generated on a near-daily basis.

'Anyway, must dash,' I lied, glancing at my watch, knocking my pace up a further gear and leaving the tubby overgrown-schoolboy trailing in my wake. He gave up the chase and regained his composure. Then wheeled round casually into a well-stocked tea trolley, decorating the corridor with fruit, canapés and two chrome pots full of hot coffee.

2

Home or Away?

I wasn't sleeping. The chatter of swooping swallows had woken me at four. And now that sunlight was streaming through the bedroom window, I was wide awake, my mind full of troubles. Most of them about the man lying next to me. Lying.

The old enamel clock ticked away while I rehearsed the previous day – awkward conversations, strained looks, barbed remarks.

The phone rang. Pete stirred. I dashed downstairs and silenced the phone. It was Mum.

'I thought I'd call now, dear. To wish you a Happy Birthday. I know you leave early for work.'

Not at bloody four thirty.

'Hi, Mum.' A whisper, hoping the phone hadn't woken Pete. Hoping that wouldn't be the trigger for another dark mood.

'Yes. Happy Birthday, dear.'

'Thanks, Mum.'

'Are you having cake?'

'I expect so. Yes.'

'Well, have a nice day. Will I see you?'

'Yes. I'll pop round later, Mum.'

'Alright, dear. I'll look forward to that.'

Poor Mum.

We were in May. My birthday was in November.

Mum was very sweet. Always had been. But, after my dad died, seven years ago now, she'd started to get ever so slightly forgetful. Now, at seventy-seven, she was rather bonkers.

She often wandered round the village in her slippers. But everyone knew Iris and everyone looked out for her. Resolutely independent and sociable to a fault, she was always inviting people round for a cup of tea. Shopkeepers, traffic wardens, people who worked in the library. But it was *Big Issue* sellers who bore the brunt of her open-handedness.

'Nobody buys their magazines, dear. Nobody. They just walk past without looking. It's so rude.'

Mum would open her purse and thrust a note on them. Then take them home for tea, refusing to take no for an answer. It was all a bit worrying. You couldn't rely on *everyone's* good nature.

And she was becoming increasingly confused.

Only the other day, her next-door neighbour had rung me at the office.

'Jennifer, I think you need to have another word with your mum.'

'What's wrong?'

'It's the postman. She's convinced herself he's Charlton Heston. I think he's scared, dear.'

So, yes, I'd be popping round later.

After the birthday wake-up call, I crept back into bed. Two hours later, I woke in a blind panic. I'd slept in. No Pete. He'd already be up and ready for work. *The sod might have woken me.*

I rushed downstairs to let the dogs out, then I filled the kettle for tea. Pete appeared. Pete always appeared at the sound of the kettle being filled. He sat himself down at the kitchen table, waiting to be served. Then, as always, he turned on the TV, taking in the headlines and giving me the benefit of his wisdom on current affairs.

But it was the weather report that really held his attention. Or rather the weather girl. A twenty-five-year-old leggy bombshell. Silky brown bob. Full lips. Figure-hugging dress. Your basic nightmare.

'She's brilliant, isn't she?'

'Mmm.'

'Don't you think?'

'Yes, she's great. Very pretty.'

'No, I mean, brilliant at the weather. Very professional.'

Professional, my arse. Except it wasn't *my* arse he was looking at.

'Heavy showers and thunderstorms are expected later,' Bombshell told us.

I didn't like the sound of that.

The Sunday papers had become a similar source of pain. The lifestyle pages. Skinny nineteen-year-olds in the latest fashions.

'What do you think of that dress?'

'Nice. If you're fifteen and a size 6.'

He slammed the paper down.

'Why do you always have to do that?'

'What?'

'Twist everything I say?'

'I'm not twisting anything.'

'You are. It's just a dress.'

'I didn't mean …'

'Forget it.'

Ten minutes of the silent treatment. Then he grabbed his jacket and left.

Sunday. Our one day together.

I stood by the long oval mirror in the hall and assessed the devastation. Time is a cruel bitch.

I tried telling myself I was pretty good for a bird pushing forty. Well, not bad. But not perfect. Better when I held my tummy in. Then, with it all sucked in, just for a few seconds, I could kid myself I was twenty-one again.

I still had the legs. But the love handles were the sticking point. The giveaway. The downside.

And they were bringing me down.

What had happened to growing old together? Was I the only one growing old? Felt like it.

My two adorable dogs, Betty and Eric, were getting a shorter walk before work. I couldn't risk being late. A conference call between us, Central London, and our partners in Akron, Ohio. My job was to open the call, make sure all the suits were dialled in, and field tetchy queries from Jonathan's manager in the London office, the famously obnoxious Gerard-Claude Heroux. Frenchie.

We passed the hedge and I slipped the leads. The dogs bounded off in pursuit of rabbits. Their favourite game.

My dogs were helping me to keep it together. I watched them having fun – Betty, the Jack Russell with the gentle, black-rimmed eyes, and Eric, the terrier-cross rescue dog horribly abused by a previous owner, a thug who'd meted out his drug-fuelled frustrations on the poor creature by hurling him at a wall so hard he'd broken both front legs. He'd been left with a permanent limp.

Ahead of me, barley that had been emerald green just a few weeks ago was now a swirling sea of gold. I breathed.

Then I looked at my watch and remembered the conference call. We sprinted back to the house under purple clouds. As I opened the front door to shout in to Pete, the air was heavy. Bombshell's storm was approaching.

'I'm off.'

Silence. Still preening himself behind the bathroom door. Some new anti-ageing product to trial.

'Pete?'

'Yep. See you later.' From behind the closed door. 'And I'll be working late tonight. Got to get that patio finished before the rain comes. If bloody Darren turns up.'

Darren was the young lad Pete paid to help him out on the odd landscaping job. A nice lad. A gentle giant. But liable to call in sick at short notice. Which wasn't helping Pete's moods lately.

'OK, bye then.'

Nothing.

That was it now. That was how we did it. *Hi. Bye. See you.*

For years, I'd never have nipped to the shop without saying *I love you*. A declaration of love had ended every conversation, punctuated every parting, however brief. It had been normal, natural, vital.

Now I didn't dare. I knew the response – the *lack* of response – would sit like a rock in my stomach.

I cuddled Betty and Eric. Their stumpy tails wagged furiously. So much affection.

You've got to get it from somewhere.

I pulled into the car park five minutes before the call. Standing outside his little hut, Nigel was glancing at his watch, a minor Mussolini in charge of national timekeeping. If I hadn't been in such a flap about the time myself, I might have laughed in his stupid face.

I reached into my handbag for my security pass. *Oh shit.* The bloody thing was still on the kitchen table where I'd left it. Now I'd got this arsehole to deal with.

Over he swaggered, with his grey uniform, his white socks and his Royal Navy tiepin. Not Allowed Nigel.

Around the office, you'd be having a conversation about work, and someone would ask what the company policy was on something – meal breaks or paper clips or something – and Nigel would pop up out of nowhere and give you the answer, a finger poised over Section 24, subsection 3a, of the little handbook he carried everywhere. It was like working in a comedy sketch.

He pulled himself up to his full five-feet seven and peered at me through his jam-jar glasses.

'Can't let you through if you haven't got your pass.'

'Nigel. How long have I worked here?'

'If you haven't got your pass, I can't let you through.'

I stared at his smug little face. His curly black hair was thick with gel, like he'd dipped his head in a deep fat fryer. I pictured the pan and my hand on the back of his neck. But time was running out, so I had to deploy the big guns. But first a little sweetness.

'You're quite right, of course, Nigel. It's great that we've got someone as thorough as you keeping us all safe.'

A wave of pride washed over him. He pulled himself up further. Five seven and a half.

'But Mr Dashwood-Silk will be *furious* if I don't open his important conference call on time.'

'Er … Right. I'll … erm …'

He scurried back to his hut and pressed the button. The barrier rose and in I swept, smiling sweetly.

The clock said 8.59 as I stepped into the boardroom with all the cool I could muster. Jonathan adjusted his cufflinks.

The meeting went well for Jonathan. He sealed some deal or other with Akron which would boost his promotion chances nicely. He was cock-a-hoop.

'What was old Frenchie like, though? Arrogant bastard.'

'Er, Jonathan …' I glanced at the green light on the mic.

'I mean, they're over the moon in Ohio. But he's never pleased, is he? The Frog Prince.'

I pointed to the light.

'Shit.'

At lunchtime, I popped out to Sainsbury's to escape the Frog Prince fallout. I needed a sachet of Colour Run. Pete's best white shirt had come a cropper. Passive voice, you'll note. I'd fired it into the washing machine before pulling out my new Next top. My red Next top. Classic Jennifer Brown.

He'd banged about the wardrobe for ten minutes, not finding it.

'Have you tried the laundry basket?'

The offending item was, in fact, lying damp and *very* pink in a Sainsbury's bag hidden at the bottom of my knicker drawer (Pete never went anywhere near my knickers these days).

He'd appeared at the bedroom door a few minutes later, smelling like the aftershave counter in Boots, his hair still damp from the shower. He was wearing the cream shirt.

I'd bought the shirt three years before, on the anniversary of the day we'd met, a landmark we'd still celebrated. We'd gone out to La Banca and I'd had the seafood linguine and he'd had the veal. We'd laughed and held hands and kissed. He'd told me I looked beautiful. Not nice. Beautiful.

Now here he was raging about having to wear an old shirt to meet a new client (*it's landscape gardening, for God's sake – not the Brits*) and I was hating myself. Too scared to tell him the truth about his precious bloody shirt.

And now here I was, skulking around trying to fix my mistake. Like some terrified kid covering up a stain on the carpet before her parents get home.

I needed a holiday but I'd stopped hinting about us getting away from it all and spending a bit of time together. Pete just banged on about how holidays were a waste of money, how he was 'booked solid', how there was no time.

Fridays had become 'work from home' day for the execs, so we merry band of minions revelled in our new favourite day of the week, Fuck About Friday, code name FAF. The perfect day to shop on line, mess about on social media and use the office phone for calls to aunties in Sydney.

I spent an hour looking online at weight-loss classes. Did I have time for a slimming programme? With a backside approaching the size of a small African nation, maybe I should make time.

The Wednesday class looked doable. I glanced at my calendar. Gosh. The 8th of May. Twelve years to the day.

Twelve years since I'd hobbled into Jonathan's office on crippling heels bought the day before. I'd walked the entire length of the car park then up two flights of stairs and along a never-ending corridor in sheer bloody agony, then collapsed into a chair in reception and pulled off my right shoe. I was squeezing life back into my big toe when a staggeringly handsome man with striking blue eyes and perfect teeth announced himself as Jonathan Dashwood-Silk and held out a manicured hand.

He spoke for ten minutes about the company and the job and what my duties would be, but I didn't hear much. I was fixated on his face. How could anyone be so handsome? Cary Grant with a dash of Johnny Depp and a sprinkle of Richard Gere.

Twelve years later, I was still his loyal assistant, always on hand. Always ready to go above and beyond the call of duty. He valued me and cared about me.

And now he'd been hearing rumours about Pete. About the way he treated me. He was far too discreet to voice an opinion, but I knew it bothered him. That made me feel good on the one hand. On the other, I didn't want his pity.

The phone jolted me back.

'Jennifer, Edward here. Just wondering if you've had any luck booking me a meeting room? For Tuesday.'

Bloody hell. Another manager. Dread Ed. He had a knack for showing me up. Catching me out. So I dreaded answering the phone when I knew it was him. And he'd done it again. I'd forgotten to book his flipping room.

'I'm waiting for Bookings to email me, Edward.' *Liar.* 'I'll chase them in the morning if I've still heard nothing.'

'Yes, pin them down tomorrow, please.'

The former army captain carried himself bolt upright and had a neatly combed, sandy-coloured quiff. This youthful affectation was matched by an annoying schoolboy penchant for salt and vinegar crisps. With all the finesse of a teenage warthog, he'd munch his way through five or six packets a day. Then, when each one was done, he'd blow up the empty packet and pop it like a balloon. These sudden explosions spilled coffee on my skirt with irritating frequency.

Another contradiction was his egregious lack of punctuality, a trait that often saw him arrive when the meeting was over, most memorably when he'd burst into the Silicon Room for a talk on online security only to find himself in a group discussion on LGBT discrimination. He'd beaten a hasty retreat.

'Yes, Edward. I will.'

Three minutes to five. Time to start the weekend. In the car park, a shock of racing-yellow lycra. Bri-Nylon Brian was climbing onto his bike.

'Have a nice weekend.'

'Thanks, Brian. You too.'

But it wouldn't be. As I pulled out my keys, the first fat drops of rain hit the car roof.

I looked up. Somewhere, behind dark purple clouds, thunder was rumbling.

3

The Text

I could hear Betty and Eric from the driveway, noses pressed up against the conservatory windows. My welcoming committee. Faithful as ever.

No sign of Pete as I dropped my bags on a chair and opened the French windows to release the critters. They darted round the garden, sniffing everything for trace elements of foreign visitors. I picked up my shopping and went into the kitchen to unpack.

As I flicked on the kettle, Pete appeared (*how did he do that?*). He had a pained expression on his face.

'I've got a terrible headache.' He untied his work boots.

'Oh, poor you. I was just going to make some tea.'

'I'm going for a lie-down.'

'Well, I'll bring you up a cup.'

'Darren phoned in sick. And now it's bloody raining.' He made for the stairs.

'I'll bring it up in a minute.'

I delivered tea to Pete, by that time sprawled half-asleep on the bed, then I went back to the kitchen to prepare myself for the latest challenge: a lemon drizzle cake.

Cooking shouldn't be so hard. It should be in the blood. But it most definitely isn't. Faced with a recipe book, I feel like the guy in the thriller sweating over whether to cut the red wire or the blue.

Moisture beading on my forehead. Impending disaster sitting on my shoulder.

As a child, I'd never been happier than sitting in the kitchen watching my mum whisk and stir and knead. The easy rhythm of it had always made me feel so relaxed and sent me into a kind of trance. And I'd loved the smells of baking. Lemon and orange and cinnamon. Childhood smells. Happy smells. *Come on. Give it a go. You can do this.*

As I was greasing the tin, I heard the beep of an incoming text. Pete's phone was on the kitchen windowsill. I turned and hit the bowl of cake mix with my elbow, sending it crashing to the floor. Betty and Eric were all over it. Pigs in muck.

Ten minutes later and I had all my ducks in a row again. Floor cleaned, cake in the oven, contented mutts dozing in their baskets. I sat down with a mug of tea.

Another beep. The screen on Pete's phone lit up. I wandered over to the window and picked it up.

A mobile number but no name. Darren, no doubt, with another lame excuse for crying off work. I opened the message.

Hi. Sorry I missed you. Had to deal with Kitty. Maybe later? xx.

Wrong number. We didn't know a Kitty, or anyone with a cat called Kitty (how unimaginative).

Definitely a wrong number. It happened all the time. My mum was constantly getting calls from guys looking for mobile mechanic services the seventy-seven-year-old lady was ill equipped to provide.

I checked the oven and went back to my tea. But something kept getting in the way. *Did* we know a Kitty? Did *Pete* know a Kitty? An aunt I'd never heard him mention? Doubt it. After ten years, didn't I know *everyone* in his life?

I heard Pete turn over on the bed upstairs. There was no Kitty, I was certain of it. Wrong number.

But I couldn't settle. Something was bugging me. Those two little kisses. I stirred my second mug of tea.

Temptation is a harsh mistress. I picked up Pete's phone and checked the call log. Then, using my own phone, I dialled the mystery number, my heart hammering under my apron.

Three rings then an unfamiliar voice. A woman's voice.

'Hello?'

'Oh, I'm sorry. I was looking for Karen.'

'You have the wrong number.' Curt. Dismissive.

'No, I don't think so. This is the number I usually get her on.'

'I'm not Karen.'

'No. You are …?'

'I'm Bronwyn.'

My head swirled. I pressed *end call*.

Not conscious that my legs were shaking until I tried to move them and found them rooted to the floor, I stared out of the kitchen window.

A noise on the windowsill. Another text beeping in.

Pete (his name this time!). I've just had a call from this number??? *(my mobile number). Someone pretending she was calling her friend???*

A thunderbolt hit me in the chest.

I blundered up the stairs. Pete was sprawled on the bed, watching the bloody weather forecast. He jumped.

'Pete!'

'What the bloody hell! I'm watching the weather.'

'Who's Bronwyn?'

'What?'

'Are you having affair?' I looked him right in the eyes.

'No, of course I'm bloody well not! Don't be stupid!'

He wanted to be firm. He wanted to be in charge. And, God, I wanted to believe him! But they gave him away. His eyes – those deep blue, ridiculously dreamy eyes I'd fallen in love with ten years ago – were now looking at the floor. Avoiding mine.

On the screen, Bombshell was pointing at clouds. In the southeast, *dig in for some pretty stormy weather ahead.*

I paced around downstairs, unable to settle, horrible scenes flashing into my head, all of them starring a faceless woman. *Bronwyn.* Where had I heard the name before?

I opened the fridge and pulled out the Sauvignon Blanc and tipped a good wallop into a glass. I took a big gulp, hoping it would stop me from shaking.

Pete appeared at the kitchen door. He looked queasy.

'I'm off to the village. To buy some cigarettes.'

I couldn't speak. Couldn't look at him.

'Need anything?'

How long had it been since he'd asked me if I needed anything? I looked up at him. He couldn't hold my gaze. He looked away.

'No.' *Well, the truth would be nice.*

I poured another generous glass and took a big mouthful, swallowing hard.

'I'll grab another bottle of wine, shall I?'

Typical. Always making light of the situation. Always that ghost of a criticism.

'If you like.' I emptied the rest of the bottle into my glass.

As his car headed down the lane, on an impulse I grabbed my phone from the kitchen table and dialled his number.

The number you have dialled cannot be reached. Please try again later.

With the best part of a bottle of wine swilling round in my head, I dialled Bronwyn's number.

The number you have dialled cannot be reached. Please try again later.

I felt sick.

I rushed upstairs to the bedroom window and peered down the lane to see if I could spot his car. The lane was empty.

I looked up. The last rays of daylight were disappearing over a dark horizon. Then a fork of lightning cracked.

I slumped to the floor. A long low roll of thunder rumbled beneath me. Another flash of lightning lit up the old pine boards of the bedroom floor. The storm had arrived.

That weekend, Pete had the perfect excuse to avoid me. He worked all day and long into the evening, trying to repair the damage the storm had wrought on his precious patio.

I walked the hedgerows and lanes with Betty and Eric, gathering my thoughts, stooping to cuddle them, wiping my cheeks.

When I hit the revolving doors on Monday morning, I could barely bring myself to step out on the other side. Maybe I could just stay inside the glass cage, circling and circling until I'd worked out what to do. What to do about my cheating bastard of a partner. That might take a while. I'd be spinning for days. Then two guys in white coats would lead me gently away by the elbow.

For now, the only choice was to paste on a false smile. No one wants to sit at a desk next to a snivelling wreck. So into the cloakroom to wipe the eyes and slather on another coat of mascara. A couple of deep breaths and I was back in the room.

Jonathan watched me from his desk. The mascara wasn't fooling him. He walked over.

'You okay?'

'Fine.'

'Good weekend?'

'Not bad. Bit too much wine last night.'

Not a lie. But not the whole truth.

He studied me for a few long seconds. Then went back to his office.

There'd been a power cut over the weekend. My computer was buggering about and I'd need to record my voicemail message again. It took more than one attempt.

I'm in the office today but my partner's been shagging some tart called Bronwyn and I'm not in the best of moods, so piss off and leave me alone!

Delete.

Another error message on my screen. Windows has encountered a critical problem and needs to shut down. Windows isn't the only one.

Bollocks. Now I'd have to deal with Carpet Slipper Craig. Our resident IT fixer. At first glance, with his grey hair and his beard and his tank tops, Craig might have passed for a high-school Geography teacher. The kind of bloke who collects stamps and gets excited about traction engines. An anorak.

But Craig was altogether more raincoat than anorak. Rather tactile. The kind of guy whose groin you might suddenly become aware of on a bus. A leaner-in. A brusher-up. Basically, a dog on heat.

I didn't need Craig now.

What I needed was an ear. A sensible male perspective.

I needed Will.

'It's just a couple of text messages, Jen. It's hardly a smoking gun.'

'But the kisses? What about the kisses?'

He leant forward and wiped my cheek with a tissue.

'And another text. Straight away another one. And my number. And the question marks. And more kisses. And him not looking me in the eye. And her phone was engaged. And …'

'Jen!'

I crumpled.

'Listen. How often do you put kisses on the end of a text?'

'I know. But …'

'Texts to acquaintances? People you hardly know?'

'Yeah. Most of the time. Nearly always.'

He held his hands in the air.

'So?'

'I know.'

'So those kisses, from Bronwyn – whoever she is – those kisses could be perfectly innocent. No?'

'I suppose.' I smiled. For the first time in three days.

Will took a big bite from his iced bun.

'Nothing else? His behaviour changed?'

'He's been a bit snappy.'

'Isn't he always?'

'Bit more than usual. And he's been buying new clothes. A new jacket. Looks expensive. *Too* expensive for the kind of places we go to. Not that we go anywhere much these days.'

'That's it? A jacket?'

'And a shirt. He's very fond of it. A pristine white shirt. Well, it's not white any more.'

I recounted my pink laundry disaster.

Will smiled and stirred his coffee.

'Don't do anything rash. See how things go. They'll probably just sort themselves out.'

I smiled a crooked smile. He wiped my cheek again.

'And remember what a special person you are.'

He was such a love.

'If Pete *is* messing you around … well, he's a complete and utter dick. And you'd be better off without him.'

Would I? Will stood up.

'I'd better be getting back.'

I stood and hugged him close.

'Thanks for listening to a stupid woman.'

I blinked back fresh tears and Will pulled another tissue from his pocket.

'I want you to promise me that you'll never call yourself stupid ever again.'

'Okay.'

'And I want you to promise me one more thing.'

'What?'

'That you'll give me that pink shirt.'

There seemed to be a slight commotion in the office. An uneasy atmosphere. Hostile glances. Harrumphing.

Over at the HRTs' cauldron, Dread Ed was sitting at Trish's desk. An immovable object. Then I remembered the memo.

Hot-desking. No personal desks anymore. More flexibility. More freedom. Just a trial. Get the lie of the land.

What a mistake. A pointless game of musical chairs. A shambolic, tension-fuelled free-for-all. A ruck. A fast track to trivial arguments of the kind developing before my very eyes.

Trish had her hands on her hips.

'So we can no longer sit together? That's what you're saying?'

She took a step forward, her slight but deadly frame now three inches from Ed's face. Her voice rose an octave.

'Is. That. What. You. Are. SAYING?'

Quite why Ed had picked on one of the HRTs' desks to prove a point was beyond me. Did he have a death wish? Didn't he understand the power of the Macbeth sisterhood?

'Not at all, Patricia,' he smarmed. *Patricia. Ooh, now he's done it.* Some people looked away. They didn't want to get caught in the crossfire. Doors were opening and people were coming out to see what the fuss was about.

Ed ploughed on, digging deeper.

'I'm merely making the point that you no longer have *exclusive* use of this desk.'

He tipped the crumbs from a packet of salt and vinegar into his smug mouth.

'And personal possessions. What about those?'

'Well, you'll all just have to cut down on the postcards and the fluffy toys and the crooked ceramic dishes made by six-year-old grandchildren.'

Trish dropped a newt's tail into her cauldron, her face livid, her frame rigid with hatred.

'I shall be lodging a formal complaint with HR. Among other things.'

Like putting cyanide in his tea.

Jonathan strolled across the office floor, looking every inch the Lion King, spreading his Dashwood-Silkness on troubled waters.

'Trish. Could I see you in my office for a second?'

Silver mane. White teeth. Blue eyes.

Worked every time. Trish was a girl again. A swooning, doe-eyed slip of a thing tripping off to his office as if she'd been invited in for a spot of tantric sex.

She emerged ten minutes later, soft, smiling, her face flushed with more than her usual menopausal blush, then clocked Ed's size elevens on her desk and, with a face like thunder, gathered her fellow witches around the boiling pot and began plotting the demise of the Salt and Vinegar King.

All I could think about was that bloody name.

Bronwyn.

I knew I'd heard it somewhere before.

Two days later, Rose came back from her lunch break in high spirits. The HRTs had begun a policy of piling their desks with personal possessions. Their little protest. In a charity shop, she'd found a vase the size of a missile silo. She plopped it down on her desk and stood back to admire its vibrant red glaze. She turned to Hilary.

'What do you think?'

'Lovely shape.'

I wasn't looking at the shape. I was looking at the colour. Red.

That was it. Red lipstick. A red car. A short blonde bob. A size-ten figure. Last Christmas. I'd answered the door.

'I've just moved in at the end of the lane. The cottage.'

She'd handed me a card, which Eric had snatched from my hand and torn to shreds, growling as he spun round and round, a little maelstrom of mock aggression.

I'd apologised profusely – I'd actually been rather embarrassed about it – and she'd laughed it off with a practised charm that had made me feel instantly inferior. She was clearly used to being liked. But I hadn't liked her.

I saw her again now. Her red lipstick. Her shitty red car. Her figure. Perfect ten.

For the next several days, I was constantly on the lookout for Perfect Ten. And every day I found myself wanting to bump into her, around the village or on my way to work, so I could take a good long look at the woman who had my head in such a spin. I was leaving the house earlier each morning, hoping to catch a glimpse of her, maybe see she wasn't so gorgeous after all, maybe see I had nothing to worry about … But it never happened.

Worst of all, my head was now full of horrible images. Them together, me walking in, them not caring and carrying on. My daydreams had become nightmares.

Will was the only thing keeping me sane.

I called him. Time for coffee. We sat in the courtyard. It was sunny and warm. But Sweet William was looking decidedly uncomfortable himself. He was fidgety. He kept sort of flapping his arms up and down.

'Feeling all right?'

'Hm. Not really.'

He raised an arm, slowly and painfully. A wounded duck.

'It's a bit embarrassing.'

'I've never seen you embarrassed in my life. What is it? Lifting too much weight at the gym?'

He leaned forward, looking over his shoulder.

'It's not muscles. It's more … armpits.'

'Armpits?'

'It's a new cologne.'

'You put *cologne* on your armpits?'

'When I shave them, yeah.'

'No wonder they're sore. Idiot.'

'It's normally fine. But I ordered this new cologne online, and … Well, let's just say it doesn't do what it says on the tin.'

'Why are you shaving your armpits anyway?'

'I got that dress. In *Aurora*. The sleeveless one.'

'Cologne. Daft sod.'

'I know.'

I stared into my cup.

'What about you?'

'Not great. This is driving me mental. I'm turning into someone I don't want my friends to know. Someone I don't want to be.'

'What do you mean?'

'Desperate. Pitiful.'

'Give over.'

'You know what I did?'

'What?'

'Went into *Ann Summers* and bought some mucky underwear. Leather. Not for him. Not really. Just to … cheer myself up.'

'Nice.'

'Except it isn't. I look like an over-inflated tyre.'

Will spat coffee onto the table. He wiped at it with a napkin.

'It's not funny! I hated myself in it. And, to cap it all, I was sweating so much, I couldn't get the bloody thing off! I had to take the scissors to it.'

'Bloody hell.'

'Thirty-nine ninety-nine! In the bin. The bottom of the wheelie bin, wrapped in newspaper. Where he won't see it.'

'Dozy cow. Don't you know the talcum powder trick? It's in all the magazines.' 'Not in *House Beautiful*, it isn't.' Will threw his head back and laughed.

I stirred my coffee.

'Will, have you ever been in love?'

He let that question hang in the air for a few seconds.

'I'm not sure you'd call it love. But there were … feelings.' He smiled at the memory.

'His name was Alexander. We were at prep school together. Nothing much happened between us. Just the odd grope in the dark. I was a good Catholic boy. Mass every Sunday. My mother made sure of that. And like a good Catholic, I carried around sackfuls of guilt. You can you imagine my confessions.'

His eyes filled up.

'I'm sorry.'

'Oh, it's fine. We were very young.'

'I didn't mean to make you sad.'

'Don't worry. It was a long time ago. You move on.'

'You didn't stay in touch?'

'No. I did have a mad moment a couple of years ago. I found his profile on Facebook.'

'Didn't you contact him?'

'He's married. He has a son. His life looks … sorted. He doesn't need reminders of some silly schoolboy dalliance.'

'And that's all it was?'

'For him, I think. For me … no. It wasn't.'

I started to fill up. Will stroked my cheek and smiled.

'Truth is, no one has ever come close. When I saw him, saw his photos – god, I'm such a bloody stalker! – my heart started racing. Again. It all came back. His hair. The smell of him. His cheeky grin that just … melted me.'

His smile wobbled. I put my arm round him.

'It's fine. I gave him up, my Prince Charming, years ago. Life's okay.'

God, love is shit! You think you've cracked it, found someone, then it's snatched away. Life moves on but you don't. It looked like my own Prince Charming was turning into an ugly frog. Maybe the single life is the best way.

Will gathered himself, looked at his watch, kissed me on the cheek and rushed off to a budget meeting. I stayed out in the courtyard and basked in the sunshine.

Love is shit. But nature can make the cruel revelation a little easier to take. The rosebeds were looking gorgeous. I walked over to a peach-coloured climber, tumbling round the boardroom window.

I closed my eyes and breathed in a deep lungful of its delicious musky scent. Eyes still closed, I took a step back. My left shoulder made contact with something firm. There was a grunt.

When I opened my eyes, a smartly dressed man I'd never seen before was kneeling on the gravel, gathering up sheets of paper.

'Oh, god, I'm so sorry.'

He turned a pair of warm hazel eyes towards me.

'It's quite all right.'

'I'm such a clumsy cow.' I crouched down and picked up a couple of sheets.

'Please. Don't give it another thought.' He smiled. He seemed thoroughly unperturbed. His voice sounded like velvet.

'I'm Jennif …'

His phone rang.

'Sorry, I'll have to …'

And he was gone.

The summer had reached its height. Haymaking was over. The fields where, three weeks ago, the grass had stood several feet high (endless fun for Betty and Eric) were now bare and yellow.

As I walked my regular morning route, the skylarks twittered and dashed. The sun had scorched the barley stubble a rich gold and I trod carefully across its prickly surface.

Pete had been treading carefully – guiltily, I thought – around me since the texts we now didn't talk about. Unable to face the truth that we were on a downward slope, I'd become silent and withdrawn around the house, which made conversation between us awkward and contrived.

'Fancy a dinner at The Feathers?' he'd say. As if nothing had happened.

'Not really.'

I was pushing him away but, for me, we'd crossed the Rubicon. Suspicion ruled my thoughts. It hung in the air like his new cologne, hours after he'd gone out.

Poor Will. I was phoning him most evenings. A bloody running commentary.

'He's out again. Another new client. Another new shirt.'

Will was indulgent and supportive.

'Reverse psychology. When he goes out, tell him to have a good time.'

'You think?'

'Well, if you're really the miserable cow you tell me you are at home, he'll find any excuse to get away from you.'

'I suppose.'

'Do you want it to work? Do you want him … back?'

'I don't know. I think so.'

'Well, the next time he suggests going out for dinner, for god's sake agree!'

'I know.'

'You're your own worst enemy.'

'I know.'

'Perhaps there really *is* nothing wrong. Perhaps he really *is* trying to make an effort to get the relationship back on track. But, if you won't let him, it's never going to happen.'

Hm. Maybe.

I'd been keeping my distance and spending more and more time on my own, outdoors with the dogs, walking the fields and the rolling hills. I'd bought myself a walking guide to the South Downs and I now knew just about every walk in the book.

One good thing to come out of all this solitude and exercise was a considerable drop in weight. I'd lost a stone. The irony of achieving something that would please Pete by spending no time at all with Pete was not lost on me. We did nothing together.

So different from the early days. The impromptu day trips. The lazy weekends away. The holidays in the sun. And the talking and planning, with guidebooks and maps over glasses of wine. That had been as much fun as the trips themselves.

An image in my head. The back seat of a taxi. On our way to Gatwick for a trip to Corfu we'd been talking about for months. His hand in mine.

As I made my way back across the fields with Betty and Eric and watched a combine harvester shoot a cloud of golden straw high into the air, I resolved to make an effort.

The heat of the day had been punishing and, by seven o'clock, it was still sitting somewhere in the top twenties. My throat was dry from the heat and the dust from the combine.

I looked through the kitchen window. Pete was on a lounger in the garden. His face and his forearms had caught the sun. A deep bronze. He looked handsome.

I took out a jug and dumped in ice, gin and vermouth and gave it a good stir. I took two champagne coupes out of the cupboard and poured the gin martinis we'd acquired a taste for in Corfu. I plopped in a couple of green olives.

Pete was on his phone as I stepped onto the grass. He spotted me. He ended the call.

'Hi!' A little too loud. A little too enthusiastic. Theatrical.

'I thought you'd like one of these.'

'Martini. Fabulous.'

'Corfu.'

'Yes.'

'You remember?'

'Yes.'

'Cheers.'

'Cheers.' A raised glass. No clinking. *When did we stop clinking?*

'Delicious. Thanks.'

'You're welcome.'

He looked down the garden and out across the fields.

'Lovely evening.'

'Yes.' I thought of Will's advice. Be positive. Make a move.

'Perhaps we could go out. Get a bite at The Feathers.'

'Er, tonight?'

'Why not?'

'It's just … I've arranged to see a client. A new job.'

'Okay.'

'She wants raised vegetable beds and a barbecue area.'

'Okay.'

'This weekend? Maybe?'

'Okay.'

'Sorry.'

'It's fine.'

I drained my glass.

'Finished?'

He knocked back the last of his martini and handed me the glass.

'Thanks. That was lovely.'

'No problem.'

The office was a ghost town for the first two weeks of August. Jonathan had disappeared off somewhere tropical. Undisclosed location. No single supplement. Lucky woman.

My days were spent arranging occasional meetings, answering the phone and trying not to care too much about my crumbling relationship and lack of holiday plans.

It didn't help that I had to field a typical above-and-beyond call from Dread Ed, sailing somewhere off Malta on his thirty-foot motor cruiser.

He bawled at me down the line. We hardly needed the phone – his voice would have carried from the Med.

'Hello there, Jennifer!'

'Hi, Edward.'

'Could you possibly go on line for me and check the weather forecast for the Eastern Mediterranean?'

'I'm not sure Met Office duties are in my job description.'

'Sorry. But do be a love. My Sirius has thrown in the towel and I can't get it fixed until I make ground in Valletta on Tuesday. So for now I'm reduced to sticking my finger in the air.'

Spooky. *I* had a finger that needed sticking somewhere.

4

The Break-Up

One balmy evening, just before the late August bank holiday weekend, I was heading out to the village shop. I called to Pete.

'Can I fetch you anything?'

He was looking over the hedge. He turned to face me.

'Sorry?'

'I'm nipping to the shop. Do you need anything?'

'Now? You're going now?'

'Yes.'

'Okay.'

'So?'

'Hm?'

'Do you need anything?'

I thought about Will's advice. Make an effort.

'How about a couple of bottles of Bishop's Finger?'

'Er, yeah. Great. Thanks.'

Bishop's Finger. Imagine if your job was coming up with daft names for beers. Gardener's Knob – a session beer guaranteed to hit the spot. Donkey's Delight – a full-bodied ale with a long finish. Blonde Bitch – a continental-style lager that went down easily.

I heard an engine. As I turned the corner into the narrow lane, I saw it. The red car. I instinctively knew it was her at the wheel. Perfect Ten.

My heart thumped as the car inched towards me. For a second I thought about hiding but I found myself rooted to the spot. The next second, defiance swelled in my chest, then anger. It had taken three months to bump into her. Why should *I* hide? *She's* the one who should be skulking around. *I* have nothing to be ashamed of.

When the shitty red car was three feet away, although it wasn't at all in my nature, I fired the stormiest glare I could muster right through her windscreen. She looked straight ahead, with an indifference that bordered on insolence. A slight smirk played at the corners of her lips. *You might as well get used to it, old girl. Your days are numbered.*

Two hours later, armed with a bottle of vodka and no beer, I flopped onto the couch and poured myself a hefty measure. No Pete. Disappeared.

I tipped in some orange juice and tried not to see her smug bitch face. But it was everywhere I looked. I flicked on the TV to erase her image. *Dinnerladies*. The one where Jean's husband leaves her for a dental hygienist. *Not Going Out*. Not funny. An early episode of *Shameless*. That's about bloody perfect.

As the evening wore on, the battle between vodka and orange juice was played out on the couch. The Russian Bear was an easy victor.

I woke up at 3am, a half empty glass of vodka on the floor. If Pete was in, he hadn't woken me.

The TV had moved onto some straight-to-video tearjerker made around 1982. Big hair.

Betty and Eric were fast asleep at my feet. My faithful friends. Always there. God. I was such a parody! The betrayed older woman reaching for the bottle.

Feeling wretchedly dehydrated, I shuffled into the bathroom and poured myself a glass of water, gulping it down so quickly half of it ended up down my shirt. I stared in the mirror. Who the hell was the pathetic creature staring back at me?

I soaked a flannel in steaming hot water and held it to my face, to rejuvenate my alcohol-sodden skin. The soft cotton felt comforting. I hid beneath its warmth for perhaps a minute, shutting out the world.

The bedroom door was open and the bed empty. He'd spent the night … somewhere else. Then I turned to the spare room. The door was ajar and I saw his head peeping out from under the covers.

Relief. Pathetic relief.

His phone was on the floor, a couple of feet inside the door. I stared at the small black device. The instrument of my torment. For an instant I thought about flushing it down the toilet. But that would be like sweeping things under the carpet. Like running.

Perhaps it was the vodka, but I just thought, *Enough.*

I crept across to the door and lifted the phone. With my hands shaking, I selected incoming calls. I scrolled down the list. Builders. Suppliers. All work stuff. Nothing from her.

Was it all off? Had it ever been on? Was it all in my head?

I felt light-headed. A mix of elation and embarrassment. Had I been imagining it all?

As I bent to lay the phone back down, Pete stirred and turned over. There was a smear of something at the corner of his mouth. Something red.

I snatched up the phone again. Texts. I hadn't looked at texts.

Hi Bron. Had a good day? Missing you, darling. See you later. If I get the chance :-) xxx

Yesterday. 6.17 pm. About the time I'd offered to go for his beer.

The hammer hit my chest again. Three times. Those three kisses.

I staggered downstairs into the living room, pulled my new best friend off the table and poured a good-sized wallop into the half-empty glass on the floor. I took a good slug.

Then I marched upstairs and grabbed the phone again. Pete didn't stir. I cocked my arm, ready to launch the phone at his head. But something made me stop. I knew exactly what I was going to do instead.

I pulled the door closed. I downed the rest of the vodka. I staggered over to the bathroom and closed the door. I plopped down onto the toilet.

Feeling unusually empowered, I dialled her number. Just two rings before she picked up.

'Hello, darling. I know you miss me, but d'you know what time it is?'

Three seconds of stony silence from my end.

'Oh. It's you. I'm calling the police. I'll have you arrested for harassment. Do you hear me? You BITCH!'

I dropped the phone. Obscenities continued to spout from the speaker. For a few seconds, I couldn't move. Then I got angry.

I picked up the phone.

'How dare you? How DARE you?!'

'… fucking harassment … in the fucking middle of the night …'

I carried the shrieking phone over to the door of the spare room, flung the door open and hurled the phone at Pete, catching him on the shoulder.

He sat up like a bomb had gone off.

'What the bloody hell?'

'I've just been speaking to your new girlfriend.'

'What? Who?'

'Your beloved Bronwyn. *Missing you, darling.*'

'At four in the morning?'

'She sounds lovely. Very wide range of vocabulary.'

'Have you gone mad?'

'Have *I* gone mad? She's bloody well threatening to have me arrested. For harassment.'

'It's the middle of the night.'

'Is that it? Is that the thing that's bothering you most about this? The bloody time of DAY?

'You're bloody mental.'

'Don't make this about me.'

'Well it IS about you. Look at you.'

'No, Pete. This is not …'

'With your saggy arse and your roots showing and stinking of bloody vodka. Is it any bloody wonder?'

'No. NO. You can't put this on me. Just because you can't keep it in your pants.'

'Is it? Is it any wonder?'

I turned away from him and caught sight of myself in the hall mirror. A thirty-seven-year-old wreck whose last drops of dignity were lying in the bottom of a glass on the floor.

I slumped onto the floor with my head in my heads.

'I mean, you're pathetic.'

I couldn't answer. Couldn't say a word. Couldn't even lift my head.

He stood up. He pulled his jeans off the chair and stepped into them. He pulled on a T-shirt. He pulled on his suede boots and laced them slowly. He stood up.

'We're finished.'

He walked downstairs, pushed past Betty and Eric, now up and yapping loudly, and lifted his car keys from the dish in the hall. He opened the door and closed it with a soft click. He started his car. He left.

For several minutes, I lay on the floor of the spare room. Not daring to look up. Numb. Then I pulled myself up and collapsed into the spare bed, which still smelled of him. I cried, quietly and steadily, and eventually fell into a restless sleep.

The sun woke me an hour or so later and, for a brief moment, I knew nothing. Then I saw the glass on the floor and remembered the whole nightmare. I saw the bedroom mirror and the image in it and looked away. *You're pathetic.*

I saw nothing of him for three days. I phoned in sick and gave an excuse that Jonathan saw right through. I sat in the house, stayed away from mirrors, and stared at my phone. After three days, I sent him a text. *Can we talk?*

Hours went by. I did some dusting. Made Heinz tomato soup and cheese on toast. Comfort food. More hours. Then came the reply.

I want you out.

Pete's house. Pete's rules.

Where would I go? Then a wave of panic. What about Betty and Eric?

A few days later, on a crisp September morning, as the mist was beginning to clear, I took my gorgeous dogs for a walk. A final walk.

The dew on the grass sparkled. A woodpecker swooped low across the field, chattering as he passed me then laughing as he banked upwards into the copse ahead of me. God! I'd been so gullible, so blind. Even the bloody birds were laughing at me.

I looked across the field at Betty and Eric, flying towards me from their rabbit hunt, and felt a rock in my heart. I had no choice but to leave them behind – it was going to be hard enough to find someone to take me in without having a couple of dogs in tow – but I was struggling to be normal with them. Saying goodbye was going to kill me.

Back at the house, my case packed with enough clothes to see me through the following week, I sat on the doorstep and stroked my two little friends.

Betty jumped up and licked the salty liquid running down my face. She knew fine well what was going on. Smart girl. Eric stared at me while I told him to be good and not run off and not be such a bloody nuisance. I told them I'd find a place. Told them we'd all be happy together. Told them I'd come back for them.

Then I walked out through the front door, for the last time. I secured the latch behind me and pushed the key through the letterbox.

The dogs whined as I walked to my car and started the engine. I pulled out of the drive and turned down the lane, not daring to look back, knowing I'd never see them again.

5

Tea in Bed with Viv

Viv and Roger Patterson were my guardian angels in the months that followed. I'll never forget their generosity. And the fact that Viv saved my life.

The lanes around our house – Pete's house – are postcard narrow, with hedgerows three feet above head height. As a driver, you can't see a thing. That morning, with Betty's and Eric's whining still ringing in my ears, I drove my little blue Peugeot at such reckless speed I deserved to die. I had no idea where I was heading, but I knew I was getting there at breakneck speed.

With my head full of Pete and his bitch, and my gut twisting in pain, I flew around every blind bend like a harpy. Then I remembered the day and the date. Tuesday, the 21st of September.

Viv.

Weeks ago, before all this, I'd arranged to see Viv for lunch. The memory, and the thought of my old friend's warm smile, made me lift my foot off the pedal. I slowed for the next bend, approaching it at a sane pace. I rounded the bend. Then I slammed on the brakes and came to rest a couple of feet from the bumper of a 44-tonne Sainsbury's truck inching its way towards the village. My heart leapt out of my chest and hit the windscreen. The truck's hydraulic brakes hissed in the silence.

No Viv and five seconds later the lights would have gone out.

Standing outside Viv's house, I tried to feel normal. It wasn't really working. I pressed the bell then immediately wanted to get back in the car and flee the scene.

Viv appeared at the door. God knows what I looked like but it clearly wasn't good.

'Jen! Goodness! What on earth's happened? You look dreadful!'

I couldn't speak.

'Oh God. Come in. Come here.'

She wrapped an arm round me and walked me inside, stroking my head with her other hand.

'It's alright. Whatever it is, it's alright.'

She lowered me onto her plump red sofa and disappeared into the kitchen, reappearing seconds later with a vase-sized wine glass half full of red.

'Here.'

'It's only half past eleven.'

'Drink it.'

I took a big gulp and almost immediately felt better. Then almost immediately thought I might have a drink problem.

'It's Pete, isn't it?'

'What? How …?'

'Just a hunch.'

Somehow that made it worse. Bloody hell. Viv knew and she hardly ever *saw* Pete. I'd seen him every day for ten bloody years and hadn't seen it coming. Bloody stupid cow.

I started sobbing. Viv put her arm round me again and pulled my head onto her shoulder.

'Oh, Viv. How can I be so bloody stupid?'

She got angry.

'Hey! Enough of that crap! It's not your fault. Why do women always think it's *their* fault?'

Then she launched into a colourful diatribe about men and vanity and midlife crises and keeping it in your trousers, using language of a kind you don't often hear on *The Archers*.

By the time she'd finished, I was feeling a good deal better.

'Right. Have you got a bag?'

'What?'

'In the car.'

'Yeah.'

'Get it.'

'What?'

'Get your bag. You're staying here.'

She waved away my protests with headmistressly authority and practically pushed me into the spare room. Then she entertained me all afternoon with stories and wine and the odd hilarious sideswipe at Pete so that, by the time Roger got in, I was feeling like a person again. More wine, a lamb and couscous dinner, then a dozy hour in their gorgeous new conservatory, candlelight flickering in its faux Gothic arches. No questions, no need for explanations, no *what are your plans?* Just the unconditional support of true friends.

There were wobbles, of course, during those first few weeks. I'd wake in the night and dark thoughts would crowd in again. And there were daily reminders. I was sleeping in someone else's bed, using someone else's shower, drinking someone else's coffee. A suitcase was all that belonged to me. Like the leaves on Viv's maple tree, the rest had slowly fallen away.

In spite of the solicitousness of my wonderful friends, a cloud was always hanging over me. Every morning, just before dawn turned the curtains in the guest room to a lighter shade of blue, I found myself hoping for rain, to match my mood.

At precisely 7am, Roger would tap gently on the door and whisper in.

'Morning, Jen. Cup of tea?'

'Great. Thanks, Roger.'

Then I'd trot through to their room and jump in beside Viv. She'd greet me with a box of tissues and a hug, while Roger fussed around us like a Victorian housekeeper, serving tea (cups, never mugs), delivering newspapers and shaking his head in mock horror while Viv put the boot into Passionate Pete and his Performing Pecker. Roger never joined in with the Pete-bashing but, seeing me standing at the conservatory window one evening, staring miserably at a gorgeous sunset, he wrapped his arms round my shoulders and kissed me on the head.

'You needed this, Jen. One day, you'll thank him.'

Work was pleasingly mindless, and Viv and Roger's home a delightful haven, but I was still moping desperately in the evenings and at weekends. My lovely friends would often drop their own numerous plans and priorities and drag me out into the country for long walks on Sundays, Roger stooping to look at a harebell or a bird's foot trefoil and Viv calculating the miles to the next tea shop. I enjoyed the fresh air and the nature and the exercise.

Their company was a beautiful bonus but, even without it, I would often feel the call of the country and started venturing out on my own, delighting in the discovery of a new route. I'd find a stream, perhaps a cute stone bridge or even a whole new village I'd never heard of. It was uplifting.

This particular Sunday, I'd struck out across a field, following the dotted line in an old pocket guide I'd lifted from the bookshelf in Viv and Roger's downstairs toilet (books in the loo – how very civilised). After about a mile, the 'well-marked path' disappeared, leaving me to make up my own route.

They say a woman's intuition is pretty reliable. They're wrong. Mine took me up hill and down dale for, by my reckoning, about seven soggy miles before I hit the outskirts of a small settlement with a familiar spire.

It was only when I saw the pantile roof of the vicarage that I realised I was back in my village. My old village.

And there, a hundred yards away, outside the Post Office, a red car. Her car. Then the pair of them, him with a bundle of newspapers, her with a bottle of something. Laughing, the way new lovers do.

I stood for perhaps a whole minute and watched them. Her. Long legs in tight jeans. Lilac polo shirt hugging a toned torso. Luxuriant bob dancing in the autumn sunshine. Then her car pulling away into the picture postcard. Love's young dream.

I leaned on the bus shelter and tried to breathe. In its perspex, the reflection of a thick-waisted frump in muddy brown boots and a grey fleece, rat-tails of sweaty blonde hair pasted to her forehead. I felt sick.

The diesel engine of the number 14 was rumbling along street. Numb with shock and self-loathing, I found myself stepping towards the edge of the pavement. *One step and it all goes away.*

I closed my eyes.

'You getting on love?'

A fat, red-faced man in his forties had his foot on the step of the bus. I opened my eyes. He was staring at me. The door of the bus was open and the driver was looking at me like I'd been let out for the weekend.

'I haven't got all day, darling.'

I couldn't speak.

The fat man got on, the doors hissed shut and the bus pulled away.

I staggered back and collapsed onto the bench in the shelter. I'd actually considered stepping in front of a bus. But I'd done it at a bus stop. The only place a bus was guaranteed *not* to run me over.

Bloody hell. I couldn't even get *that* right.

Tea in bed continued for weeks, and every day Viv would pack me off to work with gorgeous sandwiches she'd carefully constructed but I never had the strength to eat.

As she waved me off each day, I felt like a teenager being dispatched to school, but with none of the resentful hostility that is the teenager's default setting. The truth is, Viv and Roger's all-encompassing kindness was the only thing that kept me going.

My appetite had all but disappeared and weight was falling off me. I'd soon be the magic dress size. Ten.

As October neared its end, the days were growing shorter. Everywhere I looked, the colours of autumn assaulted me with memories of long walks on misty mornings with my dogs. I had one small photograph of them tucked away inside my suitcase, but I could never bear to look at it.

At work, cubicle three in the ladies' cloakroom had become my retreat. There, I could hide away and silently sob whenever I needed to. I'd started to say hello to the door. God. I was turning into my mother.

People in the office seemed to sense my pain. Nigel was strangely indulgent when I forgot my ID badge twice in one week. Craig fixed a browser problem on my desktop without attempting to brush against my breasts. I even had smiles from the coven in the corner.

I was still taking sneak peeks at the photo of Pete I'd shoved in a drawer the day I'd left. An odd compulsion. There he was, standing next to his prized JCB 801, the new mini digger that would 'revolutionise' his landscaping business. I'd seen it in action, relentlessly ripping out stumps and roots.

Then one afternoon, after lunch, I turned a corner. I pulled out the picture and laid it on my desk. I took pins from my stationery tray. I began sticking them, calmly and methodically, into the image of Pete's arms and legs. Then I took a large pin with a red head and drilled it into his groin. Then I tore the picture from the pins and slowly ripped it into little pieces and dropped it into the bin. With something approaching a sense of calm, I realised I was beginning to get over him.

I tried to recapture the fun of office Fridays by looking at travel websites. It amused me to plan trips I knew I'd never be able to afford. I looked at mountain treks, beach holidays and city breaks. Then I stumbled across the brilliantly titled Freedom Australia site, saw images of Port Jackson, the Great Barrier Reef and that iconic Opera House. And I remembered Larry.

Australian Larry and I had been an item for six months, a lifetime ago. He was one of those men who made you feel like a million dollars. We'd met when he became a regular at the Pier Grill, the restaurant in Southsea where I worked as a waitress.

Larry was short with dark brown hair that curled tightly to his head. He had terrible dress sense, all jeans and Hawaiian shirts. But there was something about him. At first, I couldn't decide if he came from South Africa or from down under, but, as our conversations grew longer, it emerged he was an Aussie.

If we were shorthanded behind the bar, I'd be drafted in to pour drinks and take money. Larry would always ask for the same drink – a large gin with a bit of lemon. When we'd started dating, weeks later, I discovered he'd been asking all along for gin and *bitter lemon*. He'd been too polite to point out my mistake. And he'd been getting pissed pretty quickly on neat gin.

A great conversationalist and a hugely well-travelled and urbane man, Larry always treated me like an equal. He didn't talk down to me like most of the male customers (I was only a waitress, and a blonde one at that). And Larry could always make me look on the bright side. That's how we'd first got talking, one lunchtime in the restaurant when I committed a 'grave' error.

I'd been given a large table to wait on. A funeral party. Eighteen sombre diners, thirteen of them ordering steak. I went round the table and remembered to ask each steak how he or she would like it cooked, then, satisfied I had the order, breezed off to hand it to the chef.

Alan looked at the ticket.

'You're missing one.'

'What?'

'Seventeen. There are eighteen covers. How many steaks?'

'Er, thirteen. I think.' I'd counted thirteen in my head. Unlucky for some.

'You've got twelve here. Go and check.'

I dashed back over to the table, glancing up and down to work out whose steak I'd missed.

It was the widow of the deceased. She'd ordered a steak. I'd missed it.

'So sorry, madam. How would you like your steak cooked?'

'Very well done, please.'

'Certainly.'

I should have stopped there. But I didn't. I tried to be chatty.

'That's how my dad likes his steak, too. Cremated.'

The table's stunned silence, and the widow's ensuing tears, sent me flying into the toilets with a scarlet face. I was quickly pulled off tables and stuck behind the bar where I could cause less trouble.

Larry was sitting at the end of the bar, reading his newspaper, a glass of gin at his elbow. I was so mortified at my *faux pas* I was practically in tears. He put his paper down and asked me what was wrong. I told him about my cock-up.

He smiled.

'It's *not* funny.'

'Come on. It *is*.'

'No it's *not*. And *they* didn't think it was either.'

'Trust me. They will. Not today. But one day, they will. They'll be talking about you for years. They'll say, *Remember that pretty waitress? Yeah. 'Cremated'. Hilarious.*

That pretty waitress.

I didn't get a tip that day. But I did get to know a really nice man. Really nice.

And here I was thinking about him again. Probably five years since I'd last thought of him, and longer since I'd heard from him. Our relationship had run its course but we'd parted as good friends. Then he'd gone back to Oz and there'd been regular contact at first, then a couple of times a year, then nothing. Last I'd heard, he was running a fancy car dealership in Sydney.

Well, Fridays were for fun. I could have a whole afternoon of fun playing detective, trying to track Larry down.

It took ten minutes. Car dealers. Mercedes. BMW. Porsche. Sydney. Larry. A handful of searches and a bit of refining and there it was. Lotus Eater Motors. An email address.

I fired off a *you probably don't remember me* email. Then I went back to work.

Seven minutes later (at 21.55, local time – Larry clearly worked long hours), I got a reply.

'Jen, how wonderful to hear from you! Business is great. I'm great. But how are you? Can I call you? How about tomorrow evening?'

Viv poured us a glass of red (Roger had upped his Wine Society order to three cases a month). She asked me about Larry.

'Any chance of a romance there?'

'No. As far as I know, he's still married. Well, he didn't say otherwise.'

'Well, you wouldn't, would you? In a quick email. Wait and see when he calls.'

'No. He's just a really nice guy. It'll be good to reconnect with him.'

'Hm.'

True to his word, Larry rang at 8. Which was 6 in the morning his time.

'How's life treating you?'

His laid-back Aussie tones made me instantly relaxed. I spoke frankly about my life, about Pete, about the break-up. For ten minutes, I poured out my heart. Like I say, he was a good listener.

'You still there Larry?'

'Yeah, I'm here.'

'What is it?'

'I'm just angry. That someone could say those things to you.'

'Larry, it's fine. I'm over it.'

'It's not fine. He wants his balls cutting off. And I'm just the guy to do it.'

'It's okay.'

'Jen. Listen. Still, after all these years …'

'What?'

'You're still … very special to me.'

'Larry, you were a very good friend to me. I have very fond memories of you.'

'Shit, Jen. Let's make some new memories.'

'What?'

'Come over. To Sydney. My treat. A little break. Tell me when and I'll fix it.'

'But …'

'No arguments.'

So it was settled. The promise of a reunion, some time in the next few months. It was something lovely to look forward to.

And, looking forward, I knew I couldn't keep leaning on Viv and Roger. After six weeks of life-saving support from my friends (*Six weeks!* God, how did they put up with me?), and despite their reassurances that I could stay as long as I wanted, I knew it was time to move on and stand on my own two feet.

My wages wouldn't cover the rent for a whole house, probably not even a whole flat. I'd have to consider renting a room.

But where?

6

Barns and Beach Huts

As November blew in with a bitterly cold wind, the shops were filling with Christmas cards and baubles and Noddy Holder's scream. I was dreading the whole phoney business.

I put aside all thoughts of the festive season and focused on my dream trip to Australia to see Larry, now fixed for the spring.

Then Jonathan mentioned the office Christmas party, and I was reminded of my historical obligation to arrange it. The most thankless of tasks.

Try pleasing everyone from the chavvy office junior to the middlebrow managing director. It can't be done. No matter what venue I suggested, there was always an objection from some quarter.

The younger teams wanted somewhere lively – sod the food, they just wanted to get slaughtered! The HRTs were angling for the elegant taster menu – six small courses with matched wines – at La Giaconda, in the nice part of town. At £55 a head, it was a non-starter. The sizeable faction of middle-aged men were happy with any place that offered cheap booze and a chance to chat up young girls.

In the end, after much deliberation and countless phone calls, I booked us onto a James Bond theme night in the faded splendour of the Royal Hotel. Martinis for the bow-tie brigade, a Shirley Bassey soundalike to blast Dread Ed out of the water, and a bevy of young beauties for the old geezers to eye up. I'd be in hot water with the HRTs, but what's new?

I took a call from a friend. Karen was Head of English at St Bernadette's. She knew I was looking for a room to rent.

'I've just bumped into my friend, Saffie. She has a room going. In her barn.'

I dropped my nail varnish. A dark red stain spread itself across my desk. I reached for my box of tissues.

'A barn?'

'Well, a conversion. It's about forty minutes away. Aldingbourne. Gorgeous little spot, not far from Chichester, close to the A27. She's in on Saturday if you want to take a look?'

'Sounds great.' I mopped up the burgundy blush on my desk.

'And, get this. You could take your dogs. Saffie's place is a bloody menagerie as it is. A couple more animals is neither here nor there.'

Oh God. I thought about how wonderful it would be to live in the country and be with my little cherubs again.

'Sounds brilliant. Too good to be true.'

'Saffie's a bit … alternative, mind. Bit of a hippy.'

'That's alright.'

'Well, see what you think.'

Karen was backpedalling a bit. But it wouldn't hurt to take a look. I lifted the bin and dropped in a clump of tissues thick with crimson varnish.

'Do you think I'd suit red hair?'

'Definitely not. If you weren't blonde, Jen, we'd have to start taking you seriously.'

On Saturday morning, I drove down to Aldingbourne with high hopes.

I'd spoken to Saffie on the phone to chat about the room and I'd got her life story instead. She sounded like a free spirit. She'd spent a few years of her childhood living in a tent with her mother at

Greenham Common in the early eighties. She'd never been entirely sure who her father was but it would have been one of the protesters who hung around the women's peace camp. Her mother said the most likely candidate was a chap called Buzz. Fond of a drink, he'd been arrested for throwing himself in front of a bulldozer. After Saffie was born, he'd buzzed off.

As I pulled into the lane that led to Saffie's barn, russet and gold leaves were doing their best to cling on to the trees. To my left, a rich brown newly ploughed field looked ready for spring cabbage.

With its high timbered roof and slatted windows, Saffie's place was impressive from the off. As was the seven-foot phallic sculpture by the front door.

I was immediately greeted by two vocal Alsatians announcing my arrival. I was now entering their territory. Hearing their welcome, a young woman appeared. She reassured the dogs that I was a friendly visitor, waved, and then walked out to meet me.

'Hi there, Jennifer. Do come in.'

Rock-star thin, Saffie had golden hair tied back in a braid that stroked her long slender back as she bent to open the latch on the heavy wooden gate. Her eyes were green, almond-shaped and utterly bewitching. Her long cotton dress brushed the floor as she glided towards me on bare feet. Her toenails were painted lilac. The sunlight caught a silver ring on the little toe of her left foot.

She held out her hand.

'Tim's out at the moment, but please do come in and take a look around. Don't mind the dogs. They're quite friendly. It's Wolfie you have to watch out for. But he's asleep. He only prowls around at night time.'

'Wolfie? Great name for a dog. Were you a *Citizen Smith* fan?'

'Sorry?'

'*Citizen Smith*. The 70s sitcom? Wolfie Smith?'

'Oh. No. He's a pure-blood wolf. Not a very imaginative name, is it?'

'Er …'

'We rescued him. A nature reserve was closing down.'

'So he's not wild?'

'No. Well, not completely. They're never really fully tame, though, are they?'

'Sorry?'

'The genus *Canis*.'

'Hm?'

'Wolves, jackals, coyotes, our so-called domestic dogs. Deep down, they're all wild.'

'I suppose.'

We stepped inside. The barn was impressively cavernous. Its vast open-plan ground floor and vaulted ceiling gave it a church-like quality. A spiral staircase led us to an expansive loft area off to the side, all air and light, that housed the bedrooms, including mine. Saffie waved a willowy hand, inviting me to take a closer look at the room, which was generously proportioned and lined with bookshelves. The roof window was open. I stood on my tiptoes and peered out onto vegetable plots and an orchard. The Darling Buds of May. Home.

'The room's lovely.'

'Isn't it?'

Saffie continued the tour. The kitchen was a timewarp, full of shelves heaving with apothecary bottles full of exotic potions and jars of homemade pickles and jams. There were bunches of herbs drying on racks above the Aga.

'We have our own witches' garden.'

'Nice.' I'd be able to pick herbs for the HRTs. They could send Dread Ed to sleep for a month.

Another spiral stair at the far end of the kitchen led down to a spacious basement with shelves packed with boxes of homegrown produce. I spotted marrows and apples and parsnips.

Back upstairs, Saffie filled an old steam kettle and popped it on the stove. We walked through to the living room. She gestured to a low armchair for me and folded herself onto a futon. I eased into the chair and surveyed the space around me.

'What do you think?'

'Gosh, yes. You have a lovely home.'

A pungent aroma of incense filled the interior which, on every surface, spoke of a fascination for Native American culture. Sofas were draped in reindeer hides. Skins decorated the polished wooden floor. Carved eagles stared down at me from walls and bookshelves. I would have been only mildly surprised to see Running Bear pop in from the garden, armed with his tomahawk, on a break from a busy morning's scalping.

'You're keen on Indians. American Indians.'

'Yes. So is Tim. Did you see his carving in the front garden?'

Ah. The giant penis. So it's a totem pole. Shame.

A large ginger cat appeared and slid its tawny fur up and down my legs, purring furiously. I bent down to return the affection and, from the corner of my eye, noticed a rug appearing to move of its own accord. Another cat, tortoiseshell, unfolded itself from the camouflage of the floor covering, wandered lazily over and turned on its little interior motor. Roused by this little flurry of activity, half a dozen other felines that had previously blended into the soft furnishings now made their presence felt, including an oatmeal kitten stretched out on a battered chaise longue and a slim black stunner on a leather cushion in the window, lapping up the sunshine.

Beneath the musky aroma of ylang ylang, I was now picking up distinct sulphurous notes.

'Lots of cats.'

'We've lost count. Aren't they gorgeous? They keep us warm on cold winter nights.'

The whole space around me seemed to be moving. I suddenly felt unnerved and slightly nauseous. The odour of urine now seemed overpowering. *They keep us warm.* Cats in my bed.

'It's rather like having an army of furry hot-water bottles.'

A furry army marching all over me while I slept. The kettle whistled. My flesh crawled.

'Do they have names?'

Saffie reeled off a list of names from Custer's Last Stand.

'That black one in the window is Little Star and over there we have Three Socks. This cheeky monkey here is White Moon.'

A kitten was merrily tearing at the curtain with his young claws.

'Crazy Bear is on the couch over there.'

'And who's that?' I pointed to a huge tabby in the corner.'

'That's Fuck Off Dave. He's a real nuisance under the bedclothes.'

Hm. I remembered a Dave just like him. Always looking to get under *my* bedclothes. Always being told to fuck off.

Before I'd finished my tea, Saffie jumped up.

'Come and meet my girls.'

She took me through to a large conservatory. Eight or nine brown hens wandered up and down, busy doing nothing. A glass menagerie. The floor was decorated with feathers. The air was filled with farmyard aromas.

This house was slipping away from me. There was no way I could bring Betty and Eric here. Within hours, the place would be littered with dead cats and chickens. And Eric would be forever cocking his leg on Tim's giant penis.

'Let me show you the garden.'

Patches of overgrown grass and lopsided vegetable beds were sprinkled with several more of Tim's sculptures. A sort of Zen allotment. Half a dozen sheep and three or four goats stood around munching and staring into space. At the far end of the garden, a swimming pool was playing host to a dozen or so ducks.

'We share the pool with the animals.'

A goat approached us. The poor thing only had three legs.

'This is Mildred.' Saffie offered a handful of oats to the bleating invalid.

'A spring trap did for her other leg.'

'That's awful.'

'The farmer said she was only fit for curry. I pleaded for her life. She manages just fine. She doesn't know how close she was to becoming a vindaloo!'

Mildred eyed me up and down with her elliptical goat eyes, to see if I had anything worth eating.

'She's really sweet.' I pulled her head away from the half-eaten KitKat in my pocket and she wandered off.

Saffie and I chatted for a while in the sunshine, sharing each other's experiences. She talked about her nomadic childhood with her hippy mother and how she'd never felt rooted anywhere. It gave her a sense of freedom, she said. How strange that I craved the exact opposite. Permanence. Familiarity. Security.

For her spiritual compass, she looked to the Native North Americans.

'They believe that everything in nature is sacred. From the mightiest mountains right down to the humblest organisms. Moss. Algae. It's about honour. Love and respect for our Creator and for Mother Earth.'

Dear Saffie. Her philosophy certainly appealed to me. But living here, in this menagerie, well … it wasn't the haven I needed. It wasn't going to mend my broken heart.

I made my excuses.

'I'll let you know in the next few days. About the room.'

I fumbled for my car keys.

'You don't want to stick around? Until Wolfie wakes up?'

'Best not. I've got a hundred and one things to do.' *Top of the list: not getting eaten by a wolf.*

I doffed my metaphorical cap to the giant penis and climbed into my blue Peugeot.

Saffie was delightful. The barn was in a lovely spot. The rent was affordable. But cats would cuddle up to me at night. My dogs would eat the hens. I'd have to share the contents of my pockets with a three-legged goat.

And how would I cope with Saffie shouting the pets in for dinner? *Fuck Off Dave? Dindins!*

On Monday, I met Will for our regular coffee.

'How was the barn?' He tipped more sugar into his latte.

'Interesting. The woman was nice, but I'd be living in the shadow of a giant penis and sharing my chocolate with a paraplegic goat called Mildred.'

'What?'

'And twenty-plus cats in the living room. And a wolf. An actual wolf.'

'Right.'

'It's a non-starter.'

'Hm.'

'What?'

'I'm just thinking.'

'What?'

'My aunt. She owns a beach house. Not far from your barn. West Wittering.'

'A beach house?'

'It's only used during the summer months. I'll call her. For a nominal rent, maybe she'd let you stay there, just until the spring.'

'Oh, Will. That sounds fab.'

'I'll give her a call later.'

'Great.'

'Just one thing.'

'What?'

'Don't mention your three-legged goat.'

'Why?'

'My aunt's name is Mildred.'

By home time he had news.

'She wasn't keen at first.'

'Oh.'

'But I told her Christians have a duty. To be kind. It's no good singing about it on Sunday and doing nothing.'

'Right.'

'Goodwill in action. We believe in life before death. Charity begins at home. All that stuff.'

Charity. Great. I'm one step away from selling the Big Issue.

The following Friday afternoon, with Jonathan off on one of his secret afternoon jaunts, Will and I bunked off early to meet Aunt Mildred.

From the moment I set eyes on the blue and white house with the white picket fence, I knew it would be the perfect place.

SandyView stood at the end of a road that ran parallel to the beach, one of only a handful of the road's original houses, most having been replaced by seventies bungalows with French windows, concrete driveways and considerable deficiencies in character.

Aunt Mildred's house was enchanting. An old wooden boat stood in the garden, upturned, faded with age, peeking out from under plastic sheeting to protect it from the weather. Beside it a plastic table and four chairs were stacked on top of each other, stowed until summer returned.

Will turned the key in the blue painted door. Smells of damp sand and seaweed greeted me, reminders of holidays as a child. The small porch was littered with buckets and spades, tennis rackets, and a kite. A faded green-striped deckchair leant against the wall. On the windowsill, a pocketful of shells and smooth pebbles from the beach had been dumped and left behind. There was a sign on the porch wall. *Happy Days.* I imagined them. A sandy beach. A clear blue sky.

The vinyl floor of the kitchen crunched under my shoes. Sand. A jumble of pots and pans, odd knives with odd forks, cups with unmatched saucers.

In the lounge, evidence of visitors past. A pile of old board games stacked in one corner, their boxes well worn with years of use. Seafaring charts on the walls. Photographs of happy smiling strangers.

I looked out to sea, its solid grey canvas splashed with the brilliant white of waves crashing onto the shore. A small yacht bobbed up and down and, further out, a hulking container ship inched along the horizon, laden with cars from Korea, electronics from Japan.

A proprietorial opening of the front door announced the arrival of Aunt Mildred, a redoubtable-looking bird with an unblinking stare. The kind of woman who, while your leg is being eaten by a shark, tells you to pull yourself together.

Her gaze started at my feet. It lingered at the ladder in my tights, just below my right knee. A loose handle on my desk drawer.

'You are Jennifer?'

I wasn't sure I wanted to be anymore.

'Yes. Hello. Pleased to meet you.' I extended a hand. She didn't take it.

'How long are you proposing to stay?' Her eyes wandered down to my tights.

'Six months. If possible.' My sweetest voice.

'Hm. How do you intend to pay the rent?'

'I'm sorry?' I crossed my left leg over my right.

'Do you work?'

'Jennifer works with me, Aunt Mildred.'

That didn't seem to reassure the old girl.

'Yes. I could manage a reasonable deposit.'

'Deposit?'

'Yes. You know. One month's rent upfront. Or whatever.'

Cogs turned. The old bird hadn't thought there'd be money upfront.

'Well, you seem like a nice girl.'

'I am.'

'She is.'

'I'm sure six months will be fine.'

'Great.' I stepped forward to hug her. Will shook his head.

'We shall discuss rent later. It will be reasonable. William has a key.'

It was agreed I'd move in at the end of the month and pay a deposit of one month's rent.

I knew I'd be happy there. It seemed like my kind of place. I had a good feeling.

Then, the following day, Will phoned me. He sounded uneasy. I had a bad feeling.

'She's changed her mind.'

'What? Why?'

'I don't know. She's been speaking to a neighbour. Someone who's has a bad experience with tenants. An awkward family. The guy kept his motorbike in the kitchen.'

'I haven't got a motorbike.'

'That's what I told her.'

'Bloody hell.'

'I told her you were solid. Dependable.'

Great. I'm a Hotpoint tumble dryer.

'But she's really got the wind up. Daft old bat. Nothing I say will budge her.'

Poor Will. He sounded close to tears.

'Don't worry. It's her place. She has a right to rent it to whoever she wants. Or not rent it.'

'I feel so shitty. She agreed. I know you didn't sign anything but she agreed.'

'Will. It's fine. It's a nice place. But there'll be other nice places.'

Bugger. Back to the drawing board. I couldn't even convince a sweet old lady – well, a prickly old cow, actually – that I was half-decent tenant material. What the bloody hell was wrong with me?

7

Secrets and Santas

So life continued and still I had no home of my own.

Each morning, wonderful Viv sent me off to work with a wave. And with a ham sandwich I didn't have the heart to tell her I never ate. I had virtually no appetite. I existed on a diet of toast and coffee. That was all I ever felt like.

The last day of the week was now 'Fretting Friday'. I scoured estate agents' websites, local papers, even postcards in newsagents' windows. And I fretted about finding nothing affordable.

Marilyn, a junior in Accounts, cornered me at the coffee machine and offered me a room in her place.

Marilyn was a biker. She wore her leather jacket to the office, ignoring Jonathan's emails about 'professional attire'. She had a broad Pompey accent that carried across the office. She had no airs and graces whatsoever and she had no time for bullshit. If someone posh and important phoned up for Jonathan, she'd delight in putting the boot in. ('No, love. He's just popped out for a quick fag.')

I quite liked her.

But I quite disliked her partner. Dave was tall and skinny and had greasy hair that sat on his shoulders. He'd sidled up to me once at some works do and locked his eyes on my cleavage. I stood next to him for about nine seconds before the stench of stale alcohol and cigarettes sent me gagging to the toilets. A definite *Fuck Off Dave*.

Besides, I'd seen Marilyn's place. It was a tiny two up, two down in the town centre. If I moved in, it would certainly be cosy. And cosy with Dirty Dave was something I definitely didn't want to be.

My next offer of accommodation came from an old pal. It was affordable, near the sea, and almost perfect. Almost. Discovering the identity of my prospective next-door neighbour was a bit of a shock.

I'd met Trevor a few years ago at a French conversation class. He was steady, reliable and kind. And therefore single for as long as I could remember. He worked for Brittany Ferries at the Portsmouth terminal and spent his days dealing patiently with customers' complaints.

He called me one evening.

'Any luck with the flat hunting?'

'I'm struggling, Trev. I did find one place, a little cottage by the sea. But it was too good to be true.'

'Fancy being my neighbour?'

Trevor lived in a holiday park.

'In a caravan?'

'Er, excuse me, Jennifer Brown! What exactly is wrong with living in a caravan?' 'Nothing.'

'We're not talking your dad's 1969 Sprite Alpine.'

'Sorry, Trev.'

'I've got central heating, a power shower, satellite telly and a sea view.'

'I know.'

'You should be so bloody lucky!'

'I know.'

Trevor took a deep breath.

'Anyway. Next door's up for rent. Do you *want* the owner's number?'

Of course I did.

I pitched up at Sunny Side Caravan Park on Friday afternoon. *Residents Only*, the sign said. *Strictly no dogs*.

I made my way along the neat rows of mobile homes with their neat gardens and tried to dispel childhood memories of fold-down formica table tops.

It didn't take me long to find number 20. White with a red roof. The owner, Jeff, was waiting to show me round.

Surprisingly spacious, it smelt of pine disinfectant (as did Jeff). It felt warm and cosy and safe. Sitting a little lower on the terrace than Trevor's place next door, it didn't have his sea view but, even on a grey day, it was full of light. And caravan parks had come on quite a bit since the discotheques and pool tables of my childhood.

For a few months, until I could get back on my feet, it would suit me down to the ground.

Jeff put the kettle on and we chatted. He was a local lad who'd made good over the years. The caravan was just one of a string of properties he owned. He spent half the year maintaining them, doing them up, checking the tenants were happy. The other half of the year he spent living it up in Spain. He showed me photos of an impressive five-bedroomed villa near Benalmadena.

In his ill-fitting khaki shorts and faded blue T-shirt pulled tight over a generous girth, he looked more plumber than property magnate. But what did I know?

'Are the neighbours nice?' I wondered what he'd say about Trevor.

'The bloke in 18 is a good egg.' Trevor had passed the test.

'But I can't tell you much about the guy in 22. He's only here once a week. Today's his day. Always Fridays. Place is empty the rest of the week.'

'Odd.'

'Stupid, more like. Two grand a year in rent, we pay. Fella must have money to burn.'

'Must have.'

'Always some leggy piece of sk… er, some tall woman, on his arm. I think it's a Love in the Afternoon job.' He chuckled and looked out of the window.

'Right on cue.'

'Is that him?'

'Have a look.'

I walked over to the couch by the window and looked over Jeff's shoulder.

'Some motor, eh? Must have wads of cash, that bloke. Must be a gentleman bank robber or something. What d'you reckon?'

He turned to me but I couldn't speak.

'You alright?'

'Fine. It's just …'

'D'you know him?'

'No. He looks a bit like someone I know, that's all.'

I smiled. Less than twenty feet away stood Jonathan Dashwood-Silk. The leggy piece of skirt at his side was Melissa Jeffrey, Handy Dick's stuck-up Sales Manager. In gold leggings, a low-cut black vest and four-inch heels, on a caravan site in November, she looked like someone who charged by the hour.

Oh dear. A girl from Handy Dick's stable sleeping with the enemy. Well, it wasn't the first time.

Melissa was copulating her way to the top. She'd started as a sales rep, all tight skirts and glossy heels. She carried her laptop in a leather Louis Vuitton case, as fake as the fake tan she sprayed on every day. Male clients loved her, of course. And so her sales figures were as impressive as her sickeningly lithe physique. She certainly was a sleek filly. A thoroughbred.

Next to her, I was the old nag who romped home last.

She'd had brief liaisons with an array of seniors, including, it was rumoured, old Gerard-Claude Heroux. Frenchie himself. But someone had tipped his wife off and she'd been quickly dumped. But that hadn't hindered her progress. She was now queen of most (not all – not yet) of what she surveyed.

And now she was jumping Jonathan. He must be the odds-on favourite in the Promotion Stakes. She must have had an inside tip.

Standing at Jeff's caravan window, watching the pair of them disappear into number twenty-two, I knew there was no way I could live next door to my boss's shag pad.

By mid December, I was losing all hope. God! What if I actually become homeless?

I began to look at people who lived on the streets. Every day I passed a woman, probably around my age but with my mother's skin, camped out on the pavement a few hundred yards from the entrance to our car park, opposite the Spar. Whenever the police came and moved her on, she gathered herself and her belongings unhurriedly and with immense poise, bade the officers good day, and strode calmly away. She carried five plastic bags.

I wondered how many bags I could carry at one time.

I couldn't stay with Viv and Roger much longer. They hadn't said anything but poor Roger would soon need a bank loan to keep me in wine. And Viv would be thinking of Christmas and having her family home and where everyone was going to sleep. I felt rather like an abandoned puppy in need of a home for Christmas.

Sometimes easy solutions to difficult problems are staring us in the face. For weeks, Helen in Sales had been telling me she was clearing out her spare room, a space piled high with the charity donations she gathered from her extensive network of family and friends. Helen was Saving the Earth for the rest of us.

'It's getting a bit ridiculous, even for me.'

'How many bags are we talking about?'

'I counted them all last weekend. Two hundred and thirty-nine.'

'Oh, Helen!'

'I know. It's probably a health hazard. I might die in a black-bag-slide. But the charities can't keep up with me. Most of them will only take half a dozen bags at a time. I can't go on like this, though.'

'What are you going to do with it all?'

'It's going to Syrian refugees. The Coats for Calais people. There's a drop-off point in the car park of Sainsbury's, this weekend. I've got a friend with a van.'

'Great.'

'I know. It'll be nice to have the room back. Don't know what I'll do with it …'

A lightbulb moment.

'How about I pay you to live in it?'

'Eh?'

'I become your lodger.'

'You need a place to live?'

'I've been looking for months! Haven't you heard me banging on about it? Seen me scouring estate agents' websites?'

'No.'

'So?'

'Yeah. Sounds great. Tell you what, if you muck in with shifting my mountain of stuff and help me smarten the room up, you can have it rent-free.'

'Helen. I'm paying you rent. No arguments.'

'No …'

'Yes. But I'll gladly help you with Operation Black Bag.'

So Helen became my Christmas angel. We lifted and loaded and swept and emulsioned and two weeks later I was saying a tearful farewell to the lovely friends who'd saved my life and asked nothing in return.

We cling to life by a system of delicate threads held by others. When most of my threads had frayed and snapped, Viv and Roger had thrown a rope around me and held on tight.

Living with Helen was good fun. We laughed a lot, with and at each other. They say opposites attract. I was a bottle blonde in high heels and Helen was a mousy vegan in an Oxfam dress. She ridiculed my high street fashions, taunting me with propping up

Third-World sweatshops and child labour and I mocked her tree-hugging habit of washing out used foodbags and hanging them out to dry next to her knickers.

'It's had a bloody chicken and mayo sandwich in it!' I'd say, as she snatched a plastic bag out of the bin.

'You can't throw plastic away. It doesn't GO anywhere, you silly cow!'

'It's covered in mayonnaise.'

'It'll be fine.'

'You're nuts.'

'And you kill baby dolphins.'

Helen was fun and sweet and energetically kind. One of her kindnesses was making linen parcels filled with lavender flowers she'd dried herself. She gave dozens of them to charity shops to sell on and handed them out to her friends to put under their pillows to help them sleep.

I was still struggling with sleep. I reckoned I'd need a whole field of lavender to get me off. I was still relying on that other purple relaxant: the grape.

Someone who shared my predilection was Helen's boyfriend, Paul, although, as a committed vegan and tree-hugger, too, he always insisted on organic wines with Fairtrade labels, which was fine by me. He was a good guy with a ratty ponytail and a penchant for cheesecloths, but he never overstayed Helen's welcome and if he despised me for being too 'of this world', he had the good grace not to show it.

Before I knew it, it was Christmas party time. What joy.

I'd successfully got the HRTs onside with the news that Jonathan would be footing the drinks bill. This peace offering had sweetened my choice of venue, a room large enough to seat them a full hundred yards away from Dread Ed. Result.

The Bond theme dress code for the evening – dinner jackets for the men, evening gowns for the women – seemed to please everyone. Apart from Will, still sulking after I'd told him he couldn't come as Ursula Andress.

The evening hadn't started well. At five thirty, I'd still been at my desk waiting for Jonathan to return from his regular Friday frolic with the cash for the open bar. As it stood, I had just over an hour to drive to Helen's, change into the black 'hope it still fits' slinky number I bought two years ago but had never had the confidence to wear, then get out to the Royal Hotel.

Fed up with waiting for Jonathan, I'd gathered the pile of Secret Santa Christmas presents dumped on and around my desk and made my escape.

'What's in those bags?' I was hobbling to my car with two bin liners full of gifts. 'It's only our Secret Santa presents, Nigel. For the party? Tonight?'

'Hm.'

'I'm already running a bit late.'

'I'll need to look in the bags.'

'Nigel …'

'Regulations.'

Deep breath Jennifer.

'Fine.'

I dropped them to the ground. He took a perfunctory peek inside and saw the festive paper.

'Presents?'

'Yes. For tonight's party. Like I said.'

'Hm.'

'Would you like me to unwrap them? All sixty-eight of them?'

He produced his clipboard.

'Just sign here, please.'

'Certainly.'

Another five bloody minutes lost.

Fifty-two minutes later, after the quickest shower in the history of bathing, and having had time to apply only the scantiest layer of makeup, I staggered into Helen's front room pulling at the shoulder straps on my little black dress.

'Wow! You look great, Jen.'

'Do I really?' I glanced at myself in the full-length mirror by the door.

'Oh yes! God! So much nicer without all that makeup.'

'D'you think? I've been wearing that black eyeliner for years.'

'Well, on you, less is most definitely more. Well, *I'd* say.'

'My eyes and lips feel a bit … bare.'

'God, your eyes look great. And you look so much better without that red lipstick.'

'I don't know.'

'Here.' She rummaged in a bag by the side of her chair. 'Try this.'

I took the lipstick from her.

'Where did you get this?'

'A freebie. Peach. Have it. I'll never use it.'

I put some on. It looked good.

'What d'you think?'

'What a difference. You look gorgeous. Right, bugger off before you turn me.'

'Yeah, right.'

'Hang on. Turn round.'

'What?'

'There's something on your dress.'

Then I remembered. Why I'd never had it on.

'That bloody security tag! The dozy cow in Next left it on.'

The pair of us went at it with pliers for ten long minutes but the offending plastic device wouldn't budge. I had two choices. I could wear the dress, but look as though I was also wearing some kind of Asbo monitor, or quickly change into my trusted old trouser suit, which I'd worn at every works do for the last three years.

'Go with the dress. Nobody will notice with the lights dimmed.'

'Really?'

'Of course. Stick this pashmina round your shoulders. And stick your lips round this glass of chardonnay.'

In spite of Nigel's clipboard and the dress faff, I still managed to look and feel composed – actually rather glamorous – as I strolled through the reception of the Royal Hotel in my four-inch heels. The young lad on the desk gave me a smile and I felt (and, perhaps pitifully, enjoyed) his eyes on my back as I made my way to the Balmoral Suite.

I thought of Pete. The critical glances. The cruel remarks. The years of self-doubt.

With its high Victorian ceilings and glittering chandeliers, the Balmoral Suite was the perfect setting for our end-of-year celebration. Although our complimentary cocktails tasted more like cough mixture than 007 Martinis, nobody seemed to care.

Dread Ed was already at the bar, sporting the Santa hat and guffawing at some comment from a suit I didn't recognise, revelling in his exalted status for the evening. Thrilled to be chosen for the top spot, he was guarding the presents with a proprietorial air, arsehole that he was.

Of the other two candidates in the Santa ballot, Craig had received just a single vote (Will being the only one willing to sit on his lap) while Jonathan, entered by the HRTs, had missed out on the honour by only three votes, in spite of the vigorous campaign fought by his demonic devotees. For their part, the three witches, dressed all in black, had never looked more infernal as, drinking deeply of Jonathan's wine, they cackled and tossed their hair.

Fashionably late and making a grand entrance as usual, Jonathan breezed into the room looking especially suave in a dinner jacket cut to perfection, his Friday afternoon frolic adding an extra glow to his golden features.

I glanced around the room at my fellow workers, all openly enjoying the festivities, and I smiled to myself. This was the one night of the year when everyone buried the hatchet, forgot their gripes and their vendettas and clinked glasses and patted each other on the back.

Life could be good, it seemed. Perhaps it was just a matter of how you chose to look at it. But in this room, on this night, I felt like I was on the outside looking in. My life was on hold. I was still looking for it. The sign that would lead me in a new direction.

Jonathan appeared at my side.

'Merry Christmas, Jen.' His glass tilted alarmingly.

'Merry Christmas, Jonathan. You look like you're having a good time.'

'But are *you*? Are *you*, Jennifer Brown?'

What is it with men when they get a drink inside them?

'I'm fine, Jonathan.'

'Are you sure?'

I wasn't in the mood for male solicitousness.

'I'm fine. Really. But thanks for asking.'

As I stepped back, the security tag on my dress hooked a length of purple tinsel wrapped around a pillar, snagging my shoulder strap and giving the assembled company a good eyeful of my strapless bra. Not without aplomb, I pulled Helen's pashmina round my shoulders, wished my colleagues a Merry Christmas and sauntered off to find myself a taxi.

I was to be spending Christmas with my mother. Since my dad passed away, the house had become dreadfully cluttered. She just couldn't walk past a charity shop. Clocks were her latest obsession. She now had five of the buggers in the front room, all with strident chimes, all slightly out of sync, which meant each hour was marked by a discordant cacophony that lasted for a nerve-jangling sixty seconds.

Clutching a case with clothes for eight days, I walked up the crooked path where I'd played hopscotch, the paving slabs now cracked and covered with weeds. The neighbours from my childhood were all long gone, apart from Mrs Jennings next door. Most of the houses in the cul-de-sac were now occupied by families from Eastern Europe, whom my mum thought were the nicest people she'd ever met.

I knocked on the door several times. No answer. I walked round to the side of the house and peered in through the kitchen window. Mum was sitting at the table in the company of a young man who looked down on his luck. I pushed the kitchen door open.

'Hello, Mum.' I kissed her powdery face and breathed the familiar aroma of sweet violets.

'I see you've acquired a new friend.'

'Yes, dear. This is Leon. He's descended from a tribe in Equatorial Guinea.'

I chatted to Leon while my mum made coffee and tipped bourbon creams onto a china plate. Leon was twenty-six, had been homeless for seven months and was now living in a hostel near the train station. He sold the *Big Issue* in a prime spot outside the new Tesco. That's where Mum had got talking to him.

He was descended from a family in Wolverhampton.

Christmas lunch went fairly smoothly, considering , although an old metal filling at the back of my mouth didn't respond too well to Mum's novel idea of using a pound coin in the Christmas pudding. But her present to me was encouraging in a way, in that it showed she'd retained at least *some* of the last conversation we'd had about Pete. It was a copy of Delia's book *One is Fun!*

With the dishes done, we settled down in front of the TV. Mum couldn't understand why the BBC wasn't showing the Morecambe and Wise Christmas Special. After all, she watched it every year.

I scoured the channels and managed to find, on Dave, a rerun of the 1972 Christmas Special, the one with Glenda Jackson, so all was not lost. Mum lapped it up. Although she was worried that Eric was starting to lose his hair.

8

A New Year

Work was like the weather – stormy, miserable and cold. And Jonathan's mood matched the current climate. Perhaps he was under pressure from London. Or perhaps the spark had gone from his Friday afternoon frolics with Melissa. People he called in to see him would stop by my desk on the way and request mini forecasts.

From her seat in Sales, Helen fired me an email.

'He wants to see me. What's the weather like today?'

'Blustery, I'm afraid. Low pressure dominating. Little chance of sunshine.'

A reply pinged back.

'Thank you for the running commentary on my state of mind, Jennifer Brown!'

Bugger. I'd sent my reply to Jonathan.

I looked sheepishly up at his window. Storm clouds gathered along his brow.

By four o'clock, the gales had calmed to a gentle breeze. Jonathan perched on the edge of my desk.

'Am I a bastard?'

'What?'

'Do you give those ridiculous weather forecasts to everyone?' He looked wounded.

'You *can* be a little difficult at times.'

'Sorry. I'll try harder.'

January gave way to February. On the 11th, I put a little asterisk on my desk calendar. Six months to the day since I'd left Pete's. Numbness had been followed by tears and self-examination. These had been replaced by a new emotion: anger.

I was beginning to understand the fine line between love and hate.

Then, before I knew it, Spring was beckoning. I was sitting at my desk, reading an article on Julianne Moore and wondering if I should dye my hair red, when an email came in. Larry.

'Hi Jennifer. How would you be fixed for Sydney at the end of this month?'

God. He was still on for it.

'Oh, Larry. That would be fantastic.'

'Great. Send me your dates and I'll make the arrangements.'

This was really going to happen. Well, it was really going to happen if I could get it past Jonathan. A three-week holiday with two weeks' notice. It was pretty unreasonable. I'd have to finesse the deal.

For three days, I arrived early and stayed late. I bought a box of pastries and made a point of giving him first pick. I watched him like a hawk and gauged his mood. By Wednesday afternoon, he was looking chipper. I waited for him to come to me.

'Jen, why are you still here?' He looked at the clock. It was 6.37.

'Oh, you know. Stuff to do.' I smiled. Just doing my job. A trouper.

'Don't bury yourself in your job. It doesn't work. You need to switch off.'

'I know …'

'When was the last time you had a break?'

This script is writing itself.

'It's been a while, I guess.'

'Don't leave it too much longer.'

'Well, as a matter of fact …' And I told him about my Australia plans.

'Sounds great. You should go.'

'Oh, Jonathan. Really?'

'Of course.'

'I know it's ridiculously short notice.'

'It's fine.'

'I really appreciate it.'

'One condition, though.'

'What's that?'

'That you promise you'll come back.'

I had a spring in my step. I had something to look forward to and my smile was genuine. I no longer ran away from mirrors. A river of tears and a diet of toast and wine had got me down to a size 10. The magic number Pete had always coveted.

Larry had always been a bit of a ladies' man. Not a good-looking smoothie like Jonathan, but he had a presence. There was an aura about him. And it sounded like he was currently unattached. I wondered if he'd still find me attractive.

I remembered a look he'd once given me. We were in his car, top down, heading into London, show tickets in his pocket, the stereo belting out Kylie's *Can't Get You Out of My Head*. Larry had turned to me. No words. Just a warm look in his eyes.

'Prick Stick?'

Jonathan's voice jolted me out of my daydream.

'Hm?'

'The chap in Supplies wants to know what it is. This item in your stationery order. Sixteen Prick Sticks.'

'Sorry. But, come on. It's obviously a typo. It's obviously meant to be Pritt Stick. Why are they even bothering to …'

'We cannot allow it, Mr Dashwood Silk!'

Not Allowed Nigel slammed his clipboard down on my desk.

'What is it, Nigel?' Silky oil on troubled waters.

'They are continuing to brew tea using their own kettle! In spite of my instructions to the contrary!'

'Who is?'

'Those ladies. The three who sit in the corner.'

'I'll speak to them.'

'It's a non-compliance. Bringing electrical equipment into the workplace.'

'I'll make that clear. A non-compliance.'

Nigel turned on his heels and strode out of the office, his little book of regulations in his hand and the confiscated kettle tucked under his arm.

I turned to Jonathan.

'You were asking about a Prick Stick?'

Prick Stick Nigel had been on *my* case as well. I'd forgotten to lock my pedestal one evening. Nigel had found the drawer unlocked on his rounds. To make matters worse, the contents weren't exactly conventional. A bottle of chardonnay and a double F cup bra.

'You'll need to explain this.' He'd stood over me, pointing at the contents of the open drawer.

There was a perfectly good explanation, of course. The wine had been a thank-you from Jonathan, for picking him up from one of his regular wine-tastings, and I'd dumped the bra in my desk after one of the wires had come loose and was digging into my ribs. Thank goodness Handy Dick hadn't been around at the time, and it had been Craig's day off.

But I wasn't about to explain myself to old chip-fat head. I refused to prop up the police state he was seeking to impose, one ridiculous regulation at a time. What next? An Explanation Form? I wouldn't put it past him. Then, clutching the completed form, I'd be summoned to his office in the bowels of the building, in some previously undiscovered Stasi-like corridor – all creams and browns – and I'd find his little window. He'd slide it back and grab the form off me. I'd look past him at the piles of buff folders on his desk, the walls lined with thousands more folders – the fruits of his snoopings – and heavy volumes of beloved regulations. His desk would be strewn with mug shots of his suspects, mine on top, my face obscured by a red stamp. *Guilty of Possessing a Red Brassiere.*

'Just what do you think there is to explain, Nigel? The wine is a present and the bra is mine. I took it off because the wire snapped.'

I lifted it out and held it under his nose.

'Perhaps you'd like to inspect it? Or put it on me. To check the fit. Establish it really *is* mine. Establish I'm telling the truth. Hm?'

'There's no need for that.'

'No.'

'Just … er …'

'Yes?'

'… er … don't let it happen again.'

'I'll have a stern word with my generous friends. And my wayward underwear.'

'What? No, I mean …'

'Are we finished?'

'Erm … yes.'

'No we're not. There's one more thing, Nigel.'

'What?'

'Your flies are undone.'

9

Down Under

May arrived with the promise of warm days. And Jonathan's weather forecasts had also grown sunnier.

Along with the blue skies, my airline ticket to Australia had arrived. I'd be flying with Singapore Airlines. Very swish. But it got better. Larry had booked me into Business Class! I checked it out online. Lie-flat comfort. Global cuisine. An onboard lounge with a bar. A bloody bar. On a plane!

I skipped along the corridor to the canteen and sat down in front of Will, waving my ticket.

'Singapore Airlines. Cool.'

'Business Class.'

'You're joking.'

'No! Look!'

'Do you know how much that costs, Jen?'

'No. Do you?'

He took out his phone, punched some keys, then showed me the screen. I felt myself blush.

'My god!'

'I think he's keen. Keen and very rich.'

'My god.'

'Just …'

'What?'

'Be careful. I don't want your heart broken again. Not after I've just fixed it.'

Will cut his iced bun in half and handed me a piece.

The Business Class lounge at Heathrow was very different from the terminal at Gatwick where my usual summer holidays began. I was fast-tracked through security then whisked into an oasis of calm by a twenty-five-year-old with matinee-idol looks. He ushered me into a comfortable leather armchair. A glass of chilled, lightly oaked chardonnay was delivered to my elbow seconds later. *Well, Jennifer Brown, you're certainly moving in exalted circles.*

A short walk from the Lounge took me directly to the door of the plane. No hanging around. No queuing. No mad rush. And on the plane, peace, comfort and champagne. I pinched myself.

Still the luxuries came. A goodie bag with an array of treats, including, incredibly, a pair of 'flight pyjamas' in cotton and silk. Black.

After a dinner of grilled lamb and several glasses of Rioja (suggested by the wine waiter as the perfect companion to lamb), I was flying high in more than one sense. Then the cabin lights dimmed, I slipped into my flight pyjamas and, seventeen seconds later, fell fast asleep.

Several hours later, my window showed me the scorched wilderness of the Arabian Peninsula. Desert later gave way to snow-capped peak then to lush green rainforest and we were soon making our descent into Singapore. Then I watched a couple of romcoms on the short hop from Singapore to Oz, refusing free alcohol so as not to arrive in Sydney on a trolley. As the plane's nose dipped, I looked at my watch and imagined Larry making his way to the Arrivals Hall.

My stomach lurched and familiar waves of self-doubt washed over me. *Come on, you daft cow! You're gorgeous!*

Perhaps just one glass of wine. To boost my confidence.

I scanned the crowd for Larry. I hoped he wasn't standing there looking at me and thinking what a mistake he'd made.

'Fifteen years and you haven't aged a day.'

A familiar voice behind me.

'Hi, Larry.'

'My god. Look at you.'

'It's good to see you.'

And it was. He'd put on a few pounds and his hair was thinner, but his eyes were the same. Laughing eyes still full of mischief.

'Welcome to Sydney.'

He stepped forward and hugged me, holding me tight for several seconds. It was nice to be in his arms. When he released me, I felt myself flush and he looked away.

Then he grabbed my bags.

'Right. Let's get you some coffee.'

We sped along the highway in his black Porsche, heading into the city, the sun already warm at eight in the morning, the low-rise buildings of the suburbs giving way to the towering hotels and office blocks of the fabulous metropolis. Commuters hurried, car horns hooted, taxis weaved frantically from lane to lane, desperate for another fare. But in all the mayhem I felt utterly relaxed, as I always had in Larry's company. The years had clearly not changed that.

The sunlight sparkled on the waters of the famous bay and danced on the white sails of the iconic opera house. Larry pulled the Porsche off the highway.

'You'll love The Rocks. Best views. And best coffee.'

We sat in the sunshine. Water lapped against the quay as the ferries and taxis sailed in and out, delivering busy people to their busy lives. They swirled around outside my bubble of relaxation. The warmth of the sun and the genuine warmth of Larry's welcome had cast a spell on me. Life felt good.

I must have looked wistful.

'Life is for living, Jen.'

'Yes.'

'You know that, don't you?'

'Yes. I do.'

'No more tears.'

'What? Never?'

'Well, not for a while. Not for him.'

'No.'

'He wasn't worth it.'

'He wasn't.'

'You've got such a lot going for you.'

'Good friends mean a lot.'

'Not just friends. You. You're a great person.'

'You're very kind.'

'I mean it. You're gorgeous. In every way. Always were.'

Such a lovely thing to hear.

'I can never thank you enough for this. Being here, with you, it's doing me the world of good already.'

'It's good for me, too. To have you here.'

My smile turned into a yawn.

'I'm so sorry!'

I checked my watch. It was only quarter past nine but I'd been awake since Riyadh and the time difference was taking effect.

Larry downed his coffee.

'Let's go. You're bushed.'

Quay West was a luxury apartment hotel overlooking the harbour. It had a recreational deck on level 24. From the sunken Roman-style pool, you had majestic views of the Bridge and the Opera House. That's what it said in the brochure on the bedside table in the one-room apartment Larry had rented for me on the fourteenth floor.

'This is too much.'

'Not for you.'

'I'll never be able to repay you.'

'You don't have to.'

'It's so good to see you.'

'You, too. To see you're still the lovely English girl who captured my heart.'

This was going too well. There was a bottle of wine – a Clare Valley Riesling – on the kitchen counter. I opened a drawer, looking for a corkscrew.

'Let's drink to friendship.'

Larry's mobile rang. He pulled it from his pocket and checked the screen.

'Sorry. I'll have to take this.'

He walked over to the window. I carried on looking for a corkscrew.

'I'll have to rush off, Jen. Catch up on some sleep and I'll call you later.'

I looked down from my lofty heights as Larry pulled away from the quay in his sleek black beauty.

I suddenly felt wide awake, so I set about exploring the luxury that was to be my home for the next three weeks.

I'd stepped straight into the glossy pages of *The World of Interiors*. Modern, simple, stylish. Soft leather sofas. White carpets. Wall-mounted Ultra HD TV.

In the kitchen, polished black units and chrome fittings. A cooker with more controls than the deck of the Starship Enterprise.

The bedroom had another deep white carpet, enough wardrobe space for Karl Lagerfeld's entire Spring Collection and, in the middle of the room, an enormous circular bed. Ample room for two.

A rush of excitement ran through my body. Did I want to rekindle my romance with Larry? Did he?

I stood at the window and gazed out at the brilliant blue Sydney morning and wondered what these three weeks would bring.

After a long shower, I stretched out on the bed and wrapped myself in its crisp white linens and raised a glass of the now-chilled Riesling to my reflection in the wardrobe mirror. *To a new life.*

I woke to total darkness. 8.34. I'd slept for nine hours. The blue morning skies had morphed into star-studded velvet framed by towers of neon.

My phone buzzed on the bedside table.

'What d'you think of the view?'

'It's absolutely amazing. Thank you.'

'Stop thanking me. Did you sleep?'

'Only all day. I've just woken up.'

'Good. Feel okay?'

'Feel great.'

'Terrific. Listen, Jen. Work's a bugger right now. Will you be okay if you don't see me for a couple of days?'

'Of course.'

'Sure?'

'Do what you need to do. I'll be fine. More than fine. Who wouldn't be?'

'I'll call you.'

Larry phoned me every day but I didn't see much of him that first week. Sydney has manifold riches to offer the sight-hungry tourist and I was feeling ravenous.

The best way to explore the city was on one of the ferries that ran from Circular Quay, a bustling centre five minutes' walk from the Opera House. I visited Darling Harbour, watched sharks glide silently over my head in the Aquarium's perspex tunnels, and wandered round the Royal Botanic Gardens marvelling at the parrots and the fruit bats in the trees and running my fingers through native tea trees and lemon-scented grasses.

I strolled down the quaint cobbled streets of The Rocks and wandered into art galleries, boutique dress shops and waterfront cafes.

The sense of space, and of having the time to enjoy it, was immensely relaxing. And it was educational. I was learning to enjoy myself. To enjoy my own company.

And it must have been showing. When I stooped to drop some coins into the hat of an aboriginal man, cross-legged on the cobbles and blowing away at a didgeridoo, he stopped playing. Instantly.

For a horrible second, I thought I'd offended him. Then his richly painted face broke into a smile.

'Thank you, sista. You are deadly sista. Murrook sista.'

'Sorry?'

'Good lady. Very good. And very happy.'

'Thank you. Yes. Yes I am.'

In the second week, Larry and I enjoyed long conversations over dinner. We reminisced about our time together in Southsea and we talked about our expectations for the future and about the cards life had dealt us during the last ten years.

There'd been some major changes in Larry's personal life. He now had a daughter. And an ex-wife. He was vague about his current romantic status. He shared a house with his best mate, John, in the suburb of Vaucluse, right on the water. I began to wonder if he was working up to telling me he was gay.

What did become clear that week was that, gay or not, Larry had no romantic intentions towards me at all. I was at my most charming, the sun was doing pleasant things to my skin, and my double F cleavage had never been displayed to better effect. And there was affection in Larry's eyes – a very deep affection – but we were always going to be just friends.

He'd moved on. I also thought he probably preferred the old me. The dim, naïve, artless Jennifer Brown who'd served him 'gin with a bit of lemon' back in the restaurant days. I wasn't that girl anymore. Larry could see that. It's not that he was your typical Aussie male – all tinnies and rugby and knob jokes – but there was part of him that liked to be in charge. To be the wise owl. The comforter.

I felt I'd moved beyond that. Gained my own wisdom. Found comfort in my own company. In just being me. The long healing process was at an end, hastened by these few days of sunshine and blissful solitude.

I looked at Larry. He was a good friend but that was it. He didn't want me as a lover. The initial twinge of disappointment, rejection even, had dissolved in the realisation that I actually didn't want to give my heart to anyone. Didn't need to. And that realisation was profoundly liberating.

And, with romance off the table, we'd be free to enjoy each other's company for another whole week.

'What about a day's sailing?

'Sounds great.'

'I keep a little boat at a marina on the North Shore.'

I remembered the last time a friend had suggested some time on the water. A booze cruise to Boulogne with three girls from the office. Force eight winds on the way back. Vomit on my gold slingbacks.

'You have your own boat?'

'Yeah. Lots of guys do here. Nothing fancy. A Jeanneau Sun Odyssey. Just a thirty-footer.'

'A yacht? A sailing boat?'

'Sure. Sail is where the fun is. Nothing like it.'

'Okay.'

'Great. Forecast for tomorrow is good. How about I get you at 7? Make the best of the day?'

Larry struggled along the jetty under the weight of a coolbox the size of a blanket chest.

'That's her. The *Lucky Lady*.'

The boat's sleek white hull was dazzling in the morning sun and her decks were all new varnish and polished brass. Larry hauled the coolbox onto the deck, climbed aboard and stretched an arm out towards me. I took his hand and stepped gingerly on after him.

'I hope she'll still feel lucky after having me onboard for the day. I'm not exactly what you'd call an experienced mariner.'

'Relax. You'll do fine. Put this on.'

He handed me what looked like an inflatable scarf.

'It's a deck vest. We always wear them.'

'A life jacket?'

'A precaution. It's the rules. You can't muck about with safety on a boat.'

'Are there sharks around here?'

'There's wine in the cooler. Let's get this stuff stowed below, have ourselves a glass of wine, and set sail for Scotland Island. Perfect place for a picnic.'

He lifted the bulk of the coolbox.

'I'm not taking any of this stuff back.'

We motored out of the marina, Larry naming the various spots we passed.

'That's the zoo, and then Clifton Gardens. And over there is Vaucluse. That's where I live.'

Comfortable-looking houses lined the waterfront. Life for Larry was good.

'We'll hoist the sails when we pass the point.'

Within minutes, Larry was cutting the motor and untying the blue canvas sail cover and stowing it in a locker. He handed me a rope.

'Here. Haul on this. You're the chief mate.'

I pulled on the rope and the crisp white sail slid smoothly up the mast. Larry took it off me and tied it up with a practised hand. Then he stood at the wheel, glanced up at the sail then ahead at the sky with an odd, bird-like motion, then turned to me with a smile.

'That's it. We can relax now. Put your feet up.'

I lay on the deck with my back against a locker and my face in the sun, listening to the swish of water against the hull and the odd flap of canvas when the wind shifted.

As we headed north along the coast, past Manly and Freshwater and North Curl Curl, the water became a little choppier and Larry clipped a safety cable to my vest. Spray hit my face as the *Lucky Lady* rode the waves. It was exhilarating.

After an hour or so, we headed inland and the waves started to subside. As we entered the shelter of a small cove, Larry dropped the mainsail in a jiffy and fired up the engine and we chugged towards the shore to drop anchor.

Larry turned off the engine and a bewitching silence reigned. We were in a gorgeous little bay with turquoise water and white sand. Above us, a hillside was covered in strange, toadstool-shaped trees. It was like another world.

'Nice, isn't it?'

'It's not too shabby at all.'

We lay on the deck, basking in the hot sun, drinking chilled wine and feasting on cold chicken and olives and cheese.

We spent a glorious afternoon in companionable silence, broken occasionally by Larry.

'It's not a bad life, Jen. What d'you say?'

'Not bad.'

Hours later, when the sun was beginning to dip seawards, we reluctantly bade farewell to this magical inlet. When life was a bugger, when dark winter thoughts crowded in on me, this is the place I'd come back to in my mind.

A biting wind had blown up as the boat headed south. It was a choppy passage down the coast. But Larry sailed expertly through the waves and we were soon rounding the point, dropping the sail and motoring past the zoo and into the marina.

The waves began to subside as the small outboard motored us back to the jetty. Larry stowed the mainsail and I made my way to the stern, ready to help Larry guide her back to her berth, feeling like a proper mariner after a few short hours on the water.

As we edged in slowly, I looked up and saw a little girl waving excitedly. Beside her stood a woman, hands placed firmly on hips. She wore wraparound shades but I didn't need to see her eyes to know they were hurling daggers in my direction. She clearly wasn't there to wish me a happy holiday. Larry hadn't spotted the welcoming committee.

'Somebody's trying to get your attention, Larry.'

'Holy shit!'

'What?'

'It's Jackie.'

The sunkissed glow drained from Larry's face. Looked like he hadn't been completely honest about his relationship with his ex.

'What do you want me to do?' Embarrassment was vying with anger for the top spot. I was on the wrong end of something that clearly wasn't my fault.

Larry's hands were shaking as he secured the final rope. That's right, mate. Tie it nice and tight or she'll have it round your neck.

He jumped across to the jetty to face his fate.

'What the HELL! On MY boat?!'

The woman I now knew as Jackie spewed forth a torrent of invective. Within seconds, a small crowd had gathered on the jetty, keen to see the Incredible Shrieking Woman.

I wouldn't have been able to escape without pushing past the sideshow and, besides, Larry looked to be in serious danger of being pushed into the drink and I didn't fancy taking an evening dip with him.

In times of stress, I always find it therapeutic to drink alcohol. There was an unopened bottle of chardonnay in the galley, which would be my refuge for now. A few large glugs would give me some

Dutch courage for the confrontation to follow. Screw top. No glass. *Oh well. I'm not proud.*

Larry suddenly appeared at my side. I put the bottle down and wiped my mouth. I smiled at him.

'So what's going on?'

He looked ashen. He spoke in a whisper.

'Look, Jen. Whatever happens, for God's sake don't mention your name.'

'To your wife?'

'My ex-wife.'

'Doesn't look very ex.'

'Just please don't tell her your name.'

'Why?'

'It's just that … over the years I've …'

'Yes?'

'… kind of talked about you a bit. A lot.'

'A lot.'

'So Jackie says. *That bloody English girl.* It seems to have … got under her skin.'

'Right.'

'So …'

'Yes?'

'Can you sort of …'

'Pretend to be someone else?'

Would you?'

I took another belt from the bottle.

'Sure.'

I pulled on my sunglasses and made an effort to stand up. *Keep cool, Jen.*

Jackie's hands were still riveted to her hips.

'Had a good day? On MY boat? With MY husband?'

The wine had made me feel I could pull off an Aussie accent.

'Oi hed no oidea. Mate.'

'I suppose you expect him to pay for a cab as well?'

The woman scorned looked me up and down, the way Melissa did when I'd been in with Jonathan.

Pay for a cab *as well!*

I looked down at myself. Short shorts. Tanned legs. Skimpy vest. Double Fs straining to get out. I have to admit that, on the evidence, it was a reasonable assumption on her part.

But the role of the hired entertainment wasn't one I was entirely comfortable playing and part of me wanted to give the game away and throw it in her face. Well if you want to pay for a cab to take me all the way back the UK love, it's gonna cost you a few bob. And, yes, I did have a great day on your boat, with your husband. But he's the one to blame for this misunderstanding. So I'll gladly help you strangle him with his mooring rope.

Then I looked at Larry. A naughty schoolboy caught with his pants down.

'No worries, mate. I'll get the bus.'

I stepped slowly past the two of them, half expecting Jackie to throw a punch. Then I tiptoed along the wooden jetty in my bare feet. Walking the plank. *Just keep going, Jen. Even if it isn't in a perfectly straight line ...*

They were still shouting at each other as I turned the corner. I looked around. Where the hell would I go from here? I reckoned it was at least fifteen miles back to the apartment. But which way?

Through my alcoholic haze, I began to feel rather sorry for Jackie. She'd been confronted with 'the other woman'. I knew how that felt. I was a bit ashamed of myself for playing along with Larry's charade. I thought about going back and telling her all was very much *not* as it seemed.

I heard an engine revving, then another. Seconds later, Larry's Porsche came flying round the corner and sped past me, closely pursued by a second sporty number, with Jackie at the wheel. Then I remembered. My handbag. Still on the boat, with my purse in it.

Stranded. No handbag, no purse, and no shoes.

I sat down on a wooden bench, overlooking the marina. I watched a couple of yachts motor in. A family, all blues and reds, like something out of a Henri Lloyd catalogue, all happy and smiling and joking with each other. A very appealing little tableau. Then a man in his sixties, weatherbeaten and fit-looking. I wondered if he had paid entertainment onboard, and an irate ex-wife on the quayside.

Evening had turned to dusk and I was beginning to feel cold. I needed a plan. But with no shoes and no money, my options were pretty limited. With the unfamiliar sounds of Australian wildlife crowding in around me, I suddenly felt like a hopeless little girl.

Then, just as I'd decided on a plan that involved knocking on someone's door and bursting into tears, a car approached and slowed in front of me. *My god! I must really look like a hooker!*

The driver wound down the window. I stood up to give him a mouthful but he spoke first.

'Jennifer? Jennifer Brown?'

'Who are you?'

'Craig. Friend of Larry's. He's sent me to take you back to your apartment.'

On the one hand, a car, a strange man, and my mother's warning. On the other, a quayside bench as my bed for the night.

Craig spent the half-hour journey defending his friend. Things had been difficult between him and Jackie. Larry had broken it off several times, but Jackie couldn't let go, and the little girl was Jackie's trump card.

I felt sorry for them both. It was a mess. But I was still furious with Larry for putting me in such an awkward position. Craig dropped me at the door.

'Don't judge Larry too harshly. He's a good guy trying to do the right thing by everyone.'

Maybe. I was exhausted. I really needed a shower. In the lift, an immaculately dressed couple looked at my bare feet and my beachwear then looked away, the image too distasteful.

I flopped onto the leather sofa with a glass of wine and thought about what Craig had said. Weariness had taken the edge off my irritation. In some ways, I was partly to blame. *I* was the one who'd initially contacted Larry. I'd made no secret of my own domestic chaos and I must have come across as a bit needy. He'd been a shoulder to cry on. A good friend. And a tremendously generous one.

And he hadn't exactly lied about his own circumstances, but he hadn't been entirely truthful either.

I suppose both of us had been looking back, remembering the good times we'd had together. A pleasant past is a seductive thing when the present's not so great.

I drained my glass and poured another. I opened the box of chocolates Larry had left by the bottle.

The next thing I knew, a phone was ringing. My watch said 3.57. I blinked, pulled myself off the couch, walked over to the window and lifted the receiver. It was Larry.

'I'm really sorry, Jen.'

'I'm still angry with you.'

'I know. I should have told you. But it really is over between Jackie and me. Has been for a good two years.'

'Didn't look over.'

'She thinks she can persuade me to go back. Give it another go.'

'Look, Larry. What you and Jackie do or don't do with your relationship is no business of mine. You and I … well, we're just mates. I thought we could be something else, but …'

'Good mates.'

'Yeah. I'm just angry at being put in that position.'

'I know.'

'A pawn. A piggy in the middle.'

'I'm sorry.'

'Playing the part of a bloody hooker.'

'Really, I am.'

I stood looking out across the city at the never-ending light show of traffic. Then I looked at my reflection in the mirror. I had chocolate-coloured drool on my chin.

'It's fine.'

'Anyway, I've told her.'

'What d'you mean?'

'Who you are.'

'Oh, Larry.'

'She was standing there, just BAWLING at me.'

I knew that feeling. Pete. Me just standing there and taking all his ridicule. His spite. His venom.

'And demanding to know how I could bring a blonde bimbo onto OUR boat. And that was it.'

'What?'

'*Bimbo*. I wasn't having that.'

'It's fine. I've been called worse.'

'No. That's not acceptable.'

'You're sweet.'

I told her, That 'bimbo' has more guts, more brains and more love in her heart than you'll ever have. And then I told her. That you're my Jennifer. From the UK.

'Oh dear.'

'She went nuts.'

'Yes.'

'I told her there was nothing going on. That you'd come over as a friend.'

'And?'

'She didn't believe me, of course. You've seen her. Seen what she's like.'

'Yes.'

'And then Lily came in. Which made it worse.'

'Why?'

'She said, Daddy's friend is nice. Isn't she pretty, mummy?'

'Ah. Not good.'

'What are you doing now?'

'Well, I *was* sleeping. Then the phone rang.'

'Can you get dressed now and leave the apartment?'

'In the middle of the night?'

'It's just a precaution.'

'A precaution. Against what?'

'Jackie.'

'WHAT?'

'Things have gone downhill a bit here. She's been digging around on my laptop and on my phone, looking at emails and texts, trying to find love letters that aren't there. She's tried calling you. I'm glad you didn't answer.

'My phone's still on your boat. And my shoes.'

'Yeah. I figured. About the phone. I've got Craig driving over to get them.'

'Craig?'

'But she did find the paperwork for the apartment. She thinks I'm keeping you there.'

'What d'you mean, *keeping*?'

'As a mistress.'

'Great.'

'She's taken my car keys and thrown them in the harbour. She's just driven off like a maniac. Jen? You still there?'

Fatal bloody Attraction. I wonder how long I have left to live.

'Yeah, I'm still here.'

'I think she's on her way to pay you a visit.'

'Oh god.'

'Don't panic, mate. Just get dressed and go for a walk.'

'Larry, you *absolute* ...'

'I know. I'm really sorry.'

I slammed the phone down. I pulled on a sweatshirt and grabbed a handful of cash. Then I sprinted out of the apartment and pressed the button for the lift. Then I had a vision of Jackie already in the building. Already riding up in the lift. Already with the knife in her hand.

I pulled up the hood of my sweatshirt and found the door to the stairs, feeling ridiculous and terrified at the same time. This wasn't a movie but it felt like one. Feeling that I was playing a part helped me to defuse the panic.

I bloody hate men.

Outside, it was beginning to get light. I stood on the pavement and scanned the street for a car driven by a homicidal maniac. Nothing. Just a taxi, a truck delivering bread, and a handful of committed runners.

The smell of bread suddenly made me feel ravenously hungry (I hadn't properly eaten since our picnic in Scotland Bay) and I headed towards the magnificent bulk of the Harbour Bridge in search of an all-night breakfast.

One hour later, with a bucket of coffee and two chocolate croissants inside me, normality returned. The awkward confrontation with Jackie, Larry's account of her flare-up, and my night-time flight, all now seemed ridiculous. If Jackie were to walk into this café now, knife or no knife, I'd be ready for her. I wasn't prepared to play the fugitive any more.

As I reached the apartment, I saw a familiar car. Craig got out to greet me.

'Your phone. And your shoes.'

'Thanks.'

'Larry's going to call you.'

'Look, Craig …'

'He's a mess, Jennifer. He didn't want any of this to happen.'

'He's not the only one.'

'He feels terrible.'

'Does he?'

'Just … let him make it up to you.'

'He's done enough.'

'Please.'

'We'll see.'

An hour later, I was loading my cases into Larry's boot. We made our way out of the city. Ten minutes of stony silence, broken by Larry.

'Got my car back.'

'So I see. Did you have to go fishing?'

'Eh?'

'For the keys.'

'Right. No. No fishing. I phoned Porsche. Guy came out with a new set. Six hundred dollars.'

'Bloody hell.'

'It's fine.'

'Larry …'

'Jen. Let me. You've been messed around enough lately, without all this. This was supposed to be a break. A chance to get your head together. That's what I wanted for you. I just want good things for you.'

'You've given me lovely things.'

'But this. All this nonsense with Jackie.'

'It's none of my business.'

'It's completely over.'

'It doesn't matter.'

'It does. It matters to *me*. That you accept I'm telling you the truth.'

'Okay.'

'It *is* completely over between me and Jackie. But, for Lily's sake, I have to see her.'

'Of course.'

'And Jackie keeps pretending we can make a go of it. But we can't.'

'No?'

'No. God! You've seen her.'

'She's gorgeous.'

'She's a nut job.'

'She can certainly be fiery.'

'She's a nightmare. Which is why it'll never work. It's over.'

'Okay.'

'I'm not some guy who gets his kicks from messing his wife around. And messing his friends around.'

'I know.'

'So. We're okay?'

'We're fine.'

'Great.'

'Where are we going?'

'You'll see.'

Manly was a lovely resort, half an hour up the road from the city's skyscrapers. Long stretches of golden sand. Rows of cute shops and cafés. A small-town atmosphere that was a refreshing change from the frantic city.

Larry had taken a few days off. We stayed in a pretty waterfront B&B (separate rooms, thank you very much) and ate gorgeous salads for lunch and lobster for dinner. I spent the days lying on the white sand reading trashy novels while Larry swam and fished. He gave me his company when I wanted it and gave me space when he could see I needed it. In short, he was a good friend. A good friend who drank too much, smoked forty a day, and had a rollercoaster personal life I didn't want any part of. How quickly things can change.

Standing at the departure gate, my eyes filled with tears.

'It's been good to see you, Jen. After all these years.'

'It's been nice.'

'I'm so sorry. I didn't mean to make you cry.'

But he'd got it wrong. I wasn't crying for him, because it hadn't worked out with him. That little daydream had evaporated very early on. I was crying because he'd been so good to me. And good *for* me. He'd given me not just a little slice of luxury but the space to think about who I wanted to be.

And I was crying because I knew I'd never see him again.

The Arrivals Hall at Heathrow was a sea of expectant faces, scanning the disgorged crowds for their friends and their loved ones. Dozens of drivers stood at the barrier waiting for their charges, names scrawled on placards, some of them illegible, some unpronounceable. One of them read, simply, 'Hurt', and I thought, yes, it does a bit, being back in this dull grey shithole. Back in my dull grey life.

Then a man brushed past me and shook hands with the placard man and I saw it was the actor, William Hurt. Looking his age.

On the train back to Helen's, the elderly man sitting next to me seemed keen to chat.

'Been somewhere nice?'

'I have, actually. I've been to Sydney. To visit an old friend.'

'A man?'

Cheeky sod. That's a bit personal.

'Yes.'

'Thought so.'

'Why?'

'Lovely lady like you. Has to be a man at the bottom of it.'

'You're an old smoothie, aren't you?'

'I try. And less of the *old*.'

'My apologies.'

'And he let you go?'

'Sorry?'

'This old friend. In Sydney. He let you go?'

'It's complicated.'

'He's an idiot.'

'Yes. He is.'

When I walked into the office on Monday, Jonathan looked like he'd spent a couple of weeks in the trenches.

'Thank goodness you're back!'

'What's up?'

'Zilla.'

'What?'

'More like bloody GODzilla!'

'What are you talking about?'

'Zilla. The bloody useless temp the agency sent me.'

'Oh. Right. No good?'

'Spends more time painting her fingernails and chatting to her boyfriend on the phone than doing any actual work.'

'Oh dear.'

'Snakeskin trousers.'

'What?'

'She wears snakeskin trousers. In the office.'

'Right.'

'Don't ever leave me again. Please.'

Within a couple of hours, I was back in the old routine. Taking phone calls, answering emails, arranging meetings. Then a sweaty presence at my shoulder.

'Hello, Jennifer. Nice to see you back.'

I bet it is, you perv. Handy Dick. Eyes on the prize.

'How was your holiday?'

'Hello, Richard. What can I do for you?'

'Nothing, dear. Nothing at all. Just came to say hello.'

'Right.'

'I think he's missed you.'

'Who?'

'Your boss.'

'Yes, so I gather.'

'He's been lost without you. He's come to rely on you, you see. We all have.'

Well, my friends, don't get too comfortable. Because, if it's one thing my little Australian foray has taught me, it's that I want more than this. That I deserve more than this. So don't get used to me being around.

It isn't going to last long.

10

The Conference

I was scrolling through an employment website when Jonathan appeared at my elbow, making me jump and immediately shut down my browser.

'Everything okay?'

'Fine, Jonathan. You just startled me.'

'Hm.'

'Do you need something?'

'I'm off to a seminar. One of the speakers is a guy I want to poach as a customer. If I get him, could be good for me.'

'Sounds good.'

'I thought you might like to come, too.'

I was only just back from Oz, but I was already fed up with the office. An awayday was just what I needed.

'Sounds good. When it is?'

'Tomorrow afternoon. Canary Wharf.'

I pulled out my entire wardrobe and gave Helen a fashion show. Pretty much everything I owned was not seminar material: too tight, too short, too low-cut. I tried on some stuff of Helen's but I just looked like an old hippy. After an hour and a half of hilarity mixed with depression and Shiraz, it came down to a straight choice between my ancient navy suit (interviews, weddings, bar mitzvahs) and a beige two-piece wool number that hadn't seen the light of day since a rather stiff garden party in 2002.

The blue suit won, tarted up with a pink silk scarf Helen had unearthed somewhere for fifty pence. The resulting ensemble was a bit Vanessa Redgrave but it'd have to do.

On the way to the station, the satnav on my new phone was trying to reroute me (*Turn left, mate*) to avoid some sort of congestion ahead. I'd set the voice to Australian Bruce to keep me in a holiday frame of mind (if I'd tuned in to Bruce *before* my trip, I might have made a better job of the Aussie accent at the marina).

Sly and the Family Stone came on the radio and I turned the volume up to eleven and belted out *You Can Make it if You Really Want*, winding the window down to give everyone the benefit of my electric performance. The traffic was slowing and Bruce was still trying to get me to turn left. Daft sod. He hadn't reckoned with the stadium-sized Gala Bingo hall thrown up in the last six months.

A line of brake lights ahead. The rental van in front of me came to a stop. I looked at my watch. Fifteen minutes until my train. The station five minutes away in normal traffic. Don't panic.

Five minutes later we hadn't budged. Some drivers were leaning on their horns (*Why do people do that?*) and others had climbed out of their cars to peer up the long line of vehicles going nowhere.

I decided to peer. Sure enough, something was blocking the road, about a dozen cars ahead. I stood on the sill of my little blue Peugeot and craned my neck to get a better view. There'd been a collision on a roundabout. I could see the drivers of both vehicles. They seemed to be having a stand-up row.

Then my blood went cold.

One of the drivers was a young man in his twenties. He was backing off with his hands in the air as the other man poked a finger into his chest and screamed abuse at the top of his voice. An irate voice I could hear quite clearly from a distance of a couple of hundred yards. A voice I knew uncomfortably well.

Seeing Pete in the flesh again hit me like a bolt of lightning. My heart started to pound in my chest. I felt sick. The sight of that face, twisted in anger, brought it all back. I could feel myself sweating through my cream silk blouse.

A siren wailed somewhere behind me, then a police car flashed past, weaving its way through the traffic. I watched as it pulled up at the roundabout. Two officers climbed out. Pete started shouting at both of them. He was still shouting as the officers ushered him back into his car and directed him and the other driver over to a lay-by.

Brucie was still urging me to turn left. I unceremoniously unplugged him and shoved him into my handbag.

The traffic began to edge forward. A minute later my car was crawling alongside Pete's. I stared straight ahead and hoped he hadn't noticed me. I needn't have worried — he was far too busy bawling at the young lad who'd put a dent in his car.

When I pulled into the station car park, I had three minutes to catch my train. As I lifted my handbag and my laptop, I checked my face in the rear-view mirror. My cheeks were lined with tear-streaked mascara. I looked like Alice Cooper.

Christ. That man still had the power to make me bloody well cry.

By the time I reached Waterloo, I needed a coffee. I grabbed a double caramel latte with extra cream and, herded along with twenty thousand other worker ants, headed down into the bowels of Europe's busiest transport network.

I find London exciting for about four minutes. Then I find it noisy, dirty, and populated by faceless robots for whom rudeness is the default setting. As if fulfilling some prophecy, I then had the misfortune to place my right shoulder in the flight path of a young pinstripe careering down the escalator as if his life depended on it. He connected with the force of a prop forward, sending a generous dose of double caramel latte all down my front.

'Thank you very much, arsehole!'

He didn't even break his stride.

At the conference centre reception, the twenty-year-old with the clipboard eyed my coffee-stained blouse with disdain as she ticked my name off the list and handed me a name badge.

'Third floor for the ladies' cloakroom. In case you need it.'

Cheeky cow. I spread Helen's scarf over the stain and strode off. Then I got in the lift and hit the button for the third floor.

Damage limitation measures involving hot water and the kind of handsoap that costs twenty pounds a bottle only served to make the stain worse. Much worse. A four-inch blemish had now metastasised into a splodge the size of Shropshire. I looked like the runner-up in a wet T-shirt contest.

Jonathan's silver mane was easy to pick out of the crowd. So was the leggy blonde with the Hollywood uplift hanging on his every word. I shuffled over to him, feeling like Nora flaming Batty, and stood for perhaps ten seconds before either of them acknowledged my existence.

'Ah, Jennifer,' he beamed. 'This is Stephanie. We've just signed a deal with her PR consultancy.'

That must have been a tough negotiation. Probably took all of three minutes. I held out my hand.

'Pleased to meet you.'

Stephanie gave me the *What ARE you WEARING?* look, flashed an ice-maiden smile, then switched her flawless skin and rosebud lips back onto Mufasa. I spent four or five minutes feeling like a spare part at a love-in then wandered off in the direction of the free coffee.

I stood at the edge of the room with my coffee and watched them all, the badgers and the bombshells, all locked in seemingly earnest conversation, all with one eye on their interlocutor and one eye scanning the room for someone more important to talk to. I'd never felt more like a fish out of water. I resolved to be out of the corporate world by the summer.

As we took our seats, Jonathan could barely take his eyes off Stephanie, sitting cross-legged on the row in front. A short man with glasses walked out to the podium, to a ripple of polite applause. I'd seen him before. I nudged Jonathan.

'Hm?'

'I recognise him.'

'That's him. David Harwood. The guy whose contract we want.'

I definitely knew that face from somewhere, but I couldn't quite place it. I turned to Jonathan. His eyes were fixed on Stephanie's lithe limbs. It wouldn't be long before the caravan was rocking to their rhythm.

The speaker with the familiar face gathered his papers and took a sip of water. Then he opened his mouth and the velvet vowels took me back to the courtyard at work, him on his hands and knees picking up papers, his warm hazel eyes.

'Good morning, everyone.'

David Harwood spoke for twenty minutes and I listened to every chocolate-coated syllable and processed not a single word. His voice sent me into a kind of trance. I floated away on a caramel cloud into a daydream: Jonathan had put my name forward for the National PA of the Year Award, the real reason he'd asked me to accompany him, and David was opening the envelope and announcing my name ...

'Turn left, mate! Stick with me and we'll be there before the first snags off the barbie!'

Bruce had come to life in my handbag.

Two hundred and sixteen pairs of eyes turned to look at me. I rummaged frantically in my bag. The satnav voice ploughed on, undeterred.

'After three hundred yards you'll reach your destination. Right, windows up, grab those sunnies, and don't let the seagulls steal ya chips!'

A few of the badgers were chortling. Not Jonathan. The livid tone of his face was clashing badly with his pale pink shirt. And I could have wiped the smirk off the face of his leggy new muse.

'If those back-seat drivers don't keep it down, we'll ditch them at the next servo.'

I fumbled for the off switch.

'Bloody hell!'

More titters and chortles from the suits. A deeper shade of purple on Jonathan's face. I finally disabled Bruce and looked up at Jonathan sheepishly.

'Sorry.'

He looked away, thunderously mortified.

By contrast, down at the podium, David Harwood was smiling. No — he was twinkling.

At the lunch break, I grabbed a glass of wine and hid in the corner behind a large yucca. I was desperate for something to eat but I didn't want to put myself in anyone's firing line, so I laid low and watched the canapés float past me. As I drained my glass, a waiter came up and handed me another glass.

'You look like you need this.'

'Is is that obvious?'

'Kind of. Rough morning?'

'Let's just say I haven't exactly covered myself in glory with my boss.'

He leant in close and whispered.

'Don't let the bastards grind you down.'

Then he turned round and beckoned a colleague carrying a tray of food.

'This lady needs some sustenance.'

The food guy proffered a platter of high-class sausages wrapped in parma ham, coated in a sort of marmalade glaze.

'Take a handful.'

I loaded my plate, thanked him, and ducked back behind the yucca. They did look delicious. I lifted one to my mouth.

'I expect you prefer your sausages cooked on the barbie.'

Velvet voice. Warm hazel eyes.

'I'm so sorry. It's a new phone, with an Australian satnav voice. I couldn't turn him off.'

'I don't wonder.'

'Sorry?'

'I mean, they're fiddly things, aren't they? Satnavs on phones?'

'Yes. Well, this one is.'

With his light brown hair and his kind features, he was quite handsome, in a corporate-badger sort of way. But it was the warm hazel eyes that I noticed again. *The man with the laughing eyes and the velvet voice.*

He held out his hand.

'I'm David Harwood. I'm very pleased to meet you, Jennifer Brown.'

'How do you know my name?'

'Your badge.'

'Of course.'

We chatted. He was a partner in an accountancy firm in the city. He lived in a village near the Surrey hills, had two grown-up children, an ex-wife, and two cats named Rough and Tumble.

'Sweet names.'

'Thanks.'

'Names tell you a lot about pets. Or perhaps about their owners.'

'Yes. Do you have pets?'

I felt a lump in my throat.

'Oh, I'm sorry. I didn't mean to upset you.'

I pulled myself together.

'No, it's fine. Yes, I have two dogs. Betty and Eric. Rescue dogs. I don't see much of them anymore. It's a bit of a custody thing.'

'That's a shame. Good names, though. Betty and Eric.'

'Yes. I love my little dogs.'

'Never had cats?'

'No. Although a woman I know lives with over twenty cats.'

'Gosh. Twenty?'

Out of the corner of my eye I spotted Jonathan sliding over, wearing the look of glazed admiration one normally deploys in the presence of Hollywood superstars. He was coming to schmooze. I ignored him.

'Yes. All with very imaginative names.'

'Oh, yes?'

'Yes. D'you know my favourite?'

'What?'

Jonathan was at my shoulder now.

'Fuck Off Dave.'

The colour drained from Jonathan's face. David Harwood roared with laughter. I waved over at the waiter with the wine.

Four hours and six cups of black coffee later, I climbed into my little blue Peugeot, turned her engine on and pointed her in the direction of Helen's. The radio played Al Green's *How Can You Mend a Broken Heart?* With hazel eyes and a velvet voice.

I drove round the roundabout where, earlier, Pete had stood and shouted down some hapless young motorist. I tried to conjure up his face and his voice. I was not entirely successful.

The following morning, I was already at my desk when Jonathan floated in, his handsome features stretched into a broad smile.

'We've got him.'

'Sorry?'

'David Harwood. The contract. He phoned me at home.'

'Great.'

'It's marvellous.'

'I'm really pleased for you.'

'Thanks. He was very impressed by what we do here.'

'Good.'

'And he asked after you.'

Did he now?

11

One Glass Too Many

The white blossom had fallen from the weeping cherries in the courtyard and Spring was shedding its cardigan and gearing up for the short sleeves of Summer. I was spending more and more office hours trawling through employment sites, tweaking my CV to suit, and firing off applications. And a lot of time opening rejection letters.

Work was stultifying. Living with Helen had also lost its appeal. What I'd chosen to see as her endearing quirks in the early weeks I now couldn't help seeing as blood-bubbling irritations. I needed a place of my own. The honeymoon period was definitely over.

Marilyn and I were in the ladies' meeting room. She was rousting up her raven hair, post-helmet.

'So, what news on the job front?'

'Nothing. But this is doing my head in. And me living with Helen isn't really suiting either of us anymore.'

Marilyn stopped plucking at her hair and went quiet. Then a cartoon lightbulb appeared over her head.

'What about a live-in job? You know, sort of two birds with one stone.'

'Like a housekeeper kind of thing?'

'Why not?'

'I can't cook. I burn baked beans.'

'Then learn. Be a smarter shade of blonde.'

I focused my online searches. Lots of vacancies, but they all wanted experience. Looked like I didn't stand a chance.

Then one particular ad caught my eye.

Urgently required. Housekeeper/Cook with a knowledge of French cuisine for domestic meals and occasional dinner parties. Light secretarial duties. Knowledge of gardening preferred. Must have a 'can-do' attitude. Good wage for the right person. Live-in accommodation provided. To start ASAP.

Hm. No mention of previous experience. Well, let's see how far a can-do attitude and a little creative manipulation of my CV can get me.

A few days later, it had got me an interview. I needed a Will session.

'Say I get offered this job? I know it's a long shot, but what if?'

'A long shot!?'

'Well ...'

'Have you forgotten the burnt beans? The dangerously raw omelette? The still-frozen sausages?'

This litany of my culinary failures wasn't helping.

'I can learn.'

'But dinner parties?'

'Well ...'

'French cuisine?'

'How hard can it be?'

'If it's French, it's hard. Trust me. I've dabbled. A lot. A *cassoulet* I can manage – it's basically a stew – but I wouldn't recommend you have a stab at a *tarte tatin*. They're bloody impossible!'

'I'll pick it up. And I'll quite enjoy the gardening. I like being outdoors.'

'It can be pretty physical, Jen. It's not all pruning. There's raking, barrowing, double-digging.'

'Enough!'

'What?'

'With the negativity.'

'It's just …'

'I know. You're worried about me. And you'd miss me.'

'No, I bloody wouldn't.' He started to well up. 'You cow.'

I smiled and took his face in my hands.

'I need this. I need a new direction in my life.'

He buried his head in my neck.

'I know.'

I also needed to be the one to act. With Pete, I'd been given no choice. He'd practically shoved me out the door while, pathetically, I'd clung on with my fingernails.

This time, I'd be the one choosing to jump.

The following week I found myself driving down through the Hampshire countryside to meet Mr G Fisher at the house I'd be running if I got the job.

New hair colour. New attitude. New life?

The plan? 1. Project self-assurance. 2. Sidestep questions I couldn't answer by asking a distracting question of my own.

In other words, blag it.

The hamlet of Singleton Ferrers was so tiny I was amazed that satnav Bruce found it. But here it was, a row of chocolate-box cottages on the twinkling River Test that wended its pretty way through lush water meadows. The sheer beauty of the place made me sit back in my seat and smile.

'You've reached your destination. Windows up, sunnies on, and don't let the seagulls steal your chips!' I thought of the seminar and David Harwood. I wondered how he was getting on with Jonathan.

The house was a mock-Tudor pile a few hundred yards from the river. The gravel path scuffed my new shoes as I approached the house, trying to calm my nerves. *This could be it.*

A painfully thin man appeared at the door. The corners of his mouth moved a fraction but Mr Gerald Fisher appeared to be a man to whom smiling did not come naturally. My first impression was of an ageing clown. His trousers were almost comically baggy and three inches too long. He had an air of sadness about him, and an unnatural pallor.

Gerald Fisher looked me up and down and I felt moved to straighten my skirt, pulling it down an inch or two. I took the hand he extended and he held onto mine for a fraction too long.

'Jennifer, isn't it?' he blinked, not waiting for an answer. 'Please come in. I'm intrigued to know more about you.'

I followed him through a musty hallway that hadn't seen a duster in a good few weeks and stepped over a box of fishing tackle at the entrance to a faded sitting room decorated in a sombre Victorian style.

My eyes instantly focused on a large speckled fish mounted in a glass case above the fireplace.

'He's impressive.'

'A deceased leviathan. I call him Alphonse.'

'Salmon?'

'Of a sort. *Salmo trutta.*'

'Sorry?'

'Brown trout to you.' A hint of a smile. 'I take it you know how to cook one?'

'Yes. And I do a good beer-battered cod.'

The smile died.

'Did *you* catch him? The brown trout?'

'Unfortunately not. One of our piscatorial members landed him and presented him to me. I'm the president.'

'Of fish?'

'Of the society. Izaak Walton.'

I must have looked gormless.

'The South Hampshire Izaak Walton Society.'

'Isaac …?'

'Fishing club.'

'Right.'

'He's something of a legend. Alphonse. Twenty-eight pounds.'

'Is that big?'

'The average is around two to three pounds. About the size you'd normally cook.' He was clearly puzzled by my ignorance.

'Right. Of course. Yes.'

He waved towards a brown velour armchair.

'So, French cuisine.'

'Yes. Love it.'

'How's your *béchamel*?'

Tactic time.

'Gorgeous. This is a lovely property. Have you lived here long?'

'It was my aunt's house.' He fell silent. The yellow eyes seemed to mist a little. 'I've lived here all my life. And I work here. I write articles for a few of the fishing magazines. It's the perfect location.'

'You're very lucky.'

'I suppose I am.' He seemed unconvinced. 'Let me show you the live-in quarters.'

He took me through the kitchen to the back of the house. The self-contained apartment was a later addition to the property and, although a little shabby and untidy, it was a place I imagined I could make my own. With a little work.

'Fully self-contained. All inclusive. No bills.' He was selling it to me.

'It's very nice.'

'And now the garden.' He opened a set of French windows that gave onto a small flagged terrace from which the garden sloped down to the river.

'I need help around the garden. How would you feel about that? Do you mind getting dirty?' Another hint of a smile. *Lecherous old bugger. You must be seventy if you're a day. I'll soon mark your card.*

'Not at all.'

'You'd be happy transplanting, cutting back, potting up?'

A pair of swans were gliding noiselessly on the water.

'Of course. Oh, I love swans!'

He looked at the river. 'Beautiful creatures, aren't they? They pair for life, you know.'

'Yes, I've heard.'

'And you?'

'Sorry?'

'Have you paired? Would there be a 'partner', living here with you?'

'I am very happily single, Mr Fisher.'

'Good. Getting used to just *one* new person in the household is hard enough.'

'Well, yes. With a position like this, you're inviting someone to share your home, I suppose.'

'Indeed. It's not good to be alone for too long.' Wistful? Or hopeful? He led me to a shed at the bottom of the garden, a stone's throw from the water.

'*This is my sanctum sanctorum.*'

'Do you write in here?'

'It's where I tie my flies.' He opened the door. Decades of dampness assaulted my nostrils. I peered inside. Every space was completely taken up with fishing gear: rods, nets, assorted boxes and trays. A wooden bench at the far end was littered with feathers, odd bits of fur and fishing line. He lifted a tray of odd-looking insects in bright colours.

'It's very therapeutic. To work with your hands after working with your brain.'

'Yes.'

A phone rang inside the house.

'Excuse me. I'll just get that. Give you a chance to look round the garden some more.'

Could I work for this man? He seemed a little odd. A little melancholy. Might be a moody sod. And he was definitely an old saucepot. But I knew I could handle that. Was this the new life I was looking for? It was certainly a beautiful part of the world.

'I'm afraid I'll have to cut our meeting short. Someone needs me.'

We walked round the side of the house back to where I'd parked my little blue Peugeot. He held out his hand again.

'I'll be in touch.'

On Monday, Will quizzed me in the canteen.

'So?' Sibilant crumbs of double-choc cookie.

'Well, he was a bit strange, to be honest.'

'Quirky strange, or serial-killer strange?'

'Quirky, I think. Odd. Definitely odd.'

'*I'm* odd! Odd can be good.'

'Yeah, but you don't stare at my thighs.'

'So he fancies you?'

'Well, I'd say he has a rich imagination.'

'Saucy old bugger.'

'I know. He *is* a bit creepy. But nothing I can't handle. And I felt sort of sorry for him.'

'You want to mother him, don't you?'

'A bit, if I'm honest.'

'You're all the bloody same.'

'He just seemed so sad.'

'It'll be bed baths at bedtime.'

'No, it bloody won't. Anyway, I probably won't get it.'

On Wednesday, Gerald Fisher sent me an email offering me the job.

Jonathan seemed genuinely hurt.

'I honestly don't know what I'll do without you.'

'There's always Zilla.'

He shuddered at the mention of her name. 'Snakeskin trousers. Brrr. You won't reconsider? We could negotiate an increase.'

'It's not about the money. And it's not you – you've been lovely. This is just something I need to do. For me.'

There was an intimidating array of cookbooks in Waterstones. Fusion seemed to be the flavour of the month, but I wasn't sure it would be Gerald's cup of tea. In the end, I plumped for the books with the most attractive chefs on the front cover: a brooding Italian, two dishy Frenchmen, and a Chinese cutie, all beaming at me in their pristine whites. Total World Cuisine!

Now I had just three weeks to teach myself to cook.

I spent every evening trying to perfect the art of French cuisine. I flambéd, I sautéed, I fricasséed. The results weren't good. My sauces split, my eggs curdled, my tarts had soggy bottoms.

Helen's kitchen, hitherto a vegetarian temple, became a charnel house. Prime sirloins sizzled alongside neck fillet of lamb and belly of pork. But with only two small electric rings and a dodgy oven that struggled to reach 160°, I made slow progress. I'd ditched the gravy granules and the cook-in sauces, but I still had a long way to go.

Helen discreetly decamped to Paul's house most evenings (doubtless aghast at the slaughter but too kind to object) and Will was pressed into service as food critic. With a free meal five nights a week, he didn't take much persuading.

And he was very sweet. He could see me sweating as I served up the latest disaster and he was careful to make his criticism constructive. 'I'd say it needs something more. A tad more paprika, maybe?' Or, 'Perhaps a bit more time in the oven?', as he masticated his way through my boeuf bourguignon like Alex Ferguson attacking a packet of Wrigleys in a penalty shoot-out.

He could see I was miserable. 'You'll be fine,' he'd say, forcing a chunk of something down with a belt of Merlot.

'I'm supposed to be a proficient cordon bleu cook.'

'And you will be. One day.' A pause. 'This Gerald Fisher. Does he wear dentures?'

Before I knew it, it was my final day at work.

Helen had decorated my desk with balloons and good luck banners, and some bright spark had sat an inflatable doll with huge breasts behind my desk. The busty bimbo. I suppose I could play that role for another few hours.

In keeping with office tradition, everyone gathered round my desk to wish me well: Handy Dick, Dread Ed, the HRTs, even Imogen from Finance (doubtless glad to see the back of me).

'Come on, Jen. Open your presents before the old silver fox gives his speech.' Will was the only one who could get away with that kind of talk in front of Jonathan.

He handed me a huge parcel wrapped in gold tissue. I tore the tissue off, revealing a box full of shredded paper. The label read: 'I'm a Secretary, Get me Outta here!'

Then I was blindfolded (Craig doing the honours. Perv.) and instructed to dip my hand inside to find the hidden, anonymous gifts. A set of wooden spoons (HRTs – affordable, and typical of a bunch of cauldron-stirring witches.) A penis-shaped jelly mould (Craig's fingerprints all over that one). A gorgeous gold bracelet that took my breath away. (Jonathan was the only one remotely in that income bracket. I looked right at him but he couldn't hold my gaze.)

Then, as master of all he surveyed, Jonathan cleared his throat for the speech.

'It's a sad day for us all when we lose a colleague who's regarded with such affection. She's certainly made life in the office very entertaining. And, as payback for all the times her memos have dropped me in it, *and* for deserting me in my hour of need, some entertaining stories of my own.'

I felt the colour in my cheeks rise. *Not the thong.*

'Always one to embrace a challenge, a few months ago Jennifer decided to try horse-riding. The day went well. She walked, she trotted, she even managed a canter. But the dismount didn't go so smoothly. She basically had to slide off the animal. Which resulted in an item of Jennifer's underwear, necessarily generously proportioned, becoming entangled round the pommel and disengaging from her body, leaving the flesh concerned in full view of the embarrassed stable hands. Quite the eye-opener for those young lads!'

Handy Dick wiped his brow and rummaged in his pockets.

'And things don't always go well for Jennifer when she ventures abroad. As most of you know, she's had occasion to mix up her words when she's typed a memo.'

Giggles from the crowd. *Dirty Rota. Tits Policy.*

'Well, it seems this tendency to mix things up is not confined to the office. She's not always terribly careful when she lifts her suitcase from a baggage carousel. As she discovered when, returning from Lanzarote a couple of years ago, customs officials at Gatwick wanted to look inside the case in her hand. As soon as she flipped open the lid, it was clear to her that this was *not* her case. Trouble was, the customs officials didn't know that. And they were in for a surprise.'

I knew what was coming.

'As they discovered not a selection of bikinis, linen blouses and Jackie Collins novels but an entire consignment of ... well, what we might call "battery-operated pleasuring devices". It seems that, submitted to X-ray imaging, these items bear a disconcerting resemblance to munitions.'

The officials had sent me on my way with nothing more than a raised eyebrow. I'd left the offending item of baggage with airport staff. It had taken the airline two weeks to locate *my* suitcase.

'But the *pièce de résistance* has to be the time when, at the office Christmas party three years ago, Jennifer decided to wear her new figure-hugging dress.'

He paused for effect and looked straight at me. *The thong.*

'Which required she deploy a new, rather brief item of underwear.'

I glanced over at Will. *Bastard.* Jonathan must have trawled round the office for these stories. Will was the only one who'd known the real reason for my limp. Will was the one who'd shopped me.

'But it was an uncomfortable evening for Jennifer. *Deeply* uncomfortable.' *Oh ground! Open up and swallow me now!*

'Sitting down seemed to be a delicate operation. She didn't dance the whole evening. And the following day, she hobbled round the office like a wounded pigeon.'

My pink cheeks tried their best to stretch into a smile.

'But the reason for her discomfort was *not* the shoes she blamed it on. The reason was altogether a different item of clothing. She'd spent the whole evening with her thong on *back to front!*' Guffaws from the assembled crowd.

Swine. But I'll get you back.

The day finished with a series of *last time ever*s: last time I'll ever close this desk drawer, last time I'll ever take this lift down, last time I'll ever swipe my security card.

At the bar, a couple of chardonnays in, I started to doubt myself. When I looked at the familiar faces gathered for a final farewell, I found myself envying them all their safe little worlds. Mine suddenly seemed risky and scary. Maybe this was a leap too far.

But I was touched by the genuine warmth shown by everyone. Well, almost everyone. A certain leggy brunette from Finance came over to shake my hand. She leaned in and whispered in my ear.

'Nice try, Jennifer Brown.'

'Nice try?'

'You were never Jonathan's type.'

The silver fox himself was making a beeline for us. This was not a time to whisper. This was a time for home truths.

'Oh, darling. You're right. I do have strong feelings for Jonathan. He's been very good to me and I love him.'

Jonathan blushed. Melissa smirked. She had me on the ropes. Victory was hers.

'I love him like a brother. And, where I come from, sweetheart, you don't shag your brother.'

Melissa squirmed.

'Especially not in some shabby caravan on a Friday afternoon.'

Little Miss Leggy didn't know what to do with herself. But she knew what to do with her Merlot. It created a striking Jackson Pollock effect on the front of Jonathan's immaculate, white, Egyptian cotton, double-cuff, Jermyn Street shirt.

I looked into his blue eyes for the last time.

'I'm going to miss you, Jonathan. I really am.'

And I meant it.

Part Two

Fishers Keep

12

Best Foot Forward

Hampshire had been wearing its Spring clothes the last time I'd made this journey, just two weeks before. But today, Winter was showing it hadn't completely given up the ghost and was flexing its muscles one last time.

The temperature gauge was showing minus four as my little blue Peugeot picked her way gingerly through narrow, icy, Hampshire lanes, piled to the gunwales with my worldly goods. And, with her broken heater, she wasn't doing much to shield me from the elements.

The cold snap wasn't doing much for my confidence, either. Was this the right move for me? Could I hack it in the country? How long would it take Gerald to work out I didn't know a Soubise from a Subo?

Will had come up trumps with a copy of *Basic French Cookery*, a long-out-of-print paperback primer on the subject, written (rather bewilderingly) by Len Deighton, the master of the Cold War spy thriller. Its recipes were presented as comic strips.

Will had hoped it would be idiot-proof. It'd need to be.

But bubbling away uneasily on the back burner was Will's question: *So he fancies you?* Was I going to deal with Gerald's trouser-based attention as well as I pretended?

The temperature was dropping with each mile. My breath was now frosting unnervingly on the windscreen. I had a vision of blue lights, my body encased in ice, my frozen hands prised off the steering wheel by a paramedic.

A dashboard light. The radiator. That couldn't be right. I'd topped up the coolant the day before. Only five miles to Fishers Keep. See to it when you get there.

Another light. Check engine. Bugger. Just plod on. Only a few miles. Then steam. Shit. Then the car whimpered and died.

I lifted the bonnet (we always do, don't we, even when we haven't got a cat in hell's chance of fixing the problem). Through the steam, I could see some sort of liquid dripping from somewhere. I opened the glove compartment and fished around under the wet wipes and the emergency knickers for my breakdown card.

'I don't *know* my location. I'm in a lay-by.'

'Penzance? Inverness?'

Cheeky sod.

'Hampshire. Singleton Ferrers. Near there. About five miles from there.'

'We'll be there in an hour, madam. Don't leave the vehicle.'

I sat and waited. In my chest-freezer of a car. My toes were numb. What would Captain Scott do? No, don't go there. What would Roald Amundsen do? He'd have emergency rations. And when they ran out, he'd have his dogs to eat. I had a half-eaten KitKat and a diet coke. What would Roald Amundsen do? He wouldn't hunker down in his tent. He'd keep moving. *Keep moving, Jen. Or you'll freeze to death.*

I paced up and down, stamping my feet. A flash of a rabbit's tail disappeared into the whitened undergrowth. Lucky bunny – he had a warm burrow to hide in. A few yards away, a pheasant scurried along the frosty verge then rose with a mad flutter of wings.

My poor broken car. Covered in snow, it reminded me of one of Will's mid-morning iced buns.

'Your radiator's blown, love.'

'Blown?'

'Porous. Did you put coolant in?'

'Yes. Yesterday.'

'Neat?'

'Yes.'

'That's your trouble. Should have diluted it. 50/50. It's corrosive, you see.'

'The coolant has corroded my radiator?'

'Well, there must have been a good few holes in it already. The coolant has opened them up and made a few more.'

'So what do we do now?'

He slapped his truck.

'We get her up on the back and I take you to where you want to go.'

Where did I want to go? Back to Intext and my cosy life? Phone Gerald? Tell him it was all off?

It was tempting.

The breakdown truck dropped me at a garage three miles from Singleton Ferrers. I booked her in for a new radiator ('How much?' 'Depends what we find.'), grabbed a couple of bags from the back seat and phoned a taxi.

With its winter coat on, Fishers Keep (was the lack of punctuation deliberate? Fishers keep *what*, exactly?) looked much bleaker than I remembered it. I stood on the gravel drive clutching a small red suitcase, a Tesco Bag for Life, and a rock in my stomach. I was carless. If I turned away now, I'd be homeless, too. I felt the urge to cry. *Stop being so bloody ridiculous, Jennifer Brown.*

Gerald came round the side of the house.

'Jennifer! How lovely.' He looked at my bedraggled appearance, then scanned around for my car. 'Did you come on foot?'

I explained about my eventful journey. He laid a bony arm on my shoulder.

'You can you use my old four-wheel drive until it's fixed.'

Perhaps he wouldn't be as bad as I'd feared. He looked at his watch.

'I've got a meeting to attend this afternoon. Perhaps I could leave you to tidy the kitchen? And I've invited a few fishing pals for supper this evening. How about *sole meunière*?'

Well, looked like I'd be hitting the ground running. Still, at least I had Len Deighton to show me the ropes.

Len Deighton who was lying in the boot of my car.

The kitchen looked as if a gaggle of boisterous teenagers had played rugby in it with crockery. I dropped my case on the floor and took a deep breath. *Right. Sleeves up.*

As I hoisted the last black bag into the wheelie bin, fresh snow had fallen, covering the lawn like a crisp, newly laundered tablecloth. I stood and watched a pair of mallards waddle up from the river, their neat webbed feet etching a crisscross pattern in the snow. A sudden gust of wind sent a shiver through me and I thought of my broken car. God knows how much the bill for the repairs would cost. My first month's pay?

I blew my nose, sending the mallards up and out over the river. Then I looked at my watch. Waitrose was six miles away. Time to fire up Gerald's jeep.

Every plate was cleaned that evening, which I considered a success of sorts, even though I'd been winging the *meunière* with only four fillets of sole, supplemented with the last five plaice on Waitrose's slab, the lot prepared without Len and only the vaguest memory of butter and lemon juice and capers from one of the dishy chefs from Waterstones. And I'd produced a passable apple crumble with a custard that didn't taste bought.

Gerald's well-to-do guests broke off from their talk of river banks and statistical reviews to thank me for the lovely meal, so that was a result.

By midnight, I'd been standing on my feet for over ten hours, as out of steam as the deceased radiator on my little blue Peugeot. I felt a bony hand on my shoulder.

'Why not leave the last lot of washing-up till the morning?'

His rheumy eyes lingered. Bloody hell.

My apartment was still chilly but I'd worked up such a sweat I didn't mind. I cranked the thermostat up another notch (mean old bugger) so I wouldn't be freezing in the morning and screwed the top off the Chardonnay-Semillon number I'd picked up in Waitrose as a housewarming gift to myself.

The following morning, I was putting the last few breakfast dishes away. Gerald bounced in, looking cock-a-hoop. A glowing review of his latest piece of fishlore.

'There's just the two of us tonight. I'll deal with dinner. Show you how it's done.'

He grinned in a way calculated to look impish. It looked maniacal. Again I thought of Will. *Quirky strange or serial-killer strange?*

After a rewarding day of organising kitchen cupboards (staples, herbs and spices at eye level, pasta makers and blowtorches near the ankles), I took my seat in the dining room and prepared myself for an evening intended to be cosy. Gerald poured Sauvignon Blanc.

'Is your apartment comfortable?'

'It's fine. Thank you.'

'It's important to be comfortable.'

'Yes.'

'And warm. Are you warm enough?'

'Fine. Thank you.'

'I've made Thermidor. The lobster dish.'

'Lovely.'

'For heat.'

'Sorry?'

'You know. Thermal, thermometer, thermos.'

'I don't follow.'

'It's named after the month in the French revolutionary calendar. The month of heat.'

'I see.'

'The second month of the summer quarter. When things are hotting up.'

'Right.'

'I thought we could do with a little heating up.'

'Erm …'

'You know. After this cold snap.'

'Right.'

'I've always been very considerate towards my employees.'

Something bony brushed against my leg.

'Could I have some water?'

'Sorry?'

'Some water. Could you get me some? Please.'

He disappeared into the kitchen and thankfully the moment was gone.

Over the next few days, he ramped up the romance. *La Traviata* bubbled constantly through the house, he placed a bouquet of exquisite orchids in my apartment, and he exchanged the aroma of the fishing shed for something in a bottle reminiscent of my dad's *Hai Karate* from 1971.

At the breakfast table, he'd drop tediously unsubtle hints about finding a woman, mumbling 'a proper wife' as he munched through his All Bran. It was exhausting.

There was no way on earth I could be attracted to Gerald: a bag of bones in baggy pants. So, at supper one evening, after a few generous glugs of the amontillado designed for trifle use, I decided it was time to put him straight. Even if putting him straight would leave me looking for another job and another home.

I served the supper and the conversation turned, as it invariably did, towards relationships.

'I had a manager at my old company who fancied me.'

'I don't doubt it. You're a very attractive woman.' Gerald munched through his green beans. An old goat grazing.

'I rather liked him actually.'

'Oh?'

'Yes. He was cultured, tall, handsome, and very charming. I was tempted. But …'

'But?'

'But there are rules I like to live by. Sensible rules. Important rules.'

'What rules?'

'Never borrow money from a friend. Be kind to people on the way up.'

'Sensible.'

'And never mix business with pleasure. NEVER.'

Gerald stopped munching. He looked at me levelly. I returned his gaze. *That's right, old man. Put it away.*

From then on, no more *Traviata*, no more orchids, and a return to eau de fishing shed. Plus a distinct huffiness in his manner, like a child denied his favourite toy.

And he became snappish. My confidence was growing in the kitchen, but he chipped away at it. When I asked if he'd enjoyed the asparagus, the *filet mignon*, or the *pommes de terre à la lyonnaise*, he'd say 'rather overcooked' or 'a little too pink' or 'rather too crispy at the edges'. Nothing was ever good.

I'd rejected his advances and now he was punishing me. But he wasn't going to win. He wasn't going to beat me. And he certainly wasn't going to Pete me.

He placed more and more demands on me, testing my ability to deal with his bad temper. I ran around, exhausted, pandering to his every whim, but never once complained. He hardly spoke and, instead, took to leaving lists of jobs that needed doing, both inside and outside the house. He had me cleaning gutters and cutting back trees, draining ponds and laying turf. Within a month, my arms had grown sinewy. Who needed the gym?

13

Continental Breakfasts

I began to get to know the neighbours, whom I gathered Gerald didn't have much to do with.

On one side was Hannah, an artist in her late sixties who smoked nearly as much as the chimney that belched out fragrant smoke from her wood-burning stove. And when Hannah was in her shed throwing paint around, I'd often detect a waft of something more exotic than tobacco. I'd wave in to her and she'd wave back, tossing her waist-length blonde hair.

On the other side of Fishers Keep, a monster of a new-money mansion dominated the riverbank, occupied by Steve and Janice Payne. 'Payne by name, Pain by nature,' I'd heard Gerald mutter at breakfast. Originally from Chingford, Steve was partial to sunbeds and gold bracelets. He'd demolished the bungalow he'd bought and replaced it with a colossal six-bedroom pile with an indoor swimming pool, a hot tub and a gym. Janice was his trophy wife. She'd found her style somewhere around 1983 and had held on tight: Kate Bush hair, *Dynasty* power jackets and, for jogging along the river, lime-green lycra. Lizzie Webb meets neon wood nymph.

If Janice was making breakfast, Wham were on full blast and we were all getting the message to *Wake Me up Before You Go Go*.

Janice owned a nail and beauty bar in Romsey specialising in extortionate manicures. In the queue at Waitrose one day, she tapped me on the shoulder.

'How you getting on with old Gerald, then?'

'Oh, alright.'

'Rather you than me, darlin'. Bit of an odd one, ain't he?' She threw her head back and guffawed.

'Mind you, always has a young lady on his arm. Fruity old bugger.'

I smiled awkwardly.

'Anyway, pop round for a coffee darlin'.'

'Right. Thanks.'

She looked down at my hands, which, after a month of dishwater and digging, now resembled those of a stevedore.

'I'll do yer nails.'

The following week my old typing errors came back to haunt me.

Gerald had asked me to send out an email to his fishing society members. As president, he'd asked them to carry out a 'statistical review of catch returns', whatever that meant. He was convening a meeting to discuss their findings.

I typed out the email in the thirteen seconds I had available between boiling his lunchtime egg and 'dipping' the net curtains. And I contrived to invite the members of the honourable South Hampshire Izaak Walton Society to a meeting about the *Sadistical* Review.

Cue numerous ribald enquiries: should I bring my whip?; what is the dress code – black leather? can arrangements for procuring a dominatrix be added to the agenda?

April twinkled on and the water birds began to hatch their young. A family of mallards hatched nine speckled ducklings who followed their mother across the lawn, cheeping their way down to the river and leaping in to swim alongside her, furiously battling the current that threatened to carry them downstream.

An attractive young woman appeared at the breakfast table one morning, looking distinctly unpiscatorial. She had shoulder-length auburn hair curled at the ends like brandy snaps, a flawless porcelain complexion, and full, cherubic lips. A niece?

She smiled. Gerald spoke up.

'This is Saskia. She's from Holland.'

'The Netherlands,' said the porcelain doll.

'Yes, Netherlands. She's an actress.'

'Hello,' I said. 'Pleased to meet you. An actress. How exciting!'

'It's okay.' She seemed unconvinced. She stood up and walked over to the toaster. I noticed she was wearing one of Gerald's Barbour cardigans. She appeared to be wearing nothing else at all.

'Will I have seen you in anything recently?'

She spread her toast with marmalade and smiled at Gerald conspiratorially.

'I wouldn't have thought so.'

Ah. Probably not a niece.

'Right. So, what do you have planned for today? Saskia.'

'I'm taking her on the water.' Gerald reached across and stroked her cheek. She deployed a professional coquettishness.

'Gezzy is teaching me how to fish.'

I hid my smile in a dish towel. *Gezzy. I'll put that one in the bank.* I reached into the breadbin.

'Toasted crumpet anyone?'

Saskia was the first in a long line of continental delights to grace our breakfast table in various states of informal attire. It was hugely entertaining. I put an old map of the world to good use by hanging it on my bedroom wall and sticking red pins in all the countries Gerald had explored. I sniggered whenever I looked at Thailand.

Nam, who'd hailed from Ang Thong, near Bangkok, had been dazzling beautiful but, from the off, something was not quite right. There was an excess of femininity that didn't ring true.

Sure enough, at breakfast the following morning, Gerald had been decidedly off colour. In a T-shirt and shorts, and with only a hint of makeup, Nam's mask of femininity had slipped. As I'd thought, there'd been an unexpected extra hidden beneath the dress. Nam. The clue had been in the name. 'She' had only visited the once. No mention of the encounter was ever made again and Gerald continued his eager search for a wife.

Although he could still be a right swine at times, I began to feel rather sorry for the master of Fishers Keep. One thing I began to notice, as I dusted and tidied each day, was the almost complete absence of family photographs. The only image visible in the whole house was a faded black-and-white snap of a small child. He was smiling and holding the hand of a woman. They were at a fairground. In the other hand, he was clutching a plastic bag, a goldfish swimming around inside it.

One evening, when he was rather in his cups and his usual snappishness had given way to dewy-eyed loquacity, I'd asked him about the photo. The woman was his aunt Emily. He'd been abandoned by his mother at birth – she'd wanted to have him adopted – and Emily, a war widow, wouldn't hear of the little boy going into care, so she'd taken him. She'd given him a good start in life, instilling in him her love of nature and an appreciation of the beauty of the English countryside, particularly its rivers. The foxed copy of *The Wind in the Willows* that Gerald kept by his bed had been a gift from her.

As Will had predicted, gardening took up a great deal of my time and I became quite the all-rounder: pruning, transplanting, double-digging and, with a huge canister strapped to my back à la *Ghostbusters*, spraying.

Fishers Keep had its own willow tree, which Gerald had christened *Gloria*. She stood proudly by the river, her leaves shimmering in the sunshine. But she was a high-maintenance girl indeed, her long summer tresses requiring my attention once every six weeks.

It was oddly rewarding but, with the household duties as well, quite exhausting. And it was a solitary existence. I missed the camaraderie of office life. I especially missed Will. The odd phone call helped.

'What's it like in the land of subserviency?'

'Not bad. But he scores me out of ten for my cooking.'

'What's your highest score?'

'Four.'

'Chin up, Jen. It's early days.'

'How's things at Intext?'

'Nuts, as usual. Zilla's all over Jonathan like a rash. She keeps sharpening those three-inch fingernails for scratching his back. He's mortified. It's hilarious.'

It sounded just as crazy as ever.

'When are you coming over to see your old pal? I could do with a night on the tiles.'

'No idea when I'll get the chance, Will. There's so much to do here.'

'He's got to give you a day off. Otherwise, it's slavery.'

'I'll give it another couple of weeks then I'll speak to him.'

Hampshire warmed up and the garden flourished. I was keeping the grounds in good shape and, with Len's help, I was scoring higher marks in the kitchen. Gerald could see I was gaining in confidence in that department and he became much less inclined to put the boot in.

But other household chores were getting on top of me. Keeping a good standard of cleanliness and tidiness across four bedrooms, three reception rooms, two bathrooms, a study, a kitchen and a walk-in pantry was, in itself, a full-time job. And Gerald was a sneaky old bugger. He'd leave fishing flies around the house, in places he thought I might omit to hoover or dust: under an armchair, behind a carriage clock, on top of Alphonse's glass case. But I was onto him. I'd always find them and place them in a neat little line on his bedside cabinet. Neither of us ever mentioned them. It was our little game.

On top of the housework, there was the laundry to attend to. For a single man, Gerald generated enormous amounts of washing, which I seemed always to be doing in such a hurry I often fired his cashmere sweaters in with the tablecloths. Then I had to coax them back to life and hope he wouldn't notice.

As I was emptying the machine one day, a small silver packet fell out of a pair of his cords. Tiny blue pills. Bloody hell! I'd sent his Viagra through on sixty degrees! Perhaps the starch would help stiffen his resolve. Out came the hairdryer.

As April turned into May, the hawthorn blossomed, dusting the hedgerows like icing sugar on cake. Gerald became excited about the arrival of another maiden. But this particular young lady didn't hail from any foreign land. She was a homegrown beauty far more important in a fisherman's life than any prospective bride, no matter how nubile.

The mayfly has a life span of only two days. It's born with no mouth, the entire purpose of its brief life being to reproduce. The male impregnates the female then flies off to die. The impregnated female skims along the top water, laying thousands of tiny eggs. Below the water's surface, juicy trout lie in wait to snatch the delicate and delicious fly. And, in their turn, fishermen lie in wait for the the trout. And when nature's mayfly have shuffled off their mortal coil, Gerald said, clever fishermen like him can fool the fish for a few more weeks with mayfly assembled in the shed.

His excitement was infectious and sweet. Men can be such little boys.

'I've hired a woman.' Goodness, Gerald, is the wife-hunt going so badly?

'A woman?'

'Some help for you. For the summer months. In the kitchen and around the house. I won't trust her in the garden.'

This was very welcome news indeed. Especially now that Gerald had announced his intention to host a Mayfly Dinner for Society members.

'Her name's Katarina. She's Romanian.'

The following morning, from the study window I spotted an elfin figure standing at the front gate, pacing nervously, smoking a cigarette like her life depended on it. She was having a heated conversation on her phone. She looked agitated. I walked out.

'Hi there. Are you Katarina?'

'Yes. I Katarina.' She stubbed her cigarette out on the gravel. In a fashionably tatty leather jacket and a pair of skinny jeans with rips in both knees, she didn't look like anyone's idea of a Mrs Mop, but she had warm eyes and a frank smile tinged with sadness. I liked her immediately. I took her outstretched hand in both of mine.

'I'm Jen. Come inside.'

I made tea and we sat at the kitchen table. I chatted to her and she pieced together a few replies in broken, guttural English. She had sleek, black hair and a way of holding herself that was proud and slightly aloof. She looked like a regal cat tossed out of the palace and onto the street after the Tsarina had died.

She was a godsend for me. The job became manageable. I could deal with the garden chores at a relaxed pace, leaving Kitty (my new name for her) with clear instructions that I was confident she'd follow. She was an able plier of hoover and duster and, in the kitchen, a solid commis chef.

But she incurred Gerald's displeasure by daring to take the cigarette breaks I gave her and by playing Def Leppard on her iPhone while we chopped veg.

'Why he so mean face, Jenni?' She tipped five spoonfuls of sugar into her tea.

'He's just lonely.'

'Hm. Men. Lonely. We all lonely. Life is lonely. Get used to it.'

'You okay?'

'My boyfriend. He call me. All the time.'

'That's nice. So *you're* not lonely.'

'No. Is not nice. If I no answer, he angry.'

'Oh dear.'

'He pay rent, Jenni. He want to knowing what I doing all the day.'

'I see.'

'He want knowing about other men. I tell him, *No other men.*'

'I'm sorry.' I knew the type. Insecure. Macho. Controlling. In short, a bully.

'I come to UK with friend. Together we hope for new life. But English no good. So no job.'

'You have *this* job.'

Kitty's eyes filled with tears. 'But Mister Gerald pay bad money for hard work.'

I wondered what slave rate Gerald was daring to pay. Bastard.

'Does your friend have a job?'

'Elena go back to Romania. But I want stay here. In UK. My boyfriend say he help. But he take all my money.'

Poor Kitty. She had a slavedriver of an employer and a bully of a boyfriend. I was the only decent person in her life. Her colleague and now her surrogate mother.

14

Slavic Roulette

It was the morning of the Mayfly Dinner, an important occasion in the fisherman's calendar.

This year, it was Gerald's turn to host a dinner for the band of musty old cronies for whom the River Test was Elysium. The menu, in keeping with the proclivities of the species, was to be schoolboy fayre strangely devoid of fish: cock-a-leekie soup, steak pie with puff pastry, spotted dick. Hardly Raymond Blanc.

But I wasn't complaining. A night off for Len meant an easy time for me. Kitty was on overtime so she could help out in the kitchen and at table.

With breakfast over, I was beginning preparations for the dinner. Kitty seemed excited to be involved.

'I write menus for guests, Jenni?'

How would I manage this situation?

'Sure. Okay. I'll write out the words on a piece of paper and you can copy them onto these cards. Is your handwriting neat?'

'I show.' She took a piece of paper and wrote out *Katarina* in gorgeous copperplate.

'That's lovely, Kitty. That'll be perfect. I'll write out the words for you. My writing's not as neat as yours, though. Hope you'll be able to read it.'

'You SMS me, no? This easier for you.'

'Good idea. I'll send you a text and you can copy it out.'

By late afternoon, the soup was made, the pie prepped and the dick spotted. I'd earned a breather. Knowing it would probably be the last time I'd get to rest my feet until midnight, I took myself off to my apartment and lay down for a twenty-minute disco nap.

I was wakened by the crunch of tyres on gravel. I glanced at the clock. Bugger! I'd dozed for two hours!

I splashed water in my face and hurried over to the kitchen.

'Sorry, Kitty!'

'Is no matter, Jenni. I do everything. Soup heating, pie in oven, dick ready, table ready.'

I glanced into the dining room. It looked marvellous. She'd even picked tulips from the garden and had three vases laid out. What a star!

'Great job, Kitty! Well done.'

What a sweet girl.

The evening was a resounding success. Almost.

'I make wrong with wine?'

She clocked Gerald's face when three bottles of his 1990 Pomerol (around £90 a throw from Wood and Winters) were breezily served as an accompaniment to the steak pie, in place of the £6.99 Australian Shiraz I'd picked up at Waitrose for the occasion. One of Bordeaux's finest appellations, clothed in one of its finest years, was slugged by the schoolboys as if it were Ribena.

'Don't worry, Kitty. Serves him right for being a skinflint.'

'Sorry, Jenni.'

'It's fine. I'll talk him round.'

Her second cock-up we didn't get wind of until later, when Norman, one of Gerald's sleazier guests (with a ninja footfall that put me in mind of Carpet Slipper Craig), staggered into the kitchen apparently in search of water. I was preparing the herring for the following day's breakfast.

'Enjoy working for Gerald?' He leaned over my shoulder with his gravy breath.

'Of course. Why wouldn't I?'

'He's a bit of an old roisterer. Not too much for you?'

I turned to meet his gaze, filleting knife in hand.

'Oh, Gerald knows that routine doesn't cut it with me.'

Norman eyed the knife nervously. 'No. Right.'

'Have you enjoyed your evening?'

'Enormously. Nice little joke on the menu, by the way. Hilarious.'

What was he on about?

'Ribs well and truly tickled. Mine, anyway. Certainly made the pie 'go down' well. Don't think Gerald approves. But don't you worry about that. He's an old stuffed shirt about protocol and all that.'

God! What the hell had Kitty done?

'Erm, I'll bring in water for everyone.'

I filled two glass pitchers and strolled into the dining room with all the aplomb I could muster. I laid the pitchers down on the table.

'Some water, gentlemen.'

A dozen pair of eyes were on me.

Someone piped up. 'Bravo with the dinner! Excellent!'

Norman resumed his seat. 'I was just telling …'

'Jennifer.'

'… Jennifer that we all enjoyed her little joke. Didn't we, Gerald?'

Gerald looked like he'd never enjoy anything ever again.

'Hm. Very droll.'

I glanced down at one of the faux vellum sheets inscribed in Kitty's beautiful hand. Once again, autocorrect had been my downfall. There it was. The Thirteenth Annual Mayfly Dinner. Second menu item:

Aberdeen Angus Steak Pie with Puff Pussy

June arrived and, with it, sunshine and clear blue skies. The old river sparkled like a sapphire and the grass on Gerald's generous lawn now needed my attention twice a week. My forearms sang with the effort of hauling round the old petrol leviathan, but my skin looked happy with its summer colour and, by and large, life was good.

But I worried about young Kitty. She had a haunted look and seemed thinner than ever. What few breaks she had were spent on the phone. Her eyes were often rimmed with red.

One morning, she seemed at the end of her tether.

'What on earth's the matter?'

'Him. He the matter.'

'You'll have to leave him, Kitty?'

'No. Not boyfriend. Him. Gerry.'

'What's he said?'

'He say me, You not work enough. You smoke like bumfire. You all the time phoning.'

Huge tears started to spill from her eyes. I put my arm round her bony shoulder and pulled her close.

'It's fine.'

But it wasn't.

One afternoon, he summoned her to his study. He laid out three A4 sheets listing her movements in the past week. Then he laid out a dozen Polaroids: Kitty sitting in the garden smoking, Kitty on the phone, Kitty laughing. All evidence, he said. Evidence of her shirking her duties. Evidence of slacking.

She was outraged by what she (rightly) saw as an invasion of her privacy.

'You Stasi, Gerald Fisher! And these, these … pictures! You PREVERT!'

She pulled off her apron and threw it at him. It wrapped itself round his head. She stormed out. He marched after her.

'How DARE you!'

'I not work at Fishers Creep no more.' She barged past me.

'I call Police! You are prevert. PREVERT!'

'Come back here this instant!'

But she never did. That was the last I ever saw of my little Romanian girl. My surrogate daughter.

Calm returned. Without my Malaprop sidekick, I was just about managing to stay on top of things horticulturally and domestically. Gerald seemed pleased.

Actually, Gerald seemed more than pleased. He seemed joyful. Animated. Excited. What was he up to?

'I'm off on a fishing trip, Jennifer. Next week. Five or six days.'

'Speyside again?'

'St Petersburg.'

One whole week without him. What bliss! It was like all my Fuck about Fridays rolled into one. I needed some Will time.

And what a glorious time we gave ourselves! Lunches in Covent Garden, drinks in Soho, a West End musical, the last train home to Will's flat in Southsea, waking up on his couch with a thick head and a thin bank account.

I went back to work for a rest.

It seemed Gerald had been busy, too. He had a permanent smile etched on his face. A spring in his step. A fishing trip, indeed.

Now, when I popped my head into the study to say goodnight, he'd be at his desk, laptop open, the light from his Skype call flickering in his glass of single malt.

'I'm having a guest, Jennifer. For a few days. Arrives this evening. Some fish, I think.'

I made an extra effort around the house: stripped the beds, cleaned the windows, put fresh flowers in all the rooms.

Gerald left for the airport with a bunch of decidedly third-rate chrysanthemums (the flower of love and hope in Britain, but the flower of death in France – and in Russia?). In his smart new brown cords, and clutching the flowers intently, he looked for all the world like the beaming boy in the photograph.

I busied myself with preparations for my steamed halibut with a spicy lemon-thyme vinaigrette (check *me*!).

Tyres on gravel announced their arrival. I pretended to be engrossed in scrubbing a chopping board as metallic heels clacked onto the kitchen tiles. I turned to see Gerald, simpering like a sixth-former, staring up at Narnia's White Witch.

'This is Tatyana.'

A fountain of luxuriant blond hair, a model's cheekbones, an athlete's body. But I focused on the blue eyes. Steel blue. Unsmiling. Cold as the North Wind.

'Pleased to meet you, Tatyana.'

'Hello.'

It was fascinating to see Gerald dance around her, proferring magazines, plumping cushions, waving me aside while he made English Breakfast Tea. Tatty Anna accepted his worship with regal indulgence and, once her comprehensive daily exercise routine had been completed, rarely shifted her fabulously toned behind from his favourite velour armchair.

She proved, unsurprisingly, to be an awkward houseguest: fruit and vegetables had to be organic and scrupulously washed, meat had to be lean, eggs free range. The fridge had to be liberally stocked with cucumber, her favourite superfood (*I love my coocumbi. Very healthy.*)

Gerald's penchant for calorie-rich cuisine was scoffed at.

'My Gerry! Such silly food!'

'You don't like French cooking?'

'All this butter, cream. No good.' She looked me up and down. 'Make people fat.'

Around eleven, they'd set off together down the lane for a 'run', Tatty Anna gliding along effortlessly in Nike lycra, Gerald limping alongside her in baggy cotton shorts and an aertex polo short from his prep school wardrobe. A sixty-eight-year-old heart attack in the making.

But Gerald was hooked. The 'few days' turned into a few weeks. Designer shopping bags appeared and deliveries mushroomed. Swatches of upholstery fabric jumped up on his desk, then books of wallpaper samples. The White Witch was going nowhere.

I took to spending as much time as possible in the garden, well away from the lovebirds. Will thought I was being unfair.

'Don't be so judgmental. She makes him smile.'

'He's sixty-eight. She's twenty-six!'

'So?'

'He's old enough to be her father. Grandfather.'

'He's entitled to a little fun.'

'I'm not sure it's fun she's after.'

'Besides, it's keeping him off your back.'

'I know. But I don't trust her.'

'You're such a cynic. Let him have his five minutes of fun.'

'Hm.'

'Enough!'

'You're right. Sorry. Anyway, what's new with you?'

'I've joined a dating site.'

'Which one?'

'Uniform Dating.com.'

'You don't wear a uniform.'

'*They* don't know that.'

The magazines piled up. *Country Living* and *Homes and Gardens* were soon joined by *Brides* and *Your Hampshire Wedding*. The Witch took to wearing Burberry and Barbour. There was talk of a dog. How long before she changed her name to Diana?

The romance was piling up. He decorated the house with red roses. She scattered saucy promises of a life of connubial bliss: a scarlet bra draped over a bedpost, a pair of burgundy string briefs on the dresser, a black lacy suspender belt on his study chair. Weapons of mass distraction.

By now feeling herself mistress of the house, she became solicitous, attentive, maternal. Serving him breakfast in bed became her thing: a tray with poached eggs, toast, tea and the *Telegraph*. I heard them trilling to each other. A couple of wood pigeons.

'You're so good to me, my darling.'

'I'll be good wife, yes?'

'You'll be a perfect wife. The best a man could have.'

'I look after you. And I look after house. Soon you no need housekeeper. I housekeeper.'

15

Oil and Sardines

With the late summer bank holiday approaching, I realised with a start that two whole years had passed since I'd left Pete.

I was standing at the kitchen sink, descaling a plump brown trout. Through the window, late summer sun had painted the sky with pinks and purples when my phone rang. It was Karen, my English-teacher friend.

'How's life?'

'I'm up to my elbows in fish scales.'

'Sounds lovely.'

'It's actually alright. The village is gorgeous, my apartment is comfortable, the work is manageable – now – and so is my boss.'

'Sounds ideal.'

'Well, not quite.' And I launched into a tirade against Tatty Anna and her plans to get rid of me.

'She sounds like a nightmare. A straight-up gold-digger.'

'She's awful. She'll take poor Gerald to the cleaners.'

'Is she jealous of you, d'you think?'

'Can't see it. She's gorgeous. The full package – legs, hair, curves.'

'Cow.'

'I know.'

Karen let that hang for a beat, then said, 'Fancy getting away for a few days?'

'What do you have in mind?'

'An old uni friend of mine has invited me out to her place in Spain. Sounds like there'll be room for two.'

I imagined another Saffie. A villa crawling with cats, their aroma sharpened by Mediterranean heat.

'Hm. Don't know. I've just had a week off.'

'Oh, go on! Sounds like old lover boy will be too 'busy' to bother. And the ice queen will likely be glad to get you out of the house.'

'Who's this friend? Is she another hippy?'

'Sharon. She and I did English together at Hull. She was a bit of a punk – well, we all were, weren't we? – then she moved out to Spain years ago with some bloke and went native. Haven't seen her for twenty years. Reading between the lines, I think the bloke's scarpered and she's trying to find herself again.'

'Does she like cats?'

'What are you on about?'

'I mean, is the place full of animals?'

'Doesn't sound like it. It's a finca. We'd fly to Barcelona. So, if it's crap, at least we get to bunk off to the big city.'

'I'll run it past Fish Face and the Witch and I'll get back to you.'

Three days later, Karen and I were in the Beehive Bar at Gatwick, on our second large glass of Pinot Grigio, watching planes fly in from Las Vegas, Dubai and Marrakech and planning how we'd spend our seven days in the sun. Karen loved the sun.

'I'll need to top up this tan.' She pulled down the waistband of her trousers to reveal a strip of flesh marginally less golden than the rest of her and I had a flashback to a nudist beach on Paros, us in our twenties being ogled by teenage boys.

'You're not getting me on another naked beach.'

'We won't need a beach. Sharon's finca has a pool.'

'You're incorrigible.'

'It's a perfectly natural thing to do.'

'If you're a rampant exhibitionist. What would your pupils say? And the principal?'

'The boys would lap it up – the fifth-year boys are all in love with me. And the principal? He'd drop his …'

'Trousers?'

'… opposition to my plan to get *Lady Chatterley* on the syllabus. Cheers!'

Barcelona was basking in 37-degree heat as we walked into Arrivals. It was immediately clear that the intervening years had not been kind to Sharon. People with a careworn countenance are often described as having a 'lived-in' look. Sharon's face was occupied by battalions of enemy troops, a fact not helped by years of exposure to a baking sun. I felt a curious mix of pity and distaste.

Karen stepped forward to give her a hug.

'God! Twenty years!'

'Twenty-two.' She turned to me. No smile.

'Nice to meet you, Sharon.'

'Hi. How was your flight?' She asked the question without seeming remotely interested in the answer.

'It was fine. So how do you find Barcelona?'

'Crowded. I try to avoid it.'

We emerged into a wall of white heat. Sharon pulled a pack of Camel cigarettes from a handbag that looked stitched together from bits of old shoe.

'Want one?'

'No, I'm fine, thanks.'

She looked at Karen. 'Do you still not indulge?'

'Only occasionally. When very drunk.'

Sharon pointed across the car park.

'We're over here.'

Sharon's tall, thin, sunbaked frame loped away in front, her mop of wispy, straw-dry, snow-white hair blowing in the breeze. A cinnamon stick dipped in white candyfloss.

With all the pleasantries apparently out of the way, we were soon speeding out of the city in Sharon's olive-green Ford Taunus, a relic from the set of *Duty Free*. When the Taunus hit the motorway and turned south, heading away from the city, Karen and I exchanged a look. Karen spoke up.

'So, we're not passing by Barcelona?'

Sharon blew smoke out of the window. 'No. Like I said, I try to avoid it. Full of tourists.'

'Good bars and restaurants, though. I'd imagine.'

'They just rip you off. And the drive's a killer. Why would I drive three hours to go to a bar?'

Another look from Karen. Three hours! *That* wasn't in the script!

'So, where exactly are you?'

'The real Spain.'

A worrying whiff of oil was mixing with the acrid stench from Sharon's Camel cigarettes. A steady orange light on the dashboard announced that the Taunus was requiring some attention I imagined Sharon was little disposed to give it. I pictured the three of us sitting at a roadside in some interior wilderness, waiting for a breakdown truck whose driver had a relaxed attitude to punctuality.

Sharon crunched the gears and Olive Oil creaked off the motorway. Within minutes, the flat, soulless scrub had given way to the foothills of impressive snow-topped peaks. Steep terraced groves of orange and lemon trees suddenly appeared, the fruits' bright skins vibrant against the clear Spanish sky. We drove through pretty sandstone villages and past inviting cafes, shady squares, and expansive villas draped with bougainvillea in pink and purple. My mood lifted. Olive Oil creaked on.

An hour later, we passed a sign – Vilanova. Sharon slowed the old Taunus to a crawl and we pulled onto a square.

'This is us. I'll show you round the village.'

Thirty yards away, a rotund man in a vest that had once been white was walking towards us, carrying a crate of wine. Sharon tooted the horn and he waved and picked up the pace.

'My mate. Manolo.'

The man in the vest laid the crate on the ground and leaned in at the window.

'Shazzer! Too long time!' She leaned forward and he planted a wet kiss on her lips.

Sharon practically groaned with pleasure and, when the man pulled away, she coloured up like a schoolgirl.

'So nice to see you, Manolo!'

'Very long time, Shazzer! Where *are* you?'

'Sorry. I've been … busy.'

'You come my restaurant!' The head leaned in again and he leered at me and Karen. 'And pretty girls also!'

Consent was given on our behalf and the crate-carrying restaurateur made off down the road, eyed with evident fluttering passion by the now-animated Shazzer. Karen glanced at me with a furrowed brow. No, I didn't get it either. In the hunk stakes, Manolo was never going to be Spain's greatest export. Antonio Banderas wasn't sweating over Barry The Vest.

A relatively pleasant couple of hours ensued, in which various delicious dishes were produced and dispatched by the hungry travellers, and wine was poured with abandon and consumed with disconcerting gusto by our driver, the proceedings presided over by the leering Manolo who waved away our attempts to pay with genuine magnanimity.

Then it was back into Olive Oil for the last leg, a terrifying ten-minute dice with death. We hugged the edge of a vertiginous ravine, our driver a good litre and a half the worse for wear. I closed my eyes.

When I opened them, we'd come to rest in a patch of waste ground. I assumed Sharon had stopped for an al fresco bathroom break, then she walked to the boot of the Taunus and began lifting out our bags.

Karen and I stood in the dim light of the still-warm evening and looked at each other. An old piece of slate was propped against a crumbling stone wall, with the words *Casa La Shaz* scratched into it.

We peered into the dusk. A few patches of worked ground marked off with stones contained the desperate fruits of an attempt at horticulture, surrounded by a scattering of olive trees badly in need of a firm hand. And, up ahead, a property with all the charm and architectural merit of a municipal toilet block in 1960s East Berlin. Karen looked like she was about to cry. Sharon, by contrast, seemed positively perky.

'Let's have another little drink before we get you settled.'

We toiled up the slope in the gloom, dragging our bags behind us. I tried to look on the bright side.

'You do a bit of gardening then, Sharon.' She looked over to the right and I followed her gaze. A small greenhouse I hadn't noticed was bursting with healthy foliage.

'Oh, that? Yeah, sort of.' We walked on up to the house.

Sharon pushed open the door. A stomach-knotting blend of tobacco and stale wine assaulted my nostrils. Sharon nursed a paraffin lantern into life and the room was revealed.

A coffee table piled with newspapers and empty wine glasses. A battered sofa with two scrawny tabbies curled up on it.

'Can't let the cats go far or the snakes'll have them.'

And, in the corner, what looked alarmingly like an open well. Karen couldn't hide the astonishment in her voice.

'Is that an *actual* well?'

'Yes. Every old house around here has one.'

'Why is it … *indoors*?'

'Water was valuable. Still is. People needed to protect it.'

'So they built their house around it?'

'Yeah.'

'And you use it?'

'Yeah. Have to.'

'So there's no running water?'

'Well, it runs under the ground.'

Karen looked at me while Sharon found wine and rinsed some glasses in a bucket by the well.

'Told you. The real Spain. Can't get more authentic than this.'

I was beginning to feel sick. I was beginning to feel that authenticity was overrated. I was beginning to feel the need for a neon sign, plastic plants, a formica reception desk …

I glanced through the only visible doorway and saw a small and chaotic kitchen. No bathroom (well, no water to put into it, I guess) and no visible sleeping quarters.

Sharon read my mind.

'This is where *I* sleep.' She indicated the sofa. 'You two are in the guest caravan, out the back. We'll have a glass of wine then I'll take you over. Get you settled.'

Deep breaths, Jennifer Brown. Maybe the guest caravan would be a cut above Casa La Shaz. In the hygiene department, anyway.

The guest caravan was an unloved relic of the nineteen fifties, doubtless abandoned by some pissed-off tourists when it gave up the ghost on the long drive south to Fuengirola somewhere around 1973, that glory time when sunshine holidays were suddenly accessible and the high streets of Britain were alive with the chart-topping sound of Al Martino's *Spanish Eyes*.

A caravan abandoned by tourists. Very small tourists.

'Come in,' said Sharon. *What, all three of us?*

The one single bed was clothed in appallingly grubby bedding and would have been a squeeze for an eight-year-old. A wide wooden plank did duty as a table and, as demonstrated by Sharon, doubled up as the second bed with a bit of Heath Robinson adjustment. Four feet away, at the other end of the bed, was a kitchenette that showed no sign of ever having been visited by a bottle of disinfectant. There was, naturally, no toilet or shower. A mosquito net, dusty from age, snagged in my hair.

'Yeah, you'll need to use that. Thousands of the little buggers up here. There's another one in the cupboard, with the bedding for the second bed. Did you bring repellent?'

Karen and I looked at each other and shook our heads.

'I'll dig out a spare bottle. There's water in the tank outside, for washing – I'll keep it full from the well – and you can use my toilet. In the shed behind the house. But take a torch. The light frightens the snakes.'

I looked around for the camera crew. This was either a pilot episode of a revamped *Candid Camera* or I was on the set of *I'm a Gullible Idiot, Get Me Out of Here!*

Tucked up in our sleeping coffins, and wearing clothes from head to toe as much to avoid contamination from the bedding as for protection from mosquitoes, we lay there like two overgrown sardines in a tiny tin can.

I did my best to put a brave face on when Karen fessed up.

'God, Jen! I'm SO sorry!'

'It's fine. You weren't to know. And everything will look a lot better tomorrow. In the sunshine.'

'And if we get lonely, there'll always be Barry The Vest for company!'

'Bloody hell! Can you imagine?'

'I'd rather not. What the hell's *wrong* with her?'

'Judging by the state of this place, I'd say *everything's* wrong with her. Karen, were you two close?'

'Not really. We did the same course, were part of the same extended group of friends. Sharon was a bit more politicised than most of us, and she had her separate *Socialist Worker* crowd that none of us really knew. But she wasn't mental. Not then. And nobody called her *Shazzer*.' Karen tittered at the thought.

'That'll just be *his* name for her. Barry The Vest.' We guffawed.

Then the mosquitoes started to gather. It was probably best if we didn't give them any encouragement.

'Lights out, d'you think?'

'Sure.'

Karen reached under her mosquito net for the paraffin lantern at her elbow, looking for all the world like a travel-weary Miss Havisham.

'Sorry. Again.'

'It'll be fine.'

'Night.'

'Night.'

16

Strictly Come Sweating

We were both a little bleary. I suspected that, like me, Karen had spent a large part of the night listening to the regular sorties flown by the squadrons of mosquitoes that had also made the caravan their home. I remember looking at my phone at 3.17 am. I must have fallen asleep not long after. Karen looked like she hadn't much more than five hours either. The sun was already high by 8.30 and Casa Sardina had reached the temperature of a blast furnace.

We breakfasted on leftover apricot tarts from Barry's and managed to rustle up some coffee on the primus stove in the kitchenette. Karen was ready to explore.

'Shall we check out the pool?'

'Do you dare?'

'What are you thinking? Alligators?'

'Maybe water snakes.'

We pulled on bikinis and shorts and T-shirts and wrestled open the door of our tin home.

You had to admit that, even viewed from the dingy environs of Casa La Shaz, the area around Vilanova was jawdropping lovely. Beyond Sharon's crumbling stone wall, the olive-lined valley descended invitingly to the village below, with a river we hadn't noticed the previous evening twinkling its way round lush fields and imposing pan-tiled properties with neat and fruitful gardens. And beyond, majestic peaks framed what was a gorgeous view indeed. I breathed it in.

'Wow!'

'The real Spain.'

'It's beautiful.'

'And look at that sky.'

'I know. Better get some cream on. I can feel it already.'

By the time I'd slathered on some factor 30, Karen was already down to her bikini and wandering round in search of the pool.

'Found it!' She giggled. Not an auspicious reaction. I followed her voice.

'Bloody hell!'

A galvanised steel water tank, about twelve feet by six, had been transformed into a leisure feature by the addition of a plastic ladder from a kiddy's slide fixed with cable ties. Karen laid a foot on the bottom rung, gingerly testing its strength.

'Go on then. She's *your* pal. Short straw.'

Karen climbed slowly up another three rungs and peered in.

'Er, no. We're not getting in that.'

'What is it?'

'I don't know. But whatever it is, it's made the water green. I don't want a swim *that* bad.'

'Me neither.'

We wandered round outside the house. No noise from within. Sharon was presumably still curled up under her grubby duvet with her tabbies, sleeping it off. We found a couple of battered wooden loungers near an ancient olive tree, by the remnants of a wire fence that marked the side boundary of Sharon's property. The spot was unprepossessing but the view into the valley was superb. Karen was ready for some rays.

'Shall we stretch out here for a while? Plan the day?'

'Sure.'

We spread our towels out on the sun-bleached loungers and settled down, me with the first of my holiday potboilers (the aptly titled *Revenge of the Best Friend*) and Karen with her ears plugged into her iPod ('I do enough reading at work.')

After about three pages, I could feel my eyelids going. I slathered on more cream and succumbed to the delicious somnolent warmth of the Spanish sun.

I was wakened by a mechanical sputter. A small white van had come to rest by the fence, a cloud of burnt oil fumes hovering round its exhaust. Barry The Vest was leaning on the fence, leering over at us.

'Nice day.'

Karen spoke up. 'Are you looking for something?'

I turned to look at Karen. True to form, she had adopted an approach to sunbathing that had its origins in the Garden of Eden, pre-snake. With no spare towel to cover her, she had positioned herself on her stomach, a posture that contained her breasts but favoured Manolo with the delicious sight of her bronzed buttocks. He was drooling.

'I look for Shazzer. I bring wine. You drink with me?' He lifted a crate off the dust. I placed my T-shirt over Karen's bottom.

'No thanks. A bit early for us. Shazzer must be inside. Try the house.'

'One glass wine. No problem.'

'No. Thank you. We were just leaving anyway. Weren't we, Karen?'

'Yes.'

She'd flattened herself on the lounger but a tantalising glimpse of breast did not go unnoticed. 'Yes. We're going for a walk. Into the village.'

'Okay. I deliver wine. I drive you to village.'

'No, no. It's fine. We'd like to walk, wouldn't we Jen?'

'Yes. We love walking. And we love olive trees. Walking *through* olive trees.'

'And *past* them.'

'Yes, we wouldn't want to miss that.'

Barry wasn't stupid. He could see we wouldn't budge.

'Okay. Perhaps you come my restaurant? I show you salsa.' He shook his considerable bulk in a way intended to be alluring.

'Yes. Perhaps.'

He disappeared inside the house and we hastily pulled on our shorts and T-shirts, grabbed our bags and set off down the hill. Five minutes later, the old lech came speeding past us in his banger, black smoke billowing out behind. He gave us a cheery wave and a peep.

For the next few days, we hardly saw Shazzer, which suited us both fine. She'd pop her head into the tin can in the mornings to say hello, fag hanging from the corner of her mouth, then leave us to breakfast on yesterday's pastries from the village while she busied herself with her greenhouse.

Karen and I became regulars in Vilanova, sitting out the fierce midday sun in a café a reassuring distance from Barry's place and spending lazy afternoons in a small but beautifully kept municipal garden with a tiny pool where, well warned by me, Karen observed a respectful modesty.

Then, out of the blue one morning, Sharon suggested a day at the coast. After a two-hour drive along motorway lined with dust and citrus groves, we pitched up in Montsià Mar, a small and fairly classy resort that, given Sharon's way of life, was a surprisingly welcome choice. A waterfront of low-rise hotels, wide whitewashed villas and shady cafés was backed by a strip of pine. This was the real Spain we'd been looking for. Spain with a bit of class.

The class act was tarnished a little when Sharon pulled a white Stetson from the boot and plonked it on her bleached head.

'I know a great little bar a bit out of the town. Manolo's cousin runs it. Dead cheap.' I imagined the place. Tatty. I wasn't having this.

'Tell you what. Karen and I have some souvenir shopping to do. We'll do our own thing for a few hours then we'll come and find you.' My gaze was level. My message was clear. *You're not ruining this for us.*

'Fine.'

Coordinates were exchanged and a time arranged. We parted company.

Mercifully Shazzer-free, Karen and I walked arm-in-arm along the stylish waterfront, drinking in the luxury.

It was lunchtime. Enticing aromas wafted from elegant, shady terraces. We found a gorgeous place with Moorish tiles and a chiselled waiter and, beneath a crisp white awning fanned by a welcome breeze, we sipped zesty Rioja blanco and gazed out over the dreamy Med. Karen was still feeling sheepish about the whole venture.

'Are you glad we came?'

'Of course. It's been lovely spending time with you again. And Vilanova is lovely. And this place is gorgeous. And Sharon's not all bad.'

'She's not all good, though.'

'Who is? I was a bombscare after Pete. For about a year. I was hell to be around. Sharon's just … looking for something. Or someone.'

The image of Barry The Vest hung in the air between us.

'She just needs to look a little harder!' We guffawed.

A few hundred yards down the road, we hit a spa hotel, all white marble and air conditioning and staff in reassuring pseudo-medical garb. On a generous tan leather sofa, we scanned their brochure and settled on the Nautilus package: steam bath to open the pores, full Turkish massage for maximum exfoliation, and hot rock relaxation to finish.

Stepping out into the mid-afternoon sun, and feeling like Jackie Onassis, I looked at my watch. Time for us to catch up with Sharon.

We scoured the waterfront looking for the bar. Then we wandered inland a couple of streets and walked around. For half an hour. Nothing. We stopped an elegant woman walking a mountainous Pomeranian that was not enjoying the heat. She pointed to a tall white spire.

'This church. Then two kilometre.' *Right. A bit out of the town.*

By the time we found it, there were chairs on the tables and shutters on the windows. No Shazzer. Just siesta.

Around us, the town's glistening waterfront had been replaced by dust and weeds. A hundred yards away, on the other side of the main road, half a dozen boys were having a kick-around on a tired-looking football pitch, baked hard by the sun. Next to the pitch, two women sat by a caravan so dilapidated it could have been the Spanish twin of Sharon's Casa Sardina. One of the women turned towards us and waved. She shouted something we couldn't hear. We crossed the deserted road and, as we got closer, it was clear the shouting woman was Sharon.

'Where did you two get to?' she bellowed.

The other woman removed her hands from Sharon's now-much-smaller head. I began to see the reason for this transformation. The woman held a mirror in front of Sharon's face.

'What do you think?'

Sharon's wispy white hair was now held tight against her scalp by a score of multicoloured threads.

'Oh, it's gorgeous. I love it!' With her mahogany tan and her exotic hairdo, she looked like the lovechild of David Dickinson and Whoopi Goldberg. 'What d'you think, girls?'

I couldn't resist. 'Yes, it's a real bobby dazzler.'

Our last night. The last night I'd sleep under a mosquito net. The last night I'd sleep on a plank. The last night I'd sit on a chemical toilet in a shed and worry about snakes.

But first, our last supper. To be partaken of, by appointment, *naturalmente*, at the establishment of Barry The Vest. Manolo had exchanged his characteristic garb for a spangly red number straight from the wardrobe department of *The Liberace Show*, circa 1977. Ah, yes. It was Salsa Night.

Even in her most decorous evening wear, Karen's firm and tanned torso was enough to drive the most restrained gentleman wild. When Barry clocked her from the bar, he practically frothed at the mouth. He sashayed over and kissed her hand.

'Thank you! My beautiful girl, thank you! So nice! So nice!'

Karen kept her nausea under control womanfully and he turned his attention to me.

'Señora, welcome!' Great. Karen was *my beautiful girl* and I was her maiden aunt. Didn't stop the mucky old sod from copping a lingering eyeful of my cleavage.

'Shazzer! Hello!' Another full-on smacker. You get it where you can. For her part, Sharon had gone to quite a bit of effort for our last night together. Glittery black leggings, a shocking pink top, five-inch heels. And the multicoloured braids. Barbie's grandmother.

The little bar was buzzing. Spurs were playing Real Madrid in the Champions League and around thirty well-oiled Real supporters were jumping up and down in front of the 52-inch TV that Barry had fixed to the wall in a room at the back. The noise was deafening. We might as well have been in the home stand of the Bernabéu Stadium.

We chose a seat outside, on the square. Barry brought out a pitcher of sangria and four glasses. He plonked himself down next to Karen.

'So! Last night. Very sad. We drink.' He poured four generous glasses. 'To beautiful ladies. Cheers! *Salud!*'

We responded with a chorus of *Salud!* and Barry leered at us.

'My bar very busy. Football. But later, football finish, we dance salsa. Okay?'

The only way out of this would be two hours of extra time. Or Karen and me faking our own deaths.

'Okay. Yes. Later.'

A seventeen-year-old waiter brought us meatballs, octopus, spicy potatoes, fried sausage and gorgeous garlicky green beans. Karen and I got through a bottle of Rioja blanco while Sharon made short work of a litre of something red and local with no label on the bottle and no questions asked. Barry would occasionally appear in the doorway and smile over at us and shake his hips before running back in to serve beer and hurl abuse at the referee.

Sharon was clearly miffed at the attention being paid to Karen and me. In some ways, this trip had been as much a bust for her as it had for us. Her default setting of morose had switched to despondent. I felt a wave of sympathy for her.

'So, how's the greenhouse doing?'

She looked up from her glass. 'Fine.'

'You spend a lot of time in there.'

'They're valuable plants.'

'Yes, I imagine.' I glanced knowingly at Karen.

'They need a lot of attention. A few hours without water in this heat and I could lose the whole lot.'

Karen joined in. 'My grandad used to spend hours and hours in his greenhouse. Tomatoes. He was mad about them. Grew all sorts of varieties. Then he got adventurous and had a go at courgettes and aubergines. He loved it. It's nice to have an interest, isn't it?'

Where was she going with this?

'What kind of vegetables do you grow?' *That's* where she was going. She really didn't get it.

'Vegetables?'

'Oh, is it fruit?'

'It's cannabis.'

A roar from the back room announced full time and a victory for Real. Barry appeared in the doorway, another pitcher of sangria in his hand.

'We win!'

'Yes.'

'And now, music and dancing and *sangría!*'

We stood up and trooped inside dutifully, while the young waiter cleared our table. The music was already on full blast. Trumpets, a saxophone, bongos. In the back room, the football crowd had thinned out and quietened down, with only a few stragglers reliving the action.

Karen bottled out and headed for the toilet. Barry fixed his eyes on my size 36 double Fs and held out his hand.

'I'm not very good, I'm afraid. I've never danced salsa.' It was the wrong thing to say.

'No problem. I show.' He grabbed my waist and pulled me close. I could smell his breath. I could feel his chest pressed into my breasts, his groin pushing into mine.

'For salsa, we are close.' We could hardly have been closer. 'For salsa, you must move this.' He placed two sweaty hands on my hips and moved them from side to side. I looked across at Sharon. She looked miserable and already three sheets to the wind. Over her shoulder, now out of the toilet but maintaining a safe distance, Karen was biting on a tissue.

'I think Sharon would be better at this than me.' I yanked myself out of his grip and grabbed my glass. I put a hand on Sharon's shoulder.

'Come on, Sharon. Show us tourists how it's done.'

Sharon slapped her glass unsteadily onto the table, recovered a modicum of composure and tottered up to grab Manolo's hips. Visibly crestfallen but thankfully too much of a gentleman to refuse, he took her hands and together they gyrated round the tiles not entirely without style or accomplishment.

I turned to Karen.

'I was Manalo-handled.'

She shuddered. 'Yes. I saw. Serves you right.'

'Eh?'

'For having great tits.'

17

Knickers and a Vicar

Back at Fishers Keep, Tatty Anna had been marking her territory good and proper while I'd been away. The English Country Lady style had acquired a certain burlesque quality around the edges. A zebra skin now adorned the back of Gerald's leather couch. A new table lamp, all chrome and cranberry glass, now lit up a once-dull corner of the hall next to the coatstand. And in the bedroom, tiger-skin scatter cushions on the bed and on a newly acquired chair fashioned in the *boudoir* style.

The only thing left untouched was old Alphonse the champion trout, gazing down from his glass case with imperious disdain.

And Alphonse was no longer the only non-human resident. In spite of the much-talked-about plans for a dog, the White Witch had acquired a feline friend, Abramovich, a huge ball of white Persian fur with his mistress's aquamarine eyes. Every inch a puffed-up pussy.

He sat on a scarlet velvet cushion on a chair in the corner of the kitchen. Like a tsar, he eyed me intently. *We Russians have taken over, lapochka – you'd better get used to it.*

But the most peculiar change of all was in Gerald himself. He appeared to have sprouted a completely new head of hair. The hairpiece, unfeasibly brown for a man of his advanced years, perched on his head at a queasy angle, looking for all the world like the unfortunate result of a boisterous game of Splat the Rat.

And there were other changes. Cashmere sweaters and Windsor corduroys had been replaced by skinny jeans and a black hoodie proclaiming the wearer to be *The Main Man*. I had to look away.

And cycling was the new fishing. Off they'd pootle down the lane, the hoodie-clad Gerald looking like ET on the run from the government agents.

Eating habits had also been adjusted. Rich, wine-based sauces and robust roasts had yielded to salads and cold, vegetable-based soups. The fridge suggested a desire to corner the world market in carrots. Or did we now have a rabbit-breeding programme in place to supply the white fur that seemed to trim every item in Tatty Anna's wardrobe?

Autumn arrived with early morning mists that lingered on the stately river and, in the hedgerows, spiders' webs that sparkled with heavy dew.

Tatty Anna continued to spin her own web tighter round Gerald, pulling him into her model of a life together, with marriage as its urgent goal. He was still entirely in her thrall, beaming up at her like a lovesick schoolboy and showering her with evermore expensive gifts – some classic, like the gold necklace and matching earrings from Cartier that she displayed pointedly whenever I was around; some a little more off-piste, like the top-of-the-range, bells-and-whistles, money-to-burn GPS training watch she flashed at me one morning after yanking the parcel out of the postman's hand.

'Look what my Gerry have bought for me!' She waved it under my nose. It had more controls than the flight deck of the space shuttle.

'New training cock.'

'Cock?'

'Yes. For time. For showing how fast my heart boom boom, how far I am running.'

'Oh, clock.'

'Yes, clock. Is what I say.'

'No, you said *cock*. That's something different. Anyway, you don't mean *clock*, you mean *watch*.'

'Cock, watch, is same. It show time, it show heart, it show how far.'

'Yes, but …'

'And it wake me.'

'It has an alarm. Right.'

'Good for waking me in night.'

'In the night? You mean in the morning?'

'Yes, morning. Also night.'

Hm.

After dinner, as I was loading the dishwasher, I overheard the lovebirds talking in the study. Tat was holding court. That was happening a lot.

'Jennifer, she no good cook. She make you fat food.'

'It's the food I've always eaten. It's very nice.'

'It make you fat. No energy. No good for making babies.'

I dropped the dishwasher liquid. A blue puddle on the terracotta tiles.

'Everything okay, Jennifer?' Gerald shouted, from the hall.

'Fine,' I shouted back. 'Just dropped something. Nothing broken. Easily wiped up.'

So that was her game. Poor Gerald. Not only was old morning glory being put to good use, but he was also being asked to stand to attention in the middle of the night. *My new training cock.* Poor old sod. I hoped he wouldn't do his back in.

One morning, when the coast was clear, and Tat had consented to jog off on her own for once (armed with the training cock), I put the mountain of ironing to one side and walked across the garden to the fishing hut, the once-favourite refuge Gerald hardly ever visited now.

He was tying new flies. I tapped on the door, which was slightly ajar. He looked up, startled, then relaxed into a rather weary smile.

'Just came over to ask if you need anything.'

'That's very kind. No, I'm fine, thank you.'

'Are you?'

He made a show of looking puzzled, toeing the party line.

'Of course. Why wouldn't I be? Life is …'

'Exhausting?'

He sneezed. Then again. Then a third time. He wiped at his nose with a handkerchief.

'I seem to be sneezing a lot. Have you changed the washing powder?' *It's not the washing powder, mate – it's that bloody cat!*

'No. No change of washing powder or conditioner or soap or shower gel. Can you think of anything else that might be causing it?' *Open your eyes, you lovesick old fool.*

'Not really.'

There's just no telling some men.

That evening, Tat appeared in the kitchen. She seemed to know I'd spoken to Gerald earlier.

'I need speak for the cooking.' Hands placed firmly on hips. 'You must make good food. Russian food. Then sneezing stop.'

'I don't think Gerald's sneezing has anything to do with his diet.'

'You don't think. Are you doctor?'

'No, but …'

'No.'

I looked over at Abramovich, recumbent on his throne. 'It's much more likely to be your cat. He's allergic to the cat. He needs medication. Or he needs no cat.'

'He need good food. Strong food.'

'Carrots?'

'Yes. Carrot. No more English skinny beans. Good strong carrot. Good for heart. Good for blood. And,' she put a thin cold finger on my face, just above the cheekbone, 'good for these lines.'

Bitch!

September brought foul weather and a foul mood in the house. Tatty Anna became more demanding. She found fault with everything I did. She'd wait till Gerald was out of earshot then she'd put the boot in.

'This house not clean. Not like my mother's.' She'd run a long finger across the top of a door. 'You need to clean better.'

She reached up.

'And this.' A filament of cobweb retrieved from the lintel of the kitchen door. 'Not clean. Delete this.' *I know what I'd like to delete.* I piled on the sweetness.

'Of course. Anything else?'

'No else. For now.'

Much as I hated to admit it, she was right. It did seem to be prime spider season. I'd never been in a house that spiders loved as much as they seemed to love this one. Had it always been like this? Or did they feel the pull of the Queen? The White Witch turned Black Widow, at the heart of a vast web, poised to gobble up her mate.

'Perhaps tonight, Jennifer, your delicious *sole meunière.*'

'I don't think Tatyana would approve.'

'She will. On this occasion.'

'Is it Society friends?'

'No. There'll just be three of us: myself, Tatyana and the vicar.'

'I see. Is he fundraising again?'

'Well, a contribution may be discussed, but he's coming over to talk about the wedding.'

I was stunned. We get *Your Hampshire Wedding* delivered to the house then ten minutes later it's dinner with the vicar.

'Gosh. I had no idea you were planning it for so soon.'

'No, well, things *have* moved rather quickly. There's now an … administrative urgency.'

'Right. Well, as long as you're happy.'

'Yes. Oh, yes. Tatyana's lovely. Of course.'

'She's very beautiful, yes.'

An administrative urgency. The language of love it wasn't. So Tatty Anna's visa was running out. What the Americans call a Green Card Wedding.

Daft sod.

St Matthews was Damian Gray's first charge as a proper vicar, so he was young. But his troubled complexion and greasy hair, coupled with a natural diffidence, belied his twenty-seven years. When he climbed into the pulpit to deliver a sermon to the blue-rinse brigade, you wondered why he wasn't veging out in front of a Playstation or propping up the bar in the student union. I imagined him needing a couple of belts of communion wine just to get him up the steps.

His skin issues weren't helped by the ladies from the WI, who force-fed him homemade Victoria sponge and macaroons. And now he was having to cope with the White Witch.

Tatty Anna was all over him like the rash on his face. She'd gone to town with her appearance, fluffing up her feline looks, straightening her hair and wearing more bling than Oxford Street at Christmas. Gerald had been allowed to revert to classic slacks and shirt for the occasion, although the errant hairpiece gave the whole ensemble a rather unsettling air. The toupee was still attracting the attention of the ever-watchful Abramovich who, when the thing was left on the bedside cabinet, was apt to pounce and subject it to a furious bout of mixed martial arts. No amount of primping could ever quite restore its form, giving Gerald the air of an ageing bass player with the New York Dolls.

Damian blushed as Tatty Anna buried him in her athletic bosom. Then she pulled him away and planted a ruby-red kiss on each cheek.

'I give Russian welcome.' Gerald tried to inject some decorum.

'This is Tatyana. My, er, fiancée.'

'Pleased to meet you, miss, er … Damian. Damian Gray. Please do call me Damian.'

Damian. The devil's child. Poor lad.

By the time I was carrying in a tray of coffee, Gerald was pouring a second glass of vodka for the vicar. Tatty Anna was brushing away his objections.

'Nonsense. This best vodka. For best vicar. For best WEDDING!'

Her strident tones startled Abramovich and he darted out of the room.

I poured coffee and offered round a plate of the titanium-strength shortbread Tatty Anna had knocked up earlier.

'You must drink. And EAT!'

Damian applied his boyish gums to the artillery but they just bounced off. He smiled awkwardly then decided on a policy of total immersion. Maybe the slab would soften and become chewable. Maybe, with an effort, he could get the whole thing down in one go.

His digestive system was rescued by the cat, who sidled in with something white and furry in its mouth. *Great. Another dead mouse for me to deal with.* Tatty Anna scooped him into her arms.

'Bad boy. Give to Mama.' She coaxed the object from his jaw and held it up. A fur-covered thong. Gerald blushed. Tatty Anna roared with laughter. Damian spat his shortbread into a napkin and rammed it in his pocket.

'Silly boy. He think it MOUSE!' She roared again. Gerald tried to look amused.

'So sorry. I have no control over pussy.'

Clutching a cheque, a fawning Damian was ushered to the door by Gerald.

'This really is incredibly generous.'

'Think nothing of it. We're grateful to you for finding us such an early slot in your busy schedule.'

'Oh, please don't think I was asking …'

'Not at all. I'm very happy to help.'

So Fishers Keep was sucked into a maelstrom of weddingness and, with military precision, a plan was set out. It was to be a private affair with only a handful of guests. A traditional church ceremony at St Matthews on December 13th (inauspicious?) followed by a glitzy reception back at the house. The theme was to be 'Winter Wonderland'. White fur and glitter. A dress embroidered with two thousand sequins, complete with matching tiara and fur-trimmed bolero jacket. And, in the wings, a snow blower and sixteen tons of fake snow, in case mother nature didn't agree to play ball.

On the guest list, Tat's mother and twin brothers shipped in from St Petersburg, and Norman and Raymond from the Society. And Abramovich. The guest of honour. At the altar. On his scarlet velvet cushion. A red ribbon round his neck.

Oh, and me.

Well, she needed someone to look after the cat.

18

The Brothers Kalashnikov

The house was in the grip of fever. Wedding fever.

With just a few days to go, the wedding spend had spiralled out of control. Bushels of flowers, gold-plated cutlery, a white horse (hired to wander around outside looking whimsical). Tatty Anna was now Queen of All She Surveyed and I was pushed further and further into the shadows. It was clear I was not long for this job.

My thoughts turned to Intext. How was Jonathan coping with Zilla? Had the HRTs boiled Ed in oil? Had Will found the man of his dreams?

I called him. A noise in the background like the Russian army rolling into Southsea.

'What on earth are you doing?'

'Oh, that. It's my new food processor. I'm trying to be a demon cook. Like you. Not.'

'Shut up. What are you whizzing? A grizzly bear?'

'It's pine nuts, Miss Sarky Knickers. I'm making pesto. Anyway, you should be ministering to the needs of your ice queen, not chatting on the phone to this old queen.'

'They've gone shopping for a fur-trimmed pageboy outfit for the cat, so I'm taking a break. Feet up. Cooking sherry on the go.'

'Seriously? A pageboy outfit for the *cat*?'

'I wouldn't be surprised. It'll be something daft like that.'

'So how is it?'

'It's fine. I won't be here for ever. She's made that very clear. And he knows which side his bread's buttered on so he won't defy her.'

'What will you do?'

'Don't know yet. Start looking around, I guess. In the meantime, I'm planning the wedding cake and the menu. A savoury buffet with Russian finger food and some sort of Russian tart for dessert.'

With the big day looming, Tatty Anna decided she needed a holiday. Cue a mini-break to Rome. Some culture for Gerald, doubtless some shopping for Tat. And a papal blessing for their union? I wouldn't have put it past her to ask.

Before the departure for the eternal city, I was briefed on Operation Wedding Cake. Carrot-cake sponge (of course) with, for the icing, a blend of sugar with fat-free cream cheese and low-fat margarine. Sounded dismally virtuous but I agreed to produce a sample for her inspection.

I scoured the internet for suitable bride and groom figures to put on top. Hamleys online offered ranges from Beatrix Potter and CS Lewis, so the choice was easy: Mr Jeremy Fisher and the Narnia Witch.

Then I decided to get a head start on cleaning the house, so I wouldn't be sweating when the wedding decorators arrived.

Gerald and I were still playing the fishing-fly game and he'd been very creative of late: behind the flex of the new hall lamp, on top of the chandelier in the bedroom (don't ask), under Abramovich's velvet cushion in the kitchen. With the reception around the corner, this week I reckoned he'd be focusing on the drawing room. That's where the guests would assemble and quaff champagne while I was seeing to the wedding breakfast.

I was on the next-to-top rung of the stepladder, feeling along the back of Alphonse's glass coffin, when I lost my balance.

The ladder juddered horribly and, in my panic, I grabbed the glass case, which promptly detached itself from the wall and slipped through my hands, shattering into a thousand pieces on the floor below my tottering ladder. I grabbed the chimney breast and steadied myself. I was still in one piece.

Alphonse, on the other hand, was now in four pieces: a body, a severed tail, and two wandering eyes. Perhaps scenting traces of fish through the clouds of formaldehyde, Abramovich appeared at the door. He glanced at the traumatised trout then stared at me: *You're in deep water now, lapochka.*

Ten minutes on Rated People and I'd found a glazier an hour away. I set to work with the superglue, restored Alphonse to a level of integrity I trusted would pass muster from behind a quarter of an inch of glass, and put the kettle on while I started clearing up the mess. The glassman was early.

'Blimey, love. What happened?'

'I had a funny turn.'

'My wife gets those. Mostly when I'm around.'

He replaced the case with ease and I rubbed some brown shoe polish into the scratches on the frame. Good as new.

'Right, let's get him back in then I'll seal the end.' The glassman picked up Alphonse.

'Has he always looked like this?'

'Like what?'

'His eye. He looks a bit … surprised. Or pissed.'

'Bloody hell!'

'What?'

'His eyes fell out. When I dropped him. I've stuck them back in.'

'No matter. We'll just pop them out and refit them.'

'We can't.'

'Why?'

'I used superglue.'

Gerald and Tatty Anna arrived back from Rome full of smiles, Tat sporting a tan not wholly ascribable to nature. They'd had a wonderful time: the Trevi Fountain, the Pantheon and the Colosseum. They'd particularly enjoyed the Colosseum. I had an image of lions, Gerald crawling in the dust in Christian rags, Tatty Anna in the imperial box, thumb down.

The house was now a hive of activity. Various hired hands had been drafted in to carry out the mistress's wishes. Tatty Anna strode round the house pointing, issuing orders, tearing workers off a strip. Gerald shuffled behind her, mending fences, pouring oil on troubled waters, sneezing. The carrots clearly weren't working.

D-Day minus one and, as I was draping white satin ribbon round the cotoneasters by the front door, I heard tyres on gravel and turned to see a long black car pull up. A tall, powerfully built blond man in a suit climbed out of the driver's seat and opened the door, giving his hand to the passenger.

Tat's mother was built like a barrel and her face, crowned with blonde frizz resembling a haystack in a force-eight gale, was deeply etched with a network of crags. Life in the old country had clearly not always been comfortable. A second well-tailored blond man, a carbon copy of the driver, moved round to take her other hand.

'Mama!'

Tatyana rushed past me to take the woman in her arms, the old lady now looking more keg than barrel in her Amazonian daughter's embrace.

Then she turned to her brothers. 'Aleksandr! Andrei!' They kissed and cuddled and slapped each other, for all the world like three strapping drinking buddies. The noise startled a flock of Canada geese into flight. They headed upstream in search of quieter environs.

The brothers stepped back and cast an appraising eye over the exterior of Fishers Keep. I looked at them. Expensive suits.

Gold watches. Gym-honed bodies. Blond lions moving in for the kill. Their latest acquisition in an extensive portfolio of dodgy dealings.

The party swept past me and into the house. I followed them into the wedding-ready drawing room and was asked to pour vodka into the crystal goblets Gerald had set out on the sideboard. Toasts were made and the visitors downed their vodka in unison. Then, one by one, they hurled their empty glasses into the fireplace. This traditional Russian gesture of good luck was not particularly welcomed by Gerald, who blanched when another round was poured into a second set of vintage crystal. I read his mind and whispered in his ear.

'I'll get some cheap ones. From Waitrose.'

'Oh, would you mind?'

'Not at all.'

'You're a treasure.' I think I'll quickly become buried treasure if I come between you and your new family.

I decamped to the kitchen to put the finishing touches to the icing. Ten minutes later, I heard Gerald's voice in the hallway.

'And these oak panels are all original. And the plasterwork cornicing has been restored in keeping with the architect's drawings of 1846.'

The brothers were getting the tour.

'Very nice.'

'And the kitchen, too, has many original features. The floortiles are early Victorian.'

One of the brothers plonked what looked like an enormous cake box on the kitchen table. I was confused. What about the carrot cake I'd been slaving over for two days?

'You brought a cake?' Tatty Anna looked at me disdainfully. 'It not cake. It BREAD!'

Gerald was in full estate agent mode. 'And look at this marble slab in the pantry. You just can't buy marble that thick these days.'

I peered inside the box. The article inside was the size of a small satellite dish and richly decorated with tiny white flowers. An impressive piece of baking.

'We break bread. At wedding. Russian wedding. In my country, bread mean life!'

'Right.'

The brothers were gazing round the kitchen approvingly.

'Very nice. Very good home for our Tanya,' said one.

'Yes.'

The other brother leaned in close. 'And you, Mister Gerald. You make very good husband. Right?'

'Yes. Of course. Right.'

They didn't exactly tie him to a chair and pull on the knuckledusters, but the effect was the same.

'Would you like to see upstairs?'

'Yes. We like.'

Gerald walked out, looking over his shoulder. A phone buzzed and one of the brothers dug into his pocket, leaving the other to continue the tour with Gerald. I strained an ear.

'Yes. One hour. We bring. You be ready.'

With the preparations all in place, I settled down in my apartment with a glass of Chardonnay. Looking out over the garden down to the river, I felt pretty relaxed, considering. It was a gorgeous, still, crisp evening and the forecast for the following day was more of the same. The wedding gods were smiling on our little Russian gathering. Maybe things would work out for the best after all.

Gerald and the brothers came into view. A tour of the grounds, with some fly-fishing tips thrown in, perhaps. One of the brothers looked at his watch and nodded to the other. He said something to Gerald, who took a step back, alarmed. I sat up. One of them gripped Gerald in a bear hug while the other produced a cloth bag and, with practised ease, pulled it over the head of my struggling employer, who was then scooped up like a child and carried round to the front of the house.

By the time I reached the front door, the long black car was pulling away down the gravel drive. I stood there for several seconds, stunned.

Then I called the police.

Detective Sargeant Bailey was a world-weary fifty-year-old in an ill-fitting suit.

'A kidnap?'

'I heard them arrange it. *Be ready in one hour*, he said.'

'And these two men, they're his brothers-in-law?'

'Well, not yet. They will be tomorrow. But there isn't going to *be* a wedding, is there? Not now.'

'Can you describe these two men?'

'Tall. Blond. Russian. Wearing suits. Black.'

'Men in black.'

'They're very dodgy-looking.'

'And this man, your employer, he's marrying their sister?'

'He's supposed to be, yes.'

'And she's where?'

'I don't know. She was here earlier, but there's no sign of her now. She's disappeared. I'm really worried about Gerald. About what they might do to him.'

'Does he have a phone? Gerald?'

'I've tried it but it's here. He left it here. He's always forgetting it.'

'What about friends? Could he be with friends?'

'He's with those two men! They've kidnapped him! I saw it!'

'Can I see his phone, please?'

I passed him the old steam-driven Nokia that Gerald was still using on pay-as-you-go. The exact same model as my mother's. The detective scrolled through Gerald's slim list of contacts.

'Norman. Seems to make lots of calls to him. A close friend?'

'One of his fishing society buddies, yes.'

'Could he be with this Norman?'

'He's been kidnapped!'

'Let's try Norman.' He pushed the call button. I heard a voice answer.

'Sorry to bother you, sir. Hampshire Police. My name's Bailey. I'm a detective sergeant. I'm trying to get in touch with a friend of yours – Gerald Fisher.'

I heard Norman answer. He babbled on for a couple of minutes. The detective listened patiently.

'Uh huh … I see … Yes, I can imagine … Right … That's all fine, sir. Thanks for your help.'

He hung up.

'Your employer's at the Boatman's Arms.'

'What?'

'He's in the bar. There's karaoke.'

'But …'

'He's getting married tomorrow, you said.'

'Yes, but …'

'He's been the victim of a stag-night prank. Not a kidnap.'

Gerald Fisher and Tatyana Brechkovsky tied the knot at 2 pm on December 13th in the Church of St Matthew, Singleton Ferrers.

The bride dazzled like a thousand-watt bulb in her sequin-encrusted gown and, as she walked up the aisle, the organist played Abba's *I Do I Do I Do* (if I'd known Abba were in the running, I'd have put a fiver on *Money Money Money*).

The ceremony went fairly smoothly but not completely without incident. Damian had never looked more in need of a slug of wine and the poor lad fluffed his lines three or four times, memorably asking Gerald if he would take Tatyana as his lawful wedded *knife*.

Photos were taken by the oak tree in the churchyard, then more under the lychgate, then, after all that Englishness, the small party headed back along the lane to Fishers Keep, where the mood was decidedly more Russian. The first official toast to the newlyweds was given by the blond boys. Vodka glasses were raised and the fiery spirit downed. Then the cry of *Gorko!* ('Bitter!') rang out, an invitation to the happy couple to enjoy a lingering kiss to drive out the bitter taste of the vodka and the bitterness of their old lives before the sweetness of married life together. A beautiful and poignant tradition.

Then bride and groom pulled a chunk each off the satellite dish and dipped it in a bowl of salt and fed it to each other. Then more vodka and more kissing. Nice touches.

Gerald looked the happiest I'd ever seen him. He walked over to me. 'Thank you for all this. I know it's been a lot of work.'

'I'm glad you're pleased.'

'And that cake! It's delicious! Ten out of ten!'

'Praise indeed.'

He looked suddenly rather sombre. 'I've not been very good, have I? As an employer, I mean.'

'Well, it took us a while to get there. Between us. It's fine now.'

'Jennifer … Tatyana feels …'

'I know. Don't worry. I'm looking already.'

'I have no complaints at all. Quite the contrary. I've been a pig and you … well, you've been marvellous. It's just …'

'It's fine. She's your wife now. She has a say. An important one.'

'But you'll stay on until you find something. I won't be moved on *that* point.'

'Thank you.'

'It's the very least I can do. And your reference will be positively glowing.'

'That's kind. I appreciate it.'

He squeezed my hand. Then he trotted back to his bride.

As the sun was setting over the Test, the long black car crunched away down the gravel, carrying Mr and Mrs Gerald Fisher and the Russian party off to Gatwick, where the eastern branch of the family would pick up a flight back to St Petersburg while the newlyweds would head out to Barbados for some summer sun. I hoped for Gerald's sake there'd be time for a spot of fishing between spa sessions.

By the time I'd got rid of Norman, it was half past two. The house was eerily silent with everyone gone, and I was wide awake. But I was in no mood to tackle the clearing-up – that would have to wait till tomorrow.

So I fired up my laptop and opened my CV.

19

A Quick Change

I'd been busy. Four days into the honeymoon and I'd bagged a handful of interviews with a variety of employment agencies. Time to dig out the faithful blue suit, which looked better on me than it had a year ago. For old times' sake, and for good luck, I dressed it up with Helen's pink scarf. At Winchester, I stepped onto the Waterloo train feeling ready for a new chapter.

As Hampshire leeched into Surrey, more and more commuters piled onto the train. It'd been a few years since I'd done the rush hour. Was I ready for it again?

I looked around. Opposite me, a pinstripe suit in his fifties reading the *Telegraph* – a barrister or a senior civil servant. Across the aisle, a pair of Next heels in her early thirties on the phone (*I know they won't settle for less than eight two five*) – an estate agent.

We judge people by their jobs, don't we? At parties, the second question is usually *What do you do?* Based on the answer, we judge, categorise, pigeonhole.

What was I? What would I say at the party? Housekeeper? Made me sound like Mrs Bridges. Also uncomfortably close to House*wife*. A woman defined by her relationship to her husband and her family and her house. A woman who doesn't do much beyond look after others. A woman who doesn't have a proper job.

'This train will shortly arrive at Waterloo.' The incantation that gets commuters on their feet, jostling for position, five minutes too soon. Pinstripe folded his paper neatly and buttoned his cashmere coat. Heels stowed her phone and grabbed her John Lewis briefcase. And, together with fourteen thousand other lemmings, the three of us filed through the ticket barriers and prepared to start the day.

I spent the morning zigzagging my way across West London on the District, Circle and Piccadilly lines. A succession of polished brass plaques on the freshly painted doors of elegant Georgian mansions. A tight schedule. Dread Ed wouldn't have stood a chance.

And all the while really not sure I wanted this again. The rushing, the suits, the straphangers' armpits in your face on the Tube. By four o'clock, I was on my knees. Last one. *Chin up, Jennifer Brown.*

'With your portfolio of experience, I do have *one* position that you'd be rather perfect for, I think, though it's perhaps not quite what you're after.'

'What is it?'

'The client is looking for a Personal Assistant, which you might think is a bit of a sideways move.'

Hm. Back to an office. Well, it'd always been on the cards, I suppose.

'Who's the client?'

'It would be something of a challenge, though. But it does play to your strengths and, in a way, your most recent experience. The client is a wealthy gentleman who runs a large estate. He's listed a variety of duties.'

I imagined someone like Norman. An overgrown schoolboy with a vivid imagination when it came to personal services.

'What sort of services? I'm not sure I'd be up for taking someone to the toilet. Or giving him bed baths.'

'Oh, no. It's nothing like that. And no nursing experience has been asked for, so you'd be perfectly within your rights to refuse any such duties. You'd have the full backing of the agency.'

'Okay. Well, that's good.'

'No, it's all secretarial, administrative stuff. There's an estate manager and you'd liaise with him. Be a sort of link between the client and the house on the one hand and the wider estate on the other.'

It sounded like a challenge the new Jennifer could rise to. With her *portfolio of experience.* 'That sounds very suitable, yes.'

'But it *is* in the country. Perhaps you were hoping for a move to the city? To a more urban environment?'

I thought of crowds and armpits and *Mind the Gap.* 'The country would suit me fine.'

'It's only for six months, I'm afraid. Initially.'

'That wouldn't be a problem. Initially.'

'One thing, though. He's looking for someone to start right away. And I should show you the salary. Perhaps a little less than you could expect in the city.'

She slid the file across the desk and pointed to a figure only slightly less than double the salary I was currently paid at Fishers Keep.

'Where is it?'

'Little Compton. Cotswolds.'

'I'll go home and pack.'

I spent my last day in Singleton Ferrers down by the water, watching the cold grey river slide past me on its journey down to the sea. A white heron stood motionless on the opposite bank. He looked content with his life of solitude. Was I with mine?

I prepared a batch of *sauce meunière* and put it in the fridge. Gerald could steam a sole to go with it when they got back later that evening, in the afterglow of their fabulous honeymoon.

Then I wrote him a note, thanking him for everything, apologising for the hasty departure but suggesting it was all for the best, wishing him well for the future.

I pulled the door to and looked back through the glass into the hall. Abramovich had followed me and now sat on the carpet like a sentinel. *I told you, lapochka. But no hard feelings, eh?*

Part Three

Thornhill Hall

20

Full-on Monty

The new year blew in with a bitter east wind, colder than Tatty Anna's heart of ice.

'You've reached your destination, windows up, sunnies on and don't let the seagulls steal ya chips!'

I wouldn't be needing Brucie's advice. Under a leaden sky, I climbed out of my little blue Peugeot, swathed in a black astrakhan coat, my recent nod to Russian fashion picked up for a song in Armstrongs Vintage in Chichester. It was the warmest garment I owned but, even with the collar up, a biting wind ripped into my cheek as I pressed the buzzer.

The gatehouse was a low, wide, stone building. Its heavy wooden door was Gothic-arched and looked capable of withstanding artillery. Tiny windows had been glazed in the Victorian style, but this building was much older than the Prussian sourpuss.

A woman's voice squawked from the box.

'Who is it?'

'Jennifer Brown. From the agency.' I was aware of shouting. *Calm down.*

'Make your way to the main house. Side entrance. On the left.'

An electrical buzz. A pair of ancient wrought-iron gates creaked open. I climbed back into the Peugeot and slipped through.

The single-track road cut through a vast area of parkland dotted with sheep and cows and stately broad-leafed trees. After a good couple of minutes, the road dipped. In the distance, the imposing Elizabethan bulk of Thornhill Hall announced itself with a fanfare.

Fishers Keep had been a bourgeois, Victorian notion of opulence. This was the real deal. A duchess, not a draper's wife.

A woman stood waiting for me at the side entrance on the left. About my height and a little older than me, she wore a light-blue uniform that suggested something medical.

'Hi. I'm Jen.'

She looked me up and down. I remembered Aunt Mildred and the beach house. 'Mr Winstanley is waiting for you. In the library.'

'Thank you, er …'

'Veronica. I'm Mr Winstanley's nurse.'

Her demeanour didn't suggest nurse. It suggested chief surgeon.

She turned on her heel. I followed her, down a dark narrow corridor, oak floorboards and painted plaster walls.

'What's it like? Working here?' She was marching on ahead but I was not inclined to trot. 'What other staff are there?'

'Just three of us these days.' She looked over her shoulder, saw I'd fallen behind, and looked at me in the manner of a schoolmistress chivvying a foot-dragging charge. I looked back and sauntered.

'Three of you.'

Her self-assurance faltered.

'Er, yes. Myself – nurse, personal carer. Rosemary – housekeeper and cook. And Robbie – gardener.'

'Just one gardener? For all that land?'

'He occasionally has help. Casual labour. For seasonal work.'

'But still.'

'A lot of the land is tenanted out to farmers.'

'Yes. I saw the sheep. And cattle.'

'That brings some income for the estate. I imagine. I guess it'll be your job to see to that.'

Hm. Where is this estate manager the agency told me about?

'So just three permanent staff and occasional seasonal help? It's a big place. Is that enough?'

'Well, four now. With you. And there's Kate.'

'Kate?'

'She comes up from the village three days a week to do cleaning.'

'She must have her work cut out.'

'She works hard. Which makes up for the rest.'

We'd passed through a door into a wide carpeted hallway with several doors leading off it. Through one of the doors, I saw a long gallery, panelled floor to ceiling. Mullioned windows with leaded glass in a diamond pattern. Flickering light from a log fire, although the room was deserted.

'A corporate shoot on Wednesday. Rosemary needs to warm the place up. The gallery's where they'll eat. Henry the Eighth.'

'*Yes.' More his daughter, surely.*

'The library's in here.' She tapped on a door and pushed it open. 'Jennifer has arrived, Mr Winstanley. Jennifer Brown.' She stood back to let me in.

I glanced around the room. Walls lined with shelves crammed with leather- bound volumes. Dark oak panels adorned with portraits of stern-looking men in military uniform, staring down at me impassively. It might have been a reading room in an Oxford college.

But there was warmth. A fireplace on the far wall, logs crackling. And above the fireplace, a portrait of a young woman, spirited and self-possessed but, unlike her frosty male companions, smiling at me with evident amiability. A timepiece ticked away somewhere, measured, peaceful. So unlike my mum's chaotic front room with its cacophonous clocks.

George Winstanley swivelled his electric wheelchair round to face me. A shock of white hair and white beetling eyebrows.

'Come in. Please.' He sounded frail, as if speech caused him some difficulty. But he had clearly been, in his time, a solidly built man. He manoeuvred the wheelchair with his right hand, the left hanging down at the side of the chair, apparently lifeless. The result of a stroke, perhaps.

'The fire will soon warm you. You look perished.'

'Thank you. Yes, it's very cold today, isn't it.' I sat down on one of a pair of leather sofas flanking the fireplace, so soft it caused me to recline more than I wanted to. I struggled to sit upright.

'Make yourself comfortable. Have you come far?' He looked at me with the steady gaze of a man used to being listened to.

'Hampshire.'

'Far enough.'

'Yes.'

'How d'you think you'll like us here in Oxfordshire?'

'The estate is beautiful. And the house.'

'They're millstones round my neck. Which is where you come in.'

'Yes.'

Right. So the Estate Manager is me. Time to blag it.

'My neck's too old to bear the weight. All of it.'

'I think I can take some of that weight from you.'

He looked at me appraisingly. 'Yes. I think you can.' A gorgeous black Labrador padded in and sat down on his left side. The old man reached his right arm over and stroked the animal's glossy coat.

'I'm an old bugger. But Benson likes me.'

'I can see that.'

'I hope we'll get along, you and I.'

'I think we will, Mr Winstanley.'

'Yes. I think we shall. I'm George. Mr Winstanley is my father.'

'George.'

'Have you met the others?'

'Only Veronica.'

'Not a bad girl. Does all the unpleasant stuff. Washing. Dressing. Injections. Stuff you need a strong stomach for. Makes you a bit sour, by the looks of it.'

I smiled.

'But she keeps me in reasonable working order.'

'Yes.'

'And you're on her turf, you see. I'm her pet project. And now you're here as my right hand – ah, the irony! – well, you've sort of ruffled her feathers.'

'I think we'll be alright.'

'Yes, I think you can sort her out. Be gentle. She doesn't have it easy with me. And neither will you.'

The Labrador padded over to me and manoeuvred his velvet head under my hand.

'He's a handsome fellow.'

'I'm afraid he's a terrible flirt. A ladies' man.'

'He seems fond of you.'

'Oh, he quite likes me. But he wouldn't fret much if I fell under a bus. My wife, on the other hand …'

'Mrs Winstanley is his favourite?'

'He is besotted with Camilla. And the fact that she ignores him makes the love stronger still.'

'She doesn't like dogs?'

'She's rather fastidious about her appearance. The nuzzling, the licking, the coat still wet from a roll in the morning dew … It's not her thing.'

'Ah.'

'Anyway. Let's get you settled. I'll have Robbie take your bags up to your room.'

'Oh, please don't bother him. I'm sure he's busy enough. I'll manage.'

'Right answer. Welcome to Thornhill Hall, Jennifer Brown.'

The room was thirty feet square and exceptionally grand. A huge double bed, as wide as it was long. A large alcove with a walnut writing desk, overlooking the gardens. An expansive bathroom with elaborate Victorian sanitaryware, the height of fashion in its time, with, in the corner, a shower cabinet in avocado, fitted around 1976, the only concession to modernity.

I dropped my bags and lay on the bed, luxuriating in its redundant space.

I remembered a posh country hotel in the New Forest. Pete and I had bunked off for the weekend to celebrate my birthday. We'd larked about, pretending to be rich and famous. We'd ordered room service – roast pheasant and champagne – and had closed our eyes as we'd paid the bill. A lifetime ago.

I heard gardening sounds and looked out of the window. A man in his fifties – Robbie, I assumed – was raking the gravel on one of an intricate network of paths bordered by rows of neatly clipped lavender bushes. By May, the bushes would look dazzling. Their heady scent would waft up through my open window.

Beyond the end wall, a lawn the size of a football pitch swept grandly down to a stretch of water bigger than most municipal boating lakes. Robbie would need a substantial tractor mower to keep that expanse of grass in such good shape. I thought of the petrol mower at Fishers Keep and felt my forearms burn again.

A voice somewhere below called out and Robbie turned his head. Then he lay down his rake and made his way inside.

A minute later, there was a tap on my door.

'Come in.'

A woman in her late fifties popped her head round the door. She had forearms like a wrestler's.

'Eleven o'clock, dear. Tea.'

'Sounds lovely.'

She took a step inside and wiped her hands on her apron. 'I'm Rosemary.'

'Jennifer.'

'Pleased to meet you, Jennifer. Come down to the kitchen and meet everyone.'

We descended the back staircase. More oak panelling. A Persian stair carpet that had seen better days. Rosemary kept up a running commentary, asking what I knew about the house and the 'master' then filling me in before I had time to answer.

His mother had died when he was nine. Packed off to boarding school in Scotland. Major in the army. Resigned his commission to take over the running of the estate from his father, Edmund, still going strong at ninety, in an apartment at the back of the house.

Had I met Robbie? Gardener. And jack of all trades. Did most of the maintenance round the house (*No money for tradesmen now*). He also bred the pheasants for the shoots.

Kate cleaned the house three days a week. Single mum. Desperate for a replacement father for her two kids. Nice girl but too fond of men (*Loose*).

What about Veronica? Bit stuck up. Didn't have an easy life with the master.

The kitchen looked like a working museum. A cast-iron range with three ovens. A huge fireplace with a roasting spit worked by a system of weights and cogs. An army of copper pots the size of bins, gleaming to perfection. Heady smells of baking.

I thought of my mum. I wondered if Leon, the *Big Issue* guy, was still sleeping in her spare room.

'Have a seat, dear. You know Veronica.'

'Yes. Hi.'

'And that's Kate and Robbie.'

Kate was as thin as Rosemary was generously proportioned. She looked late twenties but could have been younger. I imagined life had been hard. But she smiled easily – there was warmth beneath her painted mask.

Robbie was taciturn but pleasant. He nodded and munched on a piece of toast an inch thick. From my bedroom window, I hadn't noticed his earring and the Motörhead tattoo on his forearm.

He looked like the kind of guy who, if a bomb went off in his watering can, would raise one eyebrow and say, 'Well, that was close.'

I liked them both immediately.

'So, how are you settling in?' Without asking, Rosemary put a plate of hot buttered toast and a mug of navvy's tea down in front of me.

'Thank you. Fine, yes. Beautiful place.'

'It's falling to bits.'

'Well, I can see there are challenges in the house for you, Kate.'

'There are, yes. Challenges.'

'But you keep the gardens beautiful, Robbie.' He inclined his head an inch.

'And you're obviously keeping George … Mr Winstanley … in fairly good shape and good spirits, Veronica.'

'I think I do a good job, yes.'

'Seems like a very good team.'

Rosemary sat down beside me and took a big bite from a piece of toast. 'We are, aren't we?' She looked around. Nods and smiles. 'And you'll fit in just fine, dear.'

More nods and smiles.

'I think so. I'm looking forward to it.'

Veronica smirked. 'You haven't met her ladyship yet.'

'No. I gather she's not fond of dogs.'

'She can be hard work.'

Rosemary waved the comment away with her toast. 'She's fine. She's not as cut-glass as she'd have you believe. He's the real thing. Proper upper class. But Mrs Winstanley's playing at it. She thinks I don't know.'

Kate piped up. 'Thinks none of us do.'

'But I've been around the block too many times, and served with too many *real* toffs, to be fooled by the likes of her.'

'Right.'

'But she's harmless, dear. You'll be fine.' Rosemary looked at my left hand. 'No *Mister* Brown then, dear?'

'No.'

'Well, you wouldn't be taking a job like this, would you?'

'No. Not really.'

'Divorced?'

It seemed a bit early for confession, but I was too old to be coy. 'Never married.'

Robbie spoke with feeling. 'Smart move.'

'Right man just never come along?'

'No. I thought he had. But no.'

Then, before I knew it, I was giving them the whole story. The looks. The criticisms. The text. Perfect Ten. The works. It seemed to touch a chord with Veronica.

'At least you weren't married.'

'No. That's one good thing, I suppose.'

Rosemary poured more tea. 'So where were you before here.'

Hampshire. I worked for a journalist. Similar place to this. Smaller.' Early days. Cards close to your chest. She seems nice, but you don't want to be drafted into peeling spuds.

'Same type of job?'

'Yes. Estate manager. And Hampshire's lovely. But it's breathtaking here.'

Rosemary smiled and took another bite of toast.

The lady of the house was meeting me in the orangery, a later addition to the house by the looks of it. Its long, generously windowed, south-facing aspect had once nurtured orange trees and later, judging by a couple of grainy framed photographs, had also been home to pineapple bushes. Its fabulous light, bright even on a gloomy day, and its mosaic tiling made it a beautiful conservatory. A conservatory you could hold a dinner dance in.

This, Rosemary told me as she walked me over, was the mistress's favourite room in the house. It was where she held court every Wednesday afternoon, enjoying tea and gossip with lady friends carefully selected from a social circle and income bracket just a touch below her own, ensuring she occupied a position of superiority.

'She likes to be top banana.'

Rosemary went off to the kitchen. I selected a substantial cane chair and made myself comfortable.

'Bloody woman. Bloody woman.'

I looked around for the disembodied voice.

'How do I look? How do I look?'

I stood up and scanned the room. Nobody.

'Spending my money. Spending my money.'

It sounded like an old woman with Tourette's. Was the voice coming from outside? I went over to one of the windows and gazed out. A deserted terrace.

'Bloody woman. Bloody woman.'

A ruffling sound. A flash of colour caught my eye. In the corner of the room, a cage the size of a wardrobe contained a bird of some kind. I walked over.

A parrot, large and grey with a red tail, bobbed his head up and down as I approached.

'Bloody woman. Bloody woman.'

I leaned in to get a good look. 'You're a character, aren't you?'

'Please forgive Montgomery. He's incorrigible.'

I turned to face Camilla Winstanley. Ash blonde and paper thin, she had translucent skin. The whole effect was of a bone china figure, as if, dropped, she might shatter. I put her at late sixties, perhaps a few years younger than George, but in very good nick indeed. Either great genes or an extensive (and doubtless expensive) maintenance regime.

She'd clearly embraced the role of lady of the manor but, as Rosemary had implied, was trying a little too hard for it to be authentic – tweed skirt a little clichéd, Woods of Windsor perfume a little overpowering, hair a little too Duchess of Kent.

'Jennifer, isn't it?' Clipped tones channelled Edith Evans. She held out a hand. Was I expected to shake it, or kneel and kiss it?

I held out my own in return. 'Pleased to meet you, Mrs Winstanley.'

'George and I are so pleased you've come to look after us. I'm afraid you'll find the administrative side of things rather a mess. It's been several months, you see. And it's all rather too much for George, these days.'

'Yes.'

'And, well … it's just not my thing. The day-to-day.'

'No.'

'So we're rather relying on you. To straighten things out.'

'I'll do my very best.'

'Yes. Please do. Is your accommodation to your satisfaction?' She glanced down at my skirt and shoes and, based on an assessment of their merit, seemed to conclude I'd have no business *not* being satisfied.

'Very comfortable, thank you.'

'*Splendid.*' Splendid? Had I wandered onto the set of Lady Windermere's Fan? 'Well, I'll leave you to your duties.'

A pattering sound on the tiles made me turn my head.

'Coco! You naughty girl! You know this cold floor gives you a chill.'

A cream-coloured Pomeranian scurried up to Camilla and she bent down to pick it up. She straightened the red tartan bow around its tiny neck and ran her fingers through the plume of feathery hair on its tail.

'There. That's better. Isn't she a darling?'

'She's very pretty, yes. I got the impression, though, from Mr Winstanley, that you didn't like dogs.'

'Coco's a house dog.'

'Oh.'

'All that charging around outside, sniffing things, rolling in the mud. No.'

'Coco doesn't do that?'

'No. Her province is to be charming.'

Poor mutt. Never left the house. Never had fun. Never sniffed another dog's bits.

The cage came alive.

'Bloody dog. Ought to be shot.' I bit my lip.

'Shut up, Monty!'

'Your parrot talks very well.'

'He's not mine. He's George's. One of my husband's many vices, I'm afraid. But we must indulge our men, mustn't we?'

Hm. It's got to be a two-way street. And I'm sure plenty of traffic flows your way, milady.

21

The Young Wife

I developed a working routine that suited me. It seemed to suit George, too.

We were both early birds and he was as keen to get on with the day as I was. By the time I'd gathered the post and filtered out the rubbish, Veronica had him bathed and dressed and ready for the breakfast – tea with toast and two poached eggs – that Rosemary carried into the library on a tray, at eight sharp. Then, together, we'd make a plan for the day – action in the morning (phone calls to contractors, emails to creditors) and reflection and planning in the afternoon.

And I'd managed to institute a practice that gave me enormous pleasure – an early-morning walk with Benson. I'd pop my head into the kitchen around seven. From his basket in the corner, he'd open one eye, his heavy black tail would thump once, then he'd jump up and follow me down the back staircase and out onto the terrace. From there, he'd fly off down to the water and I'd stroll on after him, through the morning mist, a thick lump in my throat at the memory of barley fields and Betty and Eric.

I began to impose some sort of order on the management of the estate, previously run along principles that hadn't changed much since the Virgin Queen herself was on the throne. We abandoned the absurdly outdated institution of quarter days (when the hell is *Michaelmas* anyway?) and tenant farmers now paid their rent monthly, on the first, by direct debit.

Using web design software with ingeniously slick templates requiring no html skills whatsoever, and a handful of stylish but affordable images from an Oxford photographer, I built a website for the estate, initially to promote the pheasant shoots but later offering a wider portfolio of country pursuits designed to appeal to well-heeled corporate clients all year round: clay-pigeon shooting, quad-biking and (that talismanic licence to print money) team-building. In April alone, we had twelve bookings. Clients included an Oxford law firm, a Swiss bank, and Channel Four. All of which made the income side of the account much healthier.

The expenditure side was a little more awkward. Apart from outrageous utility bills, reflecting a heating system groaning under the weight of its advanced age, the major drain on resources was Camilla.

Keen to outshine the women in her little salon, and desperate to keep up with a cousin in Chelsea, Camilla went up to London every Wednesday to have her hair styled by the man who did all the minor royals. His salon, in Mayfair, used organic products flown in from the Seychelles. While they waited, clients were served loose-leaf lapsang souchong in Vera Wang china. A violinist was hired to play Vivaldi and Bach.

For this experience, Camilla stumped up £175. For one hour. Every week. For her hair.

Seven hundred pounds a month. On hair.

Of course, hair alone maketh not the woman. Clothes also maketh her. And, in the domain of clothes, Camilla denied herself very little. Over the past two years, the average monthly spend on frockage had been £2200. For that, she'd been getting three items, sometimes four.

I didn't think she'd been spending much time in Next.

When, feeling a little like spy *and* traitor, I laid these figures out before George, he was visibly roused. But he mastered his feelings like a gentleman. He'd have a quiet word.

It was clear that, as well as from a desire to keep up with the Joneses, Camilla's spendiness also stemmed from a desperate attempt to get George's attention. She'd often wander into the library as he and I sat poring over documents or discussing bookings, and she'd feign an interest in the running of the estate, chipping in with the odd question he'd answer with a monosyllable or a remark he'd greet with a look of bewildered exasperation.

But her main reason for being there was to be admired. And she was indeed admirable. I imagined her turning the heads of men in their forties – thirties, even. But George didn't seem to know she existed. I rather pitied her.

'You look lovely today, Mrs Winstanley.'

'Thank you, Jennifer. What do you think of this dress, George?'

'Very nice.' He didn't look up.

'Kate has one just like it.' That got his attention.

'Where does Kate get *that* kind of money?'

Camilla smiled. 'Not *our* Kate. Catherine. Duchess of Cambridge.'

George gave me a look. See. This is what I'm working with.

'Oh. Right.'

Any affection George had once had for her appeared to have evaporated into thin air.

The same fate seemed to befall portions of food in the fridge. It was an open secret that Camilla had food issues. When Rosemary had first reported food going missing from the fridge, Camilla had reacted with mock outrage (*How can anyone eat cheese in the middle of the night?*). Then Veronica had spotted her tiptoeing down the main staircase at three in the morning, one night when George's shoulder had been particularly acute and he'd needed morphine.

Now, when half a camembert had been snaffled, or serious inroads had been made in a tub of crème fraiche, Rosemary just shrugged.

'I see the mouse has been at it again.'

Camilla made a big show of eating slim at mealtimes – refusing potatoes in favour of a rocket salad, and taking fifteen minutes to eat a single slice of rye toast – but she clearly gorged at night. Kate knew as much from cleaning the ensuite. No matter how much Camilla flushed and sprayed, she could never cover her traces completely.

She wanted, and had achieved, a girlish figure. But the whole house knew she was paying a painful price.

Her illness seemed to be a source of particular irritation to Veronica. While Rosemary and Kate laughed it off, and Robbie rolled his eyes, Veronica seemed wound up by it. One lunchtime, when I was on the laptop in the library and George was enjoying early summer sun on the terrace, she came in to see me, apropos of nothing at all. Camilla must have said something to needle her and Veronica started putting the boot in about her eating. I tried to be sympathetic.

'She can't help it. It's an illness. A poor body image is a terrible affliction.'

'What does *she* have to worry about?' I walked over and closed the library door.

'I mean, she's got this beautiful house – okay, it's falling apart, but still – and she's got a husband. A *rich* husband!'

'I know. But that's just it. It's a mental illness. By definition, it makes no sense.'

'No. It doesn't.' She rubbed at her forehead with both hands.

'What is it?'

'Sorry. It's just … some days …' And Veronica told me her story.

She'd fallen for a man, years before. He was handsome. He was fun to be around. He was married.

After two years of cloak-and-dagger stuff in hotel rooms and weekend cottages, he'd had it out with his wife and had eventually left her. No kids, so not so bad. (*Did having kids make it worse? People with kids thought it did.*)

They moved to Italy together to start a new life. They bought a small hotel in Positano, on the Amalfi coast – two years of meeting in hotels and they felt they could make a go of hospitality – and they looked forward to sunshine and financial security.

But running a hotel in an Italian hotspot turned out to be a cut-throat business. It wasn't enough to paint the rooms Dulux White Cotton and put chocolates on the pillow and keep your prices keen. You had to be ruthless. You had to undercut everyone else in the town. And, to do that, you had to sack all your staff and do everything yourself and work a twenty-hour day.

After six months of not sleeping and earning no money, they hated each other and he packed up and went back to his wife in Stockport and his old job with the Department for Work and Pensions. Veronica stayed on by herself for another few months, flushing eight years' worth of savings down the toilet.

Now here she was, working as a nurse, showering an old man, wiping him.

But she could take some comfort from the fact that George, although a little sharp at times, was basically a decent human being.

The same could not be said of his father. Edmund was the object of universal and intense dislike. He was the most mean-spirited individual I had ever come across. It seemed to give him pleasure to be hurtful. You could see, in the ninety-one-year-old curmudgeon, the nine-year-old boy who'd delighted in pulling the wings off butterflies and the legs off frogs. He was vile.

He would often leave his upstairs apartment and, teetering on the brink of rage, would storm around the house looking for a fight. We'd hear his irascible footfall on the stairs and we'd all dive for cover. Then, when the strafing had ceased, we'd emerge from the trenches and get on with our work.

The only one who could stand up to him, oddly, was Camilla, whom he referred to (spitefully, if rather hilariously) as Chlamydia. She never rose to the bait, instead deploying a withering sarcasm

(*Hilarious, Edmund. I've never heard that one before. Did you think of it all on your own? Aren't you clever!*). He'd storm off, disarmed, and we'd all cheer her silently from our hiding-places.

I suspected it was Edmund, not George, who'd coached Montgomery in his litany of misogyny.

They say there are cat people and dog people. That dog people soften in the presence of the unconditional love that sickens cat people, and that cat people respect the aloofness and self-possession of the cat. It's a gross generalisation, of course, but I was not surprised to learn that Edmund's companion of choice was the cat. Two cats, actually. Hiro and Nag. Siamese. Named after Hiroshima and Nagasaki. Intelligent hunters. Which is code for little bastards.

The summer that year was the finest for a decade. Endless days of sun and skies as blue as the cornflowers in the fields around the estate. George revelled in the good weather – it seemed to ease his various pains – and he had a private spot in the garden, near the sundial, where he and I would conduct our business, the ever-faithful Benson never far from his side.

Camilla preferred to stay indoors, shunning perspiration, protecting her complexion.

Within a few weeks, my skin was in summer mode. Fixing my hair in the bathroom mirror one Sunday morning, I saw the glow of my cheeks and recalled Manly beach and those few gloriously lazy days with Larry. I wondered how he was getting on with whacky Jackie, and who he was entertaining on the *Lucky Lady*.

Sunday was my day for strolling round the estate. It gave me the chance to see how things were looking. More importantly, it let me breathe. Work at Thornhill Hall was rewarding but it could be a slog. I was usually on the go at 7 am and it was often after 7 in the evening when I switched off my laptop. Sunday was me time.

The walled garden was particularly impressive in July. The lavender had faded a little but the red campion was gorgeous against Robbie's well-raked gravel and his vegetable beds were thick with luscious beans, peas and courgettes. One of the young seasonal workers was filling a basket with courgette flowers, on Rosemary's orders. I said hello.

Robbie was in the pheasant pen and he waved me over. The chicks were two months old and coming on well. He handed me one, his fingernails still thick with grease from the motorbike he kept in the tool barn. The fluffy little creature chirped away in my hand and I felt a sharp pang in my stomach. By October, it would be little more than a terrified target, bullied into the air by a beater for the sport of some well-heeled banker. *You're still a town girl, Jennifer Brown.*

On the lake, a moorhen was leading her chicks across the lake, past a brood of Canada geese who squawked noisily at the intruders.

I'd never circumnavigated the lake, but the day was glorious and I felt like an explorer.

After fifteen minutes, the path became muddy and quite overgrown. I had to push past thick dogwood, my knees and elbows snapping its unruly red stems. Broken stems ahead showed me I wasn't the only one to come this way and, when I came to a Gothic door in a high stone wall, I could see the tracks of thin tyres in the mud.

The door opened easily and I walked through. A dozen paces and I was standing at the entrance to a tiny stone chapel.

Inside, a smell of dampness and that sense of stillness you always get in an empty church. With just four rows of pews, the walk up this aisle would be short for a bride – not much time to change your mind. The pews themselves were furnished with red leather cushions wrinkled and worn with age. I lifted a black hymn book and released a little cloud of dust into the shaft of sunlight that warmed my hand.

Off to the left, a hymn board and a tiny pulpit. I smiled at the memory of Damian and his fluffed lines. Then I looked at the altar. A simple wooden table. A carved inscription. *The word became flesh and dwelt among us full of grace and truth.*

The letters started to swim and I pulled a tissue from my pocket and wiped my eyes. What was it? The beautiful simplicity of this sanctuary? The power of the verse? The fact I was pushing forty and getting my love from a Lab?

I pulled the door to behind me. Just inside the high perimeter wall there was a headstone, not new but clearly not ancient. I walked over.

Arabella Elizabeth Winstanley
Beloved of George
1940 - 1968
Step softly. A dream lies buried here.

I knelt down to breathe in the fragrance from the yellow freesias freshly laid in a marble pot next to the stone and reached for the tissue again.

He couldn't wash or dress himself but, by a tremendous effort of will fuelled by devotion, George Winstanley had got himself to this spot to spend some time with the girl he'd lost a lifetime ago.

One of the best things about my job at Thornhill Hall was the food. Rosemary was a terrific cook. Succulent pork roasts. Rich game pies. Heavenly soufflés. And added to the pleasure of eating such wonders was the extra pleasure of not having to prepare them. Although the pressure, around the kitchen table, to pile on the portions (and the pounds) was considerable.

'Here. Have another couple of roasties. Don't want you turning into the mistress, do we?'

'I'm fine, thanks. They're delicious, though. Too delicious. Trust me, this body could all go pear-shaped very quickly.'

'Nonsense. Seen more meat on a butcher's pencil.' She'd slide another three potatoes onto my plate. I'd eat one then, when her back was turned, drop the other two into my napkin.

The evening of my discovery, I hung back to chat to Rosemary, after Veronica and Robbie had gone off. I mentioned the chapel.

She took her apron off and lifted a bottle of sherry off the shelf and poured two glasses and sat down.

'You won't find any sign of her around the house. For the mistress's sake.'

'No, I haven't seen any photos.'

'Apart from the portrait in the library.' *Ah. That's* her. 'Which the mistress doesn't know about. Nobody does. Except me.' She looked me in the eye. 'And now you.'

'I won't tell.'

'When the mistress asked about it, he told her it's just some painting he bought at an auction because he liked the colours.'

'And she believed him?'

'Or she pretended to.'

'No other memories? Apart from the chapel?'

'One.'

'What?'

'A photograph. He keeps it between the pages of a book – I don't know which one – and, when the mistress has taken a sleeping pill, he goes into the library and takes it out and looks at it. I've seen him a couple of times. He sits in the library and looks at her and reads to her. Poems.'

I went back to the empty library and stood and took a closer look at Arabella's portrait. It was easy to see how she could cast a spell on a man, a spell that would last for fifty years. Perfect skin, wonderful cheekbones, she radiated elegance. Grace Kelly, but with a Doris Day warmth in the eyes.

Poor Camilla. There was just no competition. If she suspected, it'd be killing her.

All this emotion was giving me withdrawal symptoms. I phoned Will.

'How's life in the royal household? You sound like you've poshed up a bit.' 'You're joking. There's more bad language flying around here than I ever heard at Intext.'

'That's toffs for you. Filthy bastards.'

'Not the toffs. The staff. In the kitchen.'

'So, no hunky chaps on the estate drooling over your queen-sized gazongas?'

'The field is a little thin. A middle-aged gardener with a Motörhead tattoo. And a couple of young lads with their eyes on the twenty-something maid. She keeps taking rugs outside to air. She bends over a lot.'

'Saucy cow.'

'She's young. It's fine.'

'Are *you* fine?'

'I'm alright, actually. Life's pretty good. Long days but I'm doing a good job and the boss knows it.'

'Check you! Mrs Estate Manager!'

'I know!'

'Will you stick it?'

'For now. Not sure it's where I want to be for the rest of my life, but …'

'Jennifer Brown.'

'What?'

'Will you ever be truly happy?'

'It's the perennial question.'

'Oh, by the way.'

'What?'

'Jonathan got his promotion. Finally. Director.'

'Good for him.'

'And that bloke was asking after you?'

'What bloke?'

'That client. High flyer. Jonathan's all over him.'

Mr Velvet Vowels. 'David Harwood?'

'That's him. Said to me, "You're a friend of Jennifer's, aren't you? How is she?"'

'"She's gorgeous," I said.'

'You didn't!'
'Bloody did!'
'What did *he* say?'
'He just smiled.'

Did he now?

22

Cat in the Bag

With summer on the wane and autumn knocking on the door, Robbie released the pheasant chicks from their pen and encouraged them to wander the woodland on the estate, which they were happy to do, blissfully unaware that they'd soon be target practice.

My six-month contract at Thornhill Hall had expired but George was in no mood to let me go and, with a portfolio of interesting and lucrative bookings under my belt and more challenges ahead, I was in no mood to up sticks either.

'I like having you here, Jennifer Brown.'

'That's good to know, George.'

With that, the contract was renegotiated and I got on with the day's main task – settling fifteen exectives from SmithKline into the newly renovated Pavilion for their three-day team-building experience.

Kate had made a great job of preparing the residence. She was getting the hang of the little professional touches that gave the place the feel of luxury that big-bucks clients expect – a range of bottled waters in the fridges, bathroom cabinets well stocked with Thornhill own-label products, antique davenports decorated with fresh flowers, picked that morning.

And I was making a good job of preparing Kate for life. I was now apparently of an age to be turned to for maternal advice.

'The thing is, Jen, men only want me for my looks.' *It's not a new theme, is it?*

'Well, I know what you mean.'

She gave me a look that said 'Really? You?!' then pressed on. 'Are they all bastards?'

'I might not be the best person to judge. You know *my* story. But they can't be, can they? Not *all* of them.'

'No. Don't s'pose. But how can you tell?'

'Don't think you can. Not at first. It's all a bit new and exciting, isn't it? At first. For them too, I think. So maybe you should just … be a little less … giving. At first.'

'Don't sleep with them? On the first date, you mean?'

'Yeah. Maybe not for the first *few* dates.' She seemed perplexed. What else would they *do*, then?

'Right.'

'You know. Do some stuff together first. Some other stuff.' A furrowed brow again. 'You know. Walks. The cinema. Lunch out. That sort of thing. So you can see whether you like him or not. As a person. Not just as a bloke. In the sack.'

'Right.' Eyes wide. A major discovery. Water on Mars.

'If he seems like … well, an arsehole … then you'll know. Not to sleep with him.' I felt like a primary school teacher. A Relationships module with the Year Sevens.

'Right.'

'He won't respect you for being a pushover in the bedroom. And maybe you won't respect yourself, either.' *Physician, heal thyself.* 'So let him discover who *you* really are, too. Before … you know … hopping into bed.'

Kate's generosity towards men was a popular topic of conversation at Thornhill Hall, and not just among primates. Monty had been plucked from his customary dwelling-place on Wednesday afternoons after one recent salon gathering had been entertained by a particularly earthy refrain. *Kate's shagging again* hadn't gone down well with the aspirational Camilla and now the saucy lad was banished to Robbie's toolshed for the duration of the posh pow-wow, in spite of Letty Horton's eagerness to know if Kate's current wrestling companion was 'that charming boy with the buttocks and the bedroom eyes who's just moved into the Stevenson place.'

Camilla didn't know him. Apparently.

Before I knew it, November frosts were silvering the north-facing fields and I was up with the lark to marshall a team of beaters for the first pheasant shoot of the season.

The whole house was astir. An early breakfast was being prepared for the gallery, warmed by a crackling fire set by Rosemary at the ungodly hour of three-thirty. She was now in full housekeeper mode – crisping bacon, poaching eggs, despatching Kate to lay the long refectory table. She winked at me. *That's a novelty – Kate laying something.*

We would host two groups – one shooting party who'd overnighted at the Hall and a party of businessmen arriving in the early afternoon for a quad biking session run by an Oxford company who were paying us handsomely for the use of a section of the estate that had seen better days. The businessmen were staying for afternoon tea but dining in Cheltenham.

I choked back tears as I stamped my feet in the cold courtyard that separated the shooting lodge from the main house. I was surrounded by gorgeous long-eared spaniels and thick-tailed Labradors and I was struggling. Benson's single wagging tail and soft brown eyes were enough to set me off at the best of times. This large crowd of canine beauties were pushing my Betty and Eric buttons more than I'd felt them pushed for months. This and the imminent prospect of Robbie's little birds being blasted out of the sky had me teetering on the brink of unprofessional. *Pull yourself together, town girl. Remember who pays your wages.*

George himself was in fine form for the shoot, despite a recent visible decline in his health. He looked in his element. Veronica had got him up particularly smartly for the occasion, taking extra care to straighten his regimental tie and ensuring the tassels on his shooting socks were neatly tied. Even though he wouldn't be taking a gun himself, he looked enlivened by the mere thought of being in the thick of it.

By eight, the shooting party had been breakfasted and the sun was up. No shoot could begin without a snifter in the lodge and that little ceremony was presided over by me, dispensing modest shots of George's favourite whisky, the heavily peated Jura Prophecy (notes of fresh cinnamon and spicy sea spray – that's what I'd read on the website and that's what I encouraged our shooters to appreciate before their killing spree). They imbibed the Caledonian nectar under the glassy eyes of the numerous stags' heads that adorned the lodge walls.

I thought of Alphonse. I wondered whether Gerald had ever noticed his permanently pissed look. I wondered whether Gerald was now dandling a baby on his ancient knee.

When Robbie took the shooting party off up to the woods (to do manly stuff with firearms), we women fell into the gender-sterotyped role of making the house nice and putting the lunch on for their return.

I looked round at my colleagues. It wasn't just the house they'd made nice. They'd all gone to quite an effort over their personal appearance.

Kate was doing her best to look professional but, while remaining just a whisker short of slutty, her tweedy skirt was a good three inches too short and her skin-tight silky blouse offered the combination of ribcage and creamy breast flesh that has kept Kate Moss's bank account buoyant for the past fifteen years. She'd even managed to Max Factorise some radiance into her careworn fizzog.

'Did you see him? The guy with the sports car? Bet he's loaded.' She popped the napkins down on the table while she touched up her lipstick.

Veronica had noticed him. 'It's an Aston. Ninety grand.'

'Ninety thousand pounds!'

'For the V8 Vantage, yeah.' Veronica didn't look like a *Top Gear* kind of girl, but it just goes to show you. 'Probably get one pre-owned for around seventy.'

Kate straightened her skirt and coralled her puppies into their most advantageous configuration. 'God! He's *gorgeous* as well. Did you notice a ring?'

Veronica had noticed. 'No ring.'

She was looking pretty good for an older bird. Tweed skirt, too, but elegant. And cream blouse restrained but not schoolmarmish. An attractive woman if she could keep the spikes in her character from showing.

Even Rosemary had scrubbed up well, her matronly figure sculpted into an approximation of a woman by some miracle of M&S engineering. The touch of blusher was a bit Les Dawson but, on the whole, it was a pretty good effort.

By comparison, my navy skirt and white cotton blouse looked stingy. I think I was still inclined to err on the side of straitlaced after suffering the indignity of being mistaken for a hooker by Larry's Jackie. I popped an extra button and ruffled up my hair.

At twelve thirty, the shooters returned, red-cheeked and ravenous. The house was all woodsmoke and cooking smells and they set about Rosemary's warming parsnip and cumin soup with gusto, pulling hunks of her walnut bread from baskets, clinking glasses of Gevrey-Chambertin and replaying the morning's action.

Mr Aston Martin – a thirty-year-old with floppy hair and no chin I wouldn't have looked twice at – was treated to Kate's fruitiest smiles and most attentive service and didn't seem entirely unmoved.

You couldn't see a liaison between a pharmaceutical executive and a cleaner-cum-waitress going anywhere very meaningful, but who was I to judge?

Men thrown together with other men tend to lose something in the decorum department, especially when you throw alcohol into the mix, but this shooting party seemed a decent bunch, for the most part. And it was lovely to see George letting his hair down a bit and having fun, away from spreadsheets and business plans and website updates.

While Kate and Veronica were serving Rosemary's rich lemon tarts, Camilla flounced in, looking every inch the would-be duchess – pearls, Harris Tweed skirt, powder-pink chiffon blouse from somewhere in Knightsbridge. She smiled and nodded and fiddled kittenishly with an errant strand of hair, desperate for adulation.

Aston Martin was far too preoccupied by Kate's hemline to notice poor Camilla, but she did catch the eye of one of the more mature shooters, a man in his late sixties with a luxuriant head of white hair. He put down his wine glass and furrowed his brow. Camilla moved round the table, asking the right questions, being appropriately engaged by the answers, bestowing charm and elegance.

George poured a glass of wine for her and invited her to sit down but she was having none of it. Lady Bountiful was required to circulate. Old White Hair's brow was still furrowed. Then Camilla smiled at him and a light came on.

'I think we've met before, Mrs Winstanley.'

Camilla was used to recognition in older men. She had, by all accounts, been quite something on the catwalks of swinging London.

'I don't think so, er …'

'Frederick Compton. Freddie. I used to work at Pelham's, in the West End. I was a junior accounts clerk.'

One of the younger men piped up. 'That wasn't last week, Freddie!'

'No. I left them in '69. For a job in the City. More money, but much less fun.'

There was a wobble in Camilla's aplomb. 'Pelham's? I …'

'Yes. Great place. Very sociable bunch. We worked hard but we also played very hard. We were right in the heart of Soho. And, well, when you're young and you have a bit of money ...'

George had begun to tune in. He shouted down from the top of the table. 'What's this?'

Freddie had to raise his voice. 'I was just saying to your wife that I thought I recognised her from ... somewhere.'

'Really? Where?'

Camilla's face had passed from puce to ashen. 'I think I'll ...'

The mention of Soho had raised eyebrows all round. The shooters, now lubricated, were leaning back in their seats, keen to hear more. Kate and Veronica were both smiling nervously. I was inclined to smile myself at the thought of Camilla's crown slipping to her ankles like a pair of cheap panties, then I saw the wretched look on her face, now ghastly pale, and called Robbie in and whispered in his ear.

'The duchess is having a funny turn. Would you take her outside?'

Robbie rushed over to take Camilla's elbow. 'It's rather stuffy in here, Mrs Winstanley, with that log fire. Let's get you some fresh air.'

The smiles had faded. George was looking at Freddie with something like defiance in his eyes. 'My wife was a fashion model. Camilla Crawford. She moved in celebrity circles. Jean Shrimpton. Twiggy. The Rolling Stones. People like that. No doubt you remember her face from the papers.'

Robbie bundled Camilla out through the French windows and into the courtyard. Freddie gathered up the chickens before they came home to roost.

'Yes. I think you're right. I must have seen her photo. In the newspapers.'

'Yes. You must have.'

The below stairs was abuzz for the rest of the day. We were desperate to find out Camilla's sordid secret, which George had so gallantly guarded. But the second booking was arriving within the hour and, although it was a much smaller crowd, there was still a fair amount of prepping to do and we didn't have time to be distracted.

By the time the afternoon party had whisked in from Oxford, we were all shipshape. I had Revenue matters to deal with, which also required George's attention, so Robbie was detailed to receive the party and run the quad-bike booking.

George and I were still hunched over a sheaf of papers in the library when the house came to life again at four and the patter of Kate's and Veronica's feet told me tea was being served.

George peered at me over his glasses. He looked exhausted. 'Let's take a break. I need a cup of tea and a scone.'

He wheeled out of the library and across the hall. I followed him into the gallery, which swamped the party of five now in raptures over Rosemary's eclairs. Robbie was standing at the fireplace answering a question from a shortish man who had his back to the door.

'No, sir. I'm not the estate manager. I'm the gamekeeper.' He looked up and saw me coming in with George. 'If you want the estate manager, here she is.'

The man turned to face me. 'Hello, again, Jennifer Brown.' Velvet vowels.

'Hello, David.'

David Harwood walked over and kissed me on both cheeks, *à la française*. There was a crackle of electricity in the room. Kate stood with a coffee pot poised mid-pour. Veronica put a plate of scones down on top of a butter dish. George looked up at me from his chair as David spoke again.

'*You're* the estate manager?'

'Yes I am.'

'I … don't know what to say. Except that I'm very impressed.'

George was feeling left out. 'We're glad you like it.'

David recovered his composure and held out his hand. 'Forgive me. David Harwood.'

'George Winstanley. I own the place.'

'It's beautiful. And beautifully run.'

'It is *now*. Now that Jennifer's running it.' George smiled up at me. 'I'm glad I'm not the only one who thinks she's doing a sterling job.'

'No. She is. Sterling.'

'Good. And you enjoyed the quad biking?'

'Excellent,' he said. 'Thank you. Good fun.'

'But you're not dining with us this evening, I gather?'

'I'm afraid not. Not this time.' He looked right at me. 'But I'm sure there'll be other times. I hope so, anyway.'

That evening, exhausted from the day's exertions and from the Revenue paperwork, George retired early with no dinner. He was still full from the afternoon tea. Camilla had been locked away in her apartment since the Soho business, so we'd all effectively been given the evening off.

Rosemary looked at the clock. 'We'll finish up here, Kate. You get off home.'

Kate reached into Rosemary's cupboard and took down a bottle of sherry.

'You're joking. I'm not going anywhere. I've phoned my mum. She'll watch Ryan.'

Rosemary would normally throw a cleaver at anyone laying a hand on her sherry bottles, but she could see Kate had a point. The day's events needed some mulling over.

'Quite right. Get it poured then.' And the meeting was convened. Veronica was the first to table a question.

'What the bloody hell was all *that*? Soho?'

Kate's eyes were aglow. 'D'you think she was a stripper?'

Rosemary spoke with the authority of the experienced matriarch. 'Sounds like more.'

'You don't mean …?'

'It was the sixties. They were all at it. Rock 'n' roll. Drugs. Sex. Free love.'

'It's not free if you're charging.' Guffaws.

'I'd love to get the full story.'

I reached into my bag and pulled out my iPad. 'Google is a wonderful thing.'

Within five minutes, we had the full story. A much fuller story than any of us had expected. Camilla had been quite the celebrity.

The Cat's Tail had been one of Soho's busiest nightspots, entertaining gentlemen from all walks of life, from junior accounts clerks to government ministers. Glamorous 'Cat Girls' entertained clients in see-through body stockings adorned with long feline tails which they'd wrap around their sexed-up charges while plying them with champagne cocktails at inflated prices. It was an open secret that the girls could be expected to offer a little extra service for the right price.

The *Daily Mirror* of the day had carried a report with the headline *The Cat in the Bag*. This phrase, when Googled, threw up a sheaf of articles on what had been, in January 1970, a national scandal.

The *Mirror* had the most to say about Camilla herself. The photo that accompanied the article showed a girl of around eighteen, of quite dazzling beauty, smiling into the new decade as if she owned it. Two days later it had all gone horribly wrong.

Referring to her throughout as Camilla the Alley Cat, the article went on to detail the special services that Camilla had offered a minister in the Home Office, a minister with a family-values image and a line in parliamentary rhetoric to match. The amorous activities in question – which had involved cream and licking – had been witnessed by a *Mirror* reporter posing as a wealthy businessman. His cover had been blown by another MP who'd seen his face in the Westminster press corps. Things had turned ugly.

Camilla had ended the night smuggled out of the club inside a laundry sack and bundled into the back of a car. The minister had resigned in disgrace. The by-election that followed had done no favours to an already shaky Wilson government and, by June, Ted Heath was smiling from the steps of Number Ten.

We stared at each other around the table. I felt very sorry for Camilla.

'Poor cow.'

Rosemary topped us all up.

'Well, the cat's out of the bag now!'

Kate choked on her sherry. When she'd caught her breath, I stood up.

'Bedtime, I think.'

Veronica waved me back. 'Not for you, it isn't.'

'Yeah, come on,' said Kate. 'Spill.'

'What?'

'You know bloody well what.' Three pairs of eyes turned on me.

'He's just … someone I bumped into – literally – a couple of years ago.'

Kate wanted details. 'Did you two ever …?'

'No we didn't, thank you, Katherine!'

'He's keen.'

'No, he isn't! Is he? D'you think he is?'

Rosemary weighed in with the authority of the Oracle at Delphi. 'If he's not keen, I'm the bloody Queen of Sheba! Now, get out, the lot of you. Cluttering up my kitchen!' Pause for effect. 'There's not room in here to swing a bloody cat!'

23

Out of the Blue

Christmas morning. I rubbed my eyes and looked at my phone. A voicemail in the inbox. I opened it. My mum.

'Jennifer, it's mother. I just wanted to wish you a Merry Christmas. It won't be the same without you this year, dear. Hello? Can you hear me, dear? I could hear you for a bit but now it's all gone quiet. Hello?'

It's a bloody recording, Mum. You just leave a message. She pressed on.

'Don't worry about me, though. Leon's here, keeping me company. I've given him your old room, by the way. He's been in a spot of trouble with the authorities. For smoking. Shocking what you can get into trouble for these days. Poor lad. Good job your dad isn't still with us. That pipe of his might have got him arrested.'

I didn't imagine Leon had fallen foul of the police for a meerschaumful of Old Holborn.

'We're just having a quiet Christmas Day. What are you doing today? Hello? You've gone again, dear.'

We were having a quiet day, too. But it was the calm before the storm. The Pavilion had been booked by a private party from Minneapolis who'd made a speculative enquiry in October. George wasn't initially minded to open over the festive season, so I'd gone back to them with a polite refusal. Then they'd made us an offer we simply couldn't refuse. The word 'Cotswolds' weaves a magic spell over the Pond.

But they weren't arriving until Boxing Day. Which meant that, with the accommodation ready and the menu all planned, the household could more or less relax for the day. Veronica wasn't due at her friend's until the afternoon and Rosemary had no family to attend to. I was needed to see to the Americans, so I was effectively stuck. Kate had the day off to spend with Ryan before she put her pinny on again tomorrow.

Camilla was still in reclusive mode, doubtless aware we'd have pieced it all together by now, but George gathered us all into the drawing room and, over sherry, distributed gifts. Very thoughtful ones.

Veronica, who'd been talking for months about looking up an old French penfriend, got a subscription to an online French course and a fine bottle of Crozes Hermitage. And Rosemary, whose feet were always giving her 'gyp', was treated to a foot massage and pedicure at a swish Cheltenham spa, with a champagne tea to follow. She'd enjoy being served for a change.

Then George pressed a small rectangular box into my hand. It contained the most exquisite antique brooch I'd ever laid eyes on. Silver, with emerald green enamelwork. My eyes filled with tears.

'I'm sorry if I've upset you. I could only think of jewellery.'

'Oh, no! It's absolutely beautiful. Stunning. Thank you.'

'It's art nouveau. *Ecole de Nancy.*'

'It's gorgeous. You're very kind.'

Rosemary stood up. 'I'll go and put the roast potatoes on.' She drained her sherry. 'Can you give me a hand, Veronica?'

'Of course.'

The two of them trooped off to the kitchen. I was still stunned by the beautiful gift. George wheeled over to me. He lowered his voice.

'It belonged to my wife. Arabella. It was her favourite piece.'

'Oh.' It seemed too much. To take his love's favourite object away from him. I filled up again.

'I'm sorry. I've offended you.'

'No. Not at all. It's just … well, it seems too much.'

'As a gesture of thanks for the way you've turned this place – this household – around, it seems to me to be a very modest gift indeed.'

'Oh, no. It's beautiful. But I can't. I can't take your wife's … Arabella's …'

'Please. It needs to be worn. Camilla wouldn't wear it – it's not fancy enough – but I thought you might like it. Arabella appreciated beauty, not value. And you remind me of her, in many ways.' An awkward silence. 'I don't mean …'

'No, I know. But … well, I'm very flattered.' And I could say no more. He wheeled himself out of the drawing room and across to the library.

When I'd recovered myself, I made my way through to the kitchen to see if I could help the girls. Veronica was already getting ready to head off to her friend's house, so I pulled on an apron and stepped in as Rosemary's sous chef.

'You don't have to do that.'

'It's fine. I'm a champion carrot-peeler.' Thanks to Tatty Anna's obsession with the buggers.

'Well, thanks.'

There'd only be four for Christmas dinner – George, Camilla, Rosemary and me – but Rosemary had given me two kilos of carrots to skin. Enough for a Scout camp.

'Isn't this a bit much for four?'

She didn't look up.

'Rosemary?'

'Huh?'

'The carrots. Do we need this many?'

She lifted her head. Her eyes were red and swollen.

"You OK?'

'Not really.'

'What can I do?'

'Nothing. Unless you can turn the clock back forty years.'

'Here. Come and sit down.' I pulled out a chair then went into the sherry cupboard and poured a couple of glasses. Not yet midday and we were on our second glass. *Well. It's Christmas Day.*

Rosemary pulled an envelope out of her apron pocket and handed it to me. Inside was a Christmas card. Standard religious theme. The Virgin Mary holding the infant Jesus in her arms. Madonna and Child.

I opened it.

Merry Christmas, mother. Love from your son James.

'I don't know what to do.'

'You have a son?'

'I've always known this would happen. That he'd find me.'

I looked at the envelope. American stamp. Boston postmark.

'I've always secretly hoped he would, to be honest. But, now it's happened ...'

'So ... you've never met?'

'No. Not since ...' And her face crumpled.

Then she gave me the whole story. She was seventeen. Didn't have a clue about men. Was never the most attractive girl in the village. Was flattered by this man's attention. It had happened after a party.

'I didn't protest. I wanted it to happen. Wanted to know what it would be like. To be touched by a man. To be intimate. And it was ... lovely. Then two months later, I was pregnant.'

'What happened then?'

'He was older. He sent me away. He wanted me to have the baby in secret.'

'He was married?'

'Widowed. Young. Thirties. He paid for everything. Arranged the adoption.'

'Was that what you wanted?'

'I didn't know. I didn't want to tell my parents, that's for sure. But giving him away. My baby ...' Her lip trembled again and she turned away.

I put my arm round her. 'You were so young, Rosemary. It was too much for anyone to deal with.'

'I know. But there's always a part of you that thinks ...'

'Well, *now* there is. But you're so much older and wiser and better equipped for life now. Then, you were just ... a girl.'

'What if he hates me? What if he's tracked me down so he can look me in the eye and tell me he hates me? That his life's been miserable?'

'I doubt it. If his early life had been terrible, he'd want to put it all behind him and start again. He'd want to forget you, not look you up.'

'Do you think?'

'I think he's just curious. It's a basic desire, I imagine. To know who your birth mother is. To talk with her. To see what she looks like.'

Rosemary laughed through her tears. 'Poor sod! Wait till he sees this wreck! That'll make him wish he hadn't spent the airfare.'

'Nonsense. You're his mother.'

She wiped her eyes. 'Am I?' She looked at her hands.

'When's he coming?'

'Not till the summer.'

'Well, that gives you a bit of time to get your hair done.'

January was crisp and February wet and windy. Then along came March and the estate began to put its glad rags on. Out came the crocuses and the daffodils and in flooded the bookings. Life was busy, but in a good way.

A party of sixth-formers and their teachers were being treated to a tour of the estate, as part of a programme to connect with the community. A bit of nature, a bit of architecture and art history, a tour of the kitchen, a nice lunch. Camilla couldn't stand the sight of teenagers marauding round her house so she'd gone up to London, out of the way, for an overnight stay with one of her salon friends.

I went back into the house to report to George, but couldn't find him. Instead I found Rosemary in the kitchen.

'Have you seen the old man?'

'Try the walled garden.'

Not somewhere I would have thought to look. The steps down from the terrace were a barrier to his wheelchair – a ramp was on my hit list for April – and the long way round via the gravel path was doable but not easy.

But there he was, in the little arbour tucked away at the back. As I approached, I saw he wasn't alone. An impeccably dressed woman in her fifties, with legs a woman half her age would have coveted, was sitting with him. George was in his manual wheelchair. The pair of them were laughing at something. The woman tossed her hair back, setting her noble profile into sharp relief against the early spring sky. He turned to me, initially a little startled, I thought, but he quickly mastered himself.

'Jennifer. Hello. Everything alright?'

'Fine. They seem to be enjoying themselves. They're about to come inside. I thought you might want to …'

'Yes. I'll pop in. Can you give me ten minutes?'

'Of course.' I looked at the woman. She was smiling at me in a frank way that I immediately warmed to. George wasn't going to introduce me, but she was too polite not to. She stood up.

'I'm Cécile. I'm delighted to meet you. George has told me so much about you. About how you've turned Thornhill Hall into a thriving business. It's very impressive. Congratulations.'

A soft French accent but a confidence in English that spoke of years in the UK.

'Thank you. I think we've built a good programme here and a good team.'

'You certainly have.'

The three of us stood looking at each other in silence for three or four seconds.

'Well, I'll get back to them. Very nice to meet you, Cécile.'

'It's been very nice finally to meet you, too, Jennifer.'

George shouted after me. 'I'll be there shortly.'

'Right.'

So George has told you all about me. Hm. Well, he's told me nothing about you.

In the evening, with the sixth-formers gone, the following day's schedule squared away, and dinner over with, I went into the kitchen to find Rosemary.

'You're late.'

'What?'

'Expected you an hour ago.'

'Why?'

'I knew you'd want to talk. About her.'

'The woman in the garden? How did you …?'

'What? Know she'd be there? I saw her step out of a taxi earlier. I've seen her once or twice before. Never when Madam is around, though.'

'And you think she's his …?'

'His friend. Companion. Mistress.'

'Mistress? How do you know?'

'Camilla let it slip, one night when she'd had a few and George was out at some regimental do. The Scarlet Pimpernel. That's what Camilla called her. It was all very *there are three of us in this marriage.*'

'Good god.' For the first time in a long time, I thought about Bronwyn. Saw her scarlet lipstick and her scarlet car.

'She, the French woman, was married to an old pal of George's. Charles. Died twenty-odd years ago. Used to run marathons for charity. Fit as a fiddle. Then, bam! Heart attack.'

'God! How awful!'

'It was. She was a mess. And George was pretty cut up. He comforted her. And, well …'

'Poor Camilla.'

'I think she can cope as long as her nose isn't rubbed in it. And George is too much of a gentleman to do that.'

A gentleman? I'd always thought so. Until now.

I went back to my apartment feeling as if a rug had been pulled out from under me. I wasn't at all sure how I felt about this revelation.

I needed Willpower.

'So, is it because you feel sorry for *her*? The wife?'

'Well, yeah. She's a bit of an idiot, but ...'

'She doesn't deserve that.'

'No. She doesn't.'

'But, if there's no love there anymore.'

'I know. I'm not sure there ever was.'

'Then why marry her in the first place? Is that what you're thinking?'

'A bit.'

'All sorts of reasons. Companionship. Affection. Sex.'

'You don't have to be married to have sex. You particularly didn't need to be married to have sex in the seventies.'

'Well, maybe you did if you were of a certain class.'

'Nah. People of a certain class please themselves. Always have. I think it was just a rebound thing. Blinded by grief. Then, ten minutes later, he realised Camilla couldn't ever replace his first wife. His love.'

'So what about this new woman? The Scarlet One.'

'Seems nice. Very nice. And she's stylish. And gorgeous.'

'What's she doing with an old geezer in a wheelchair, then?'

'Well, I've only seen them together for a few minutes, but you could tell. That they just ... love each other.'

'Well, there's your answer.'

'What do you mean?'

'To the question, "How do I feel about this?" You feel happy.'

'But what about Camilla?'

'The woman scorned?'

'Exactly. I bloody well know how *that* feels!'

'I know. But it was different with you.'

'Was it?'

'You and Pete had a great thing going for a while. Then …'

'Then I became a fat pudding.'

'Then *he* became an arsehole. Then you walked away. Which was absolutely the right thing for you. Which is all we care about.'

'What would I do without you?'

'You'd be a basket case. A fat one.'

When I went down to the library the following morning, I knew there was something wrong the moment I walked in.

George was sitting near the fire, staring at the rug. He spoke without looking up.

'He's gone.' And then he dissolved into tears, his broad shoulders heaving with each silent sob. I walked over to his chair and knelt down beside him, my eyes moist, my thoughts flitting between memories of the slow thump of Benson's heavy tail and images of Betty and Eric and fields of barley stubble.

'I'm very sorry.'

'He was such a good lad.'

'He was. Very good.'

George dabbed at his eyes with a handkerchief.

'I'll miss him terribly.'

'I know. I can understand that.'

'I'm sorry. You've lost a dog, too?'

'Yes.' I felt my face crumple at the thought of my little lovelies.

'I've lost two. Good friends.' I wiped my wet cheeks with my fingers. George reached up and put a hand on my shoulder.

'I didn't mean to upset you.'

'I'm sorry. It always gets me when it's dogs. But this is not about me.'

George took a deep breath and wiped his eyes again.

'Oh, I'll be fine. I'll just … miss him.'

I put my arm round his shoulder and we sat in silence. I wanted to make him feel better.

'Can I get you a cup of tea?'

'Yes. Thank you. Shout Rosemary.'

'It's fine. I'll make it.'

A pause.

'About yesterday. In the garden.'

'You don't have to explain. Not to me.'

'We're very old friends. Who just happen to love each other very much.'

'Please. I don't ...'

'But I want you to understand. You're not just an ... employee – God! You're running the bloody place! – but I also have the honour, I hope, of regarding you as a friend.'

'George. I just can't ...'

'I would never do anything to embarrass Camilla.'

'But everyone knows. Everyone.' I looked away.

'That's not my fault. That was not meant to happen. And we rarely meet here. And never – absolutely never – when Camilla is around.'

'It's none of my business.'

'But I want you to understand.'

I looked at him. 'I'm trying to.' I wiped my eyes. 'Tea? I'll see Rosemary.'

'That would be lovely. Thank you. May I invite Cécile to join us?'

'It's your house.' He looked wounded. 'I'm sorry. That was uncalled-for. I'll see to the tea.' I stopped at the door.

'I'm very sorry. About Benson.'

'Thank you.'

Rosemary and I returned to the library with a tray. A pot of Earl Grey and a plate of her melt-in-the-mouth shortbread. Four cups. George was still by the fire. Standing next to him was Cécile, looking effortlessly fabulous in a light-grey knitted dress, as if breakfasting on the Place Vendôme.

Rosemary was pouring the tea when we all saw Camilla's blue Jensen come over the brow of the hill. George looked at me.

'She's not due back for hours.'

We had about three minutes. 'Never mind.' I looked at Cécile. 'If you'd like to come with me.'

I led her across the hall, down past the kitchen and through into my apartment. I closed the door behind us and invited her to take the armchair in the corner, away from the window.

'Thank you. It's important we be discreet.'

'Yes.'

Ten seconds of silence.

'I know you must hate me.'

'I don't.'

'No?'

'No.'

'You seem to disapprove.'

'Wouldn't you? In my shoes?'

'Yes. Probably. If I didn't understand.'

'I don't need to understand. It's not my job.'

'But George wants you to. He wants your approval.'

'He doesn't need my approval.'

'No. But he thinks he does. He wants it. But you're not ready to give it. I can see that. I can understand why.'

'Can you?'

'Of course. A man you respect has proved himself unrespectable. And a woman you like has been betrayed. It's simple.'

'It doesn't feel simple.'

'It's not, of course. I lied.'

'Ah.'

'It's complicated. Because, when Arabella died, George couldn't cope. He needed someone. Camilla wanted him. He thought he wanted her. They married. He found out he didn't want her. But he knew it was his duty to make her happy. She was his wife.'

'When did he decide to stop doing his duty?'

'He hasn't stopped. He gives her a very good life. Gives her everything she wants.'

'Except love.'

'He can't give it if he doesn't have it.'

'He has it for you.'

'Yes. And I understand how fortunate I am. And how terribly unfortunate Camilla is.' She looked at her shoes. 'Not to be loved.'

'I know.'

Cécile looked up. There were tears in her eyes. 'Please try to understand. Neither of us wanted this. To hurt another person with our happiness.' The tears started to run down her cheeks. I stepped forward and put my hand on her shoulder. She laid a hand on mine and looked up at me with red-rimmed eyes. 'I'm sorry. For coming into your home and crying.'

'I invited you. And I'm glad I did.'

'Thank you.' She wiped her eyes.

I glanced at my watch. Eleven twenty-two. 'Is it too early for wine?'

She smiled. 'Do you know the French saying, '*Il est toujours l'heure du vin*'?

'Does it mean 'cheers'?'

'Yes. Pretty much.'

I went into my kitchen and returned with a bottle of white and two glasses. Cécile lifted the bottle and studied the label.

'I'm impressed. A Montrachet. Grand Cru Burgundy. You know your wine.'

'It was a gift from George. I know nothing. Well, a little. I know what I like. I know this is gorgeous. But I'd like to know more.'

'Then fate has brought us together.'

'What do you mean?'

'It's what I do. Wine. Import it. Promote it. Teach people about it.'

'Really?'

'Yes. Here.' She handed me a business card. 'I'll send you our spring tasting programme. Pick a course. Or two. I always keep a place for friends. Don't look at the price. Friends don't pay.'

'But I couldn't …'

'Please let me. It's the least I can do. And I'd enjoy seeing you again.'

24

My Cup Runneth Over

George was sheepish at breakfast. I still wasn't sure how I felt about the whole thing with Cécile. She seemed lovely, and I genuinely liked her, but I couldn't get past the betrayal of Camilla. And he could see that. His wheelchair rolled over eggshells for a couple of hours. When we'd settled the day's business, I went outside to salute the sun.

Edmund was on the drive, leaning over his car. As I got closer, I saw he was wiping the wing mirror with his handkerchief and muttering something to himself. He looked up as I approached the gleaming burgundy beauty.

'That young Robbie never cleans the chrome properly. If a job's worth doing, it's worth doing well! Don't you agree, young lady?'

'It's a Bentley, isn't it?'

'No, it's not A Bentley, it's THE Bentley. A coach-built Mulliner Park Ward. Great British craftsmanship. Not like those bloody Kraut-built monstrosities they churn out these days.'

'She's lovely.'

My enthusiasm seemed to soften his mood. 'Look at this.' He walked round to the back of the car and opened the boot.

'A full Fortnums hamper and three cases of wine and there'd still be room for the campaign table.'

'That would be a fine picnic indeed.'

He walked round to the front and lifted the bonnet, warming to his theme. '4.9 litres. Electrically operated rear dampers. Like riding on air.'

'I'm sure it is.'

I'd lit a small fire in his eyes. 'Fancy a spin?'

'Now?'

'No time like the present.'

I looked at my watch. George would be settling down for a nap. I had nothing pressing to attend to.

'Sounds great.'

I went to open the door, but he nipped round to the passenger side and took the handle himself. A man from a different generation.

Soft cream leather interior. Burr walnut dashboard. Inch-thick carpeting. Climbing in was like stepping back several decades and stepping up several social ranks. He started the engine and it purred quietly. A coiled panther.

We slid effortlessly down the drive towards the main gate.

'It's a lovely ride.'

'Not out of third gear yet. Wait until we're on the main road.'

As we swept through the gates and turned left towards Little Compton, Edmund opened her up. With the windows down, he had to raise his voice.

'Father used to race these at Brooklands. In the twenties. Bugattis couldn't touch him.'

I was aware of him not paying particularly close attention to the road.

'I've had a hundred and twenty out of her before.' *Not on this road, I hope.*

We sailed past high hedgerows, the Bentley's coachwork brushing against low-hanging branches. I glanced over at Edmund. He looked like a boy with a new train set.

'Isn't she a beauty?'

I looked at the speedometer. Eighty-five. I looked up. A crossroads a hundred yards ahead. We reached it in one point three seconds, just as a red van, nosing out from the left, slammed on its brakes and stared as the Bentley flew over the junction. The sound of its outraged horn faded in an instant as we sped onwards to certain death.

Oblivious to all around him, Edmund turned to face me, pointing at the dial.

'Ton up! The old girl's still got it!'

I gripped the central console with my right hand. It sprang open, revealing a gleaming cut-glass decanter and four matching tumblers. The amber liquid rippled. 'Tudor Frobisher. Superb crystal.'

I'd never needed a whisky more in my life. Edmund nudged the wheel and the Bentley moved out, passing a cyclist in lime-green lycra at one hundred and six miles per hour. I looked down at my hand. It was welded to the walnut woodwork. *Oh well. If this is my last day on earth, at least I'm going out in style.*

Rosemary sat me down and poured me tea.

'You look like you've been dragged though a hedge backwards.'

'I've been out for a spin. In Edmund's Bentley.'

'With him driving?'

'Yeah.'

'That explains the haunted look on your face.'

'You've experienced it too, then?'

'You're joking. Nobody – NOBODY – gets to ride in his Bentley. Not even George.'

'I must have caught him on a good day.'

'I think he's just taken a shine to you.'

'That must be why he tried to kill me.'

'He didn't tell you he was banned? From driving?'

'Banned?'

'He hasn't got a licence. His age for one thing. He failed the new test at eighty-five. Eyesight. And there's his speeding. Been banned twice for speeding. Doesn't stop him. As you've seen.'

In the evening, I sat in my armchair by the window, a glass of red at my elbow, and flicked through the brochure Cécile had given me. All the upcoming tasting events were in London, in the kind of hotel where you might bump into Angela Merkel at the bar. I wasn't sure it was my kind of thing.

My phone screen lit up. Will.

'How's the queen of pastry?'

'Bloody brilliant! How's the queen of tarts?'

'Good, yeah.'

'Don't sound it.' *Nothing gets under that bugger's radar.* 'You're not still moping about his nibs and the scarlet woman?'

'I can't help it.'

'Bloody hell! Look at the big picture!'

'What d'you mean?'

'*They're* happy, but not completely – he's in a wheelchair and they have to skulk around. Her *ladyship's* happy, but not completely – she gets access to the money and the big house but not his trousers. *I'm* happy, but not completely – last week, my coconut macaroons were stonkingly good, but this week's sticky toffee pudding was a DISAHSTER, darling.'

'What are you on about?'

'Welcome to life! It's a bit shit. But not always.'

'It *is* a bit shit. And this situation is a bit shitty. But I'll stop moping. Tell me about you.'

'I've told you. Great macaroons, crap pudding.'

'Dating. Uniform.com. What gives?'

'What *gives*? You been listening to Tiny Tempah?'

'Shut up and spill.'

'One date. Overpriced wine bar. Airline pilot.'

'Sounds good.'

'It wasn't. *Very* no-frills. Definitely more Easyjet than Emirates.'

'And you didn't fancy his bumpy landing?'

'Does your boss know you're a mucky cow?'

'He knows I'm a high-class lady. Speaking of which …'

'Yes?'

'I've been invited to a wine tasting.'

'Who by?'

'The scarlet woman.'

'Ha! Quaffing with the enemy! Traitor!'

'Very grand affair, by the look of it.'

'Go.'

'Not sure I want to.'

'Why not? Because it's with *her*?'

'It's not really *with* her. She's running it. It's her business. Bordeaux Wine Group. Importers. And anyway – I quite like her. Really like her, actually. Even though part of me feels I shouldn't. No, it's just that it looks … incredibly posh.'

'Remember what Jonathan always says. *Wine greases the wheels of commerce.* It's where the movers and shakers do their best business. So what if it's posh? You're Mrs Professional Estate Manager these days. Posh is your middle name.'

A couple of days later, I was whizzing through the Oxfordshire countryside on an express bound for Paddington, the course brochure in my bag.

The train was heaving with England rugby supporters on their way to Twickenham for a match against Australia. The handful of Australians in the carriage were taking the Ozzie-bashing on the chin. I tried to tune the banter out, but some of it was too entertaining.

'Heard this one? Three rugby fans on their way to a game. One notices a foot sticking out of the bushes. A dead woman. Naked. Awful. Out of respect, the Springboks fan takes his cap off and places it over her right breast. The All Blacks fan takes his cap off and places it over her left breast.'

I pulled the collar of my jacket up and sank an inch lower in my seat.

'Following their lead, the Wallabies fan takes his cap off and places it over her crotch. The police officer arrives. He lifts the Springboks cap, replaces it, and writes a note in his book. Then he lifts the All Blacks cap, replaces it, and write another note. Finally, he lifts the Wallabies cap. Then he replaces it. Then he lifts it again, and replaces it. He does this a third time. The Australian gets his hair off. 'What are you, mate? Some kind of pervert?' The copper turns to him. 'No, I'm just a bit surprised. Normally, when I look under an Australian hat, I find an arsehole.'

The carriage erupted with laughter. I turned my head to the window so they wouldn't see me smile.

One of the guys saw me turn away.

'Sorry. They don't know how to behave in polite company.'

'It's fine.'

'Going to the game yourself?'

'No. A wine tasting.'

'*Lovely. In vino veritas.*'

'Sorry?'

'The Latin phrase. *In wine there is truth*. In other words, people under the influence are more inclined to speak their mind.'

'Right. This lot'll be heading to confession then.'

'Yeah, maybe they should be. It's all good-natured stuff, though. That's the great thing about rugby. No hard feelings. The Aussies are taking it all in good part. They just put up with it.'

I thought about Larry. What was he putting up with?

The Premier Inn in Kensington was quite nice. But being so far south made me think of my mum. Made me feel guilty for not seeing her more often. I called her. She was having one of her bad days.

'Hello, Joan.'

'Mum, it's me. Jen.'

'Joan, dear. How are you?'

'No, Mum. It's Jennifer. Your daughter.'

'Jennifer. I told you not to go out until you'd done your homework. And now you've gone and I've given Leon your room. You shouldn't have gone.'

'No, Mum. I'm sorry.' I filled up.

'Don't cry, love. Just come in when you're hungry. I'll make you some toast. And watch the roads.'

The assistant had assured me that the knee-length dress in pale blue wool brought out the colour in my eyes. It certainly seemed to meet with the approval of the young man at the reception of the Palazzo Odoni Hotel.

'Good evening, madam.'

'I'm here for a wine tasting.'

'The San Marco suite is through those double doors.'

'Thank you.'

'My pleasure, madam.'

I scanned the room. Quite a few people already there. Good. I wasn't the first. I ran through the checklist in my head. Hold the stem. Swirl and sniff. Sip and spit. Don't neck. *Don't neck!*

Good-looking youthful staff circulated with glass trays of tiny but exquisite-looking canapés. Not a vol-au-vent in sight.

'Jennifer! It's really nice to see you.'

Cécile looked like the cover of *Vogue*. She dripped elegance and aplomb.

'It's good to see you again, too. This is a gorgeous venue.'

'It *is* nice, isn't it. For the money I'm charging, I have to give them something other than just me.'

'I honestly think, with you looking as lovely as you do, that the men would pay the ticket price just to stand near you. Some of the women, too.'

'You're very kind.'

'So, how does the evening work?' *Sip and spit.*

'I'll get them seated in a few minutes. I'll tell them a bit about the business, give an introduction to the region generally, then talk about the particular chateaux whose wines we'll be tasting. I'll talk a bit about what flavours to expect. Then guests will move to the various exhibitors' tables to taste the wines on offer. We'll come together at the end and I'll open up a group discussion about the wines. Feel free to join in – it's very informal. Informative but fun.'

'Sounds good.' *Don't neck!*

'Then I stand back and wait for them to order a hundred cases of each.'

'A hundred cases!'

'I'm joking. I'll expect big orders from the trade buyers, but just the odd case from the private buyers. Above all, it's about communication. Brand visibility. For me and for the exhibitors.'

A twenty-year-old beauty walked up to Cécile and whispered something in her ear and her brow furrowed.

'Oh dear.'

'Problem?'

'One of our exhibitors has only just landed at Heathrow.'

'Ah.'

She thought for a couple of seconds then gave me a sidelong glance. 'How would you feel …?'

'Oh, Cécile. I don't …'

'It's just pouring wine and smiling. And looking good. And you look very good indeed.'

'Flattery. Nice try.'

'You'd be marvellous.'

'I know nothing.'

'I'll give you my notes. You can scan them while I drone on about *terroir*.'

I could feel my armpits moistening. 'I'm not up to it.'

'Sorry. You're right. I shouldn't have asked.' She scanned the room in a blind panic.

I sighed. 'Right. Give me the notes.'

By the time they stood up, I knew my Médoc from my Saint Emilion and my 2014 (good now but not for long-term 'cellaring') from my 2009 (stonking now and great for 'laying down').

I must have been doing something right. The queue at my table was twice as long as at any other. I could hardly keep up with the demand.

Then a hand wearing a slim gold wristwatch stretched towards me holding a glass.

'It's been a long time, Jennifer Brown.'

I looked up to see a familiar pair of intense blue eyes and a familiar set of perfect white teeth grinning at me broadly.

'Jonathan! How lovely to see you!'

He stepped forward and kissed me on the cheek. 'You look … lovely.'

'Thank you. You're still as charming as ever.'

A thirty-year-old blonde with legs appeared at his elbow. 'You remember Steph?'

I remembered her immediately. The stick insect in the skirt from the Canary Wharf conference.

'Yes. Hello again.'

The same daggers in the eyes. 'Hello.' *Hands off. He's mine.*

'And perhaps you remember David Harwood?'

Mr Velvet Vowels stepped forward with his hand outstretched. I shook it warmly.

'Hello again. Nice to see you.'

I felt Jonathan watching us. Waiting to see how the chemistry experiment would turn out. There was a pause, broken by Jonathan.

'So, you're a wine expert now?'

David smiled. 'There seems to be no end to your expertise.'

'Well, I wouldn't say expert.'

Steph's alpha female hormones were kicking in. 'So, would you recommend this?' She picked up a 2014 Chateau Bleufontaine and waved it at me.

'Well, like all Médocs, the 2104 is drinking well now.' I glanced at Jonathan then back at her. 'Will you be laying it down?'

'Sorry?'

'Cellaring it?'

'Er … no. I'll be drinking it.'

I pulled on my haughtiest mask. 'I see. Then it probably doesn't matter which of these you choose. They're all delicious now.'

Jonathan chipped in. 'Could I try the 2009?'

I gave him my best winning smile and leaned forward, aware the new dress was displaying my girls to good effect. 'Of course.' I filled his glass. Legs tried hard to look bored. She turned to David.

'Shall we try the whites?' She grabbed his elbow.

'I'll be there in a sec.' Legs glared at me, then turned on her impressive heel and wandered off to another table.

David pulled a business card out of his jacket pocket and handed it to me. 'I'd be delighted to hear more about your expertise. Perhaps I could buy you lunch sometime.' He smiled then walked off to find Legs.

Jonathan was trying hard to keep his eyes on the glass in front of him. He studied the colour. He sniffed. He sipped and slurped. He spat.

'Mmm. That really is very good. Thank you.'

'You're very welcome.'

He leaned in, took my arm and whispered. 'Is this your first time?'

'What?'

'At a wine tasting?'

'How did you know?'

'Your measures. They're four times as big as anyone else's.'

'God! Are they? I'll be costing my friend a fortune!'

He stood back. 'It really has been lovely seeing you again.' He kissed me on the cheek. 'Take care.'

After he'd gone, I looked at David's card. Was he offering me a job? Was he asking me out? I turned it over. He'd scribbled a mobile number on the back. *Please call me if you're interested.*

I was none the wiser.

Cécile waved off the last guests and the exhibitors and paid the young hired hands. She reached into a box, pulled out a bottle and came over and poured two glasses. She handed one to me.

'A 1990 Saint-Estèphe. Chateau Montrose.'

I sniffed it. 'Oh god. That smells gorgeous.'

'Take a small sip and let it sit on your tongue. Then let it spread to the inside of your cheeks and breathe.'

I followed her instructions as best I could. The effect was stunning. It was like discovering a sense of taste for the first time.

'That is the most delicious wine I've ever tasted.'

'I thought you'd like it. That's why I've sent a case over to the house. For you.'

'Oh no, Cécile. That's too much. Too generous.'

'This session has generated enormous amounts of trade business for me. Double the usual orders. Most of them for the wines at your table.'

'Really?'

'Really. The exhibitors will be very pleased. My commission will be very handsome.'

'I'm amazed.'

'And some huge private orders, too.' She looked through a couple of A4 sheets. 'One from a Mr … Dashwood-Silk is the biggest order I've ever had from a private buyer. Thirty-five cases.'

Three years on and he was still fighting my corner.

25

George

We were discussing the development of the woodland for field archery when it struck. By the time the paramedics had arrived, the sudden and massive bleed in George's brain had taken him, leaving the house in stunned and silent disbelief.

Thirteen minutes of mayhem. Now I could only remember snapshots. A slurred word making me look up, the mouth already slipping, and his right eye. Then me pulling out my phone. So many questions! *Just send a bloody ambulance!* Then George, now a ghastly, waxy white, falling forward in his chair. Then a paramedic – a girl with a Birmingham accent – asking me for his name but telling me, with her eyes, that there was no point. That she was going through the motions. That he'd already gone.

The only thing I wanted to do was be outside. Not in this room. Not in this house.

Outside. Outside with the cluck of the brown hens, the giant-bee buzz of a light aircraft overhead, the updraft of a phalanx of Canada geese. Outside in the glorious sunshine. On this twelfth of August. This unglorious twelfth.

We were all numb. Veronica sat staring at the Persian rug in the library. Rosemary stood in the kitchen with her hand on the handle of an open cupboard then, forgetting why she'd opened it in the first place, closed it again. Kate, belonging as she did to the Queen of Hearts generation, wept openly and unashamedly, while Robbie rearranged the tins in his tool shed, a man taking refuge in his cave.

Edmund seemed chastened, his sharp edges rubbed off, and suddenly looked every day of his four score years and ten. The death of his son had called time on his spitefulness. The game was over. He sat in the orangery and stared at the shadows on the sunny terrace.

Camilla took to her bed and refused all human contact. I could only imagine the swirl of emotions in her head. After two days of no food or water, I called the doctor, who diagnosed nervous exhaustion and prescribed rest and chicken soup, which he'd browbeaten her into accepting using the powerful threat of imminent hospitalisation.

The mood was sombre beyond words and the air heavy with grief but also with unspoken musings about our collective future. What would happen to the house now? With no nominal employer, would any of us have a job this time next week?

Camilla's knees buckled when George's coffin, draped in his regimental colours, was carried into the Church of St Mary The Virgin in Little Compton. She leaned heavily on my arm throughout the service, with, on her other side, Edmund standing bolt upright, every inch a soldier, dropping the mask now and then during the eulogy to stroke Camilla's hand and wonder, dewy-eyed, at the seemliness of a fate that had allowed him to outlive his own son.

After the service, the small family gathering made the journey back to Thornhill and the tiny private graveyard beyond the lake, daring not to look at Camilla as the coffin was lowered into the plot beside his beloved Arabella, then dispersing in rather rag-tag fashion to regain the house, there to drink a glass of Prophecy to George's memory, leaving Robbie with the grim task of filling in his master's tomb.

I hung back to be with my own thoughts and caught a glimpse of an impossibly elegant figure slip in through the Gothic door in the wall. She touched Robbie's arm, then knelt and placed a single red rose on the headstone while Robbie bowed his head.

I walked over to meet her as she came out. She looked stricken. She held onto my arm, tears staining her flawless cheek.

'It's silly, I know.'

'Not at all.'

'I mean, it's not as though we didn't know it was bound to happen soon.'

'Doesn't make it any easier to bear.'

'No.'

'How's … Mrs Winstanley?'

'Dreadful. As you can imagine.'

'Yes. I can. And you?'

'I'm okay. Holding it all together.'

'That's what you do, isn't it?'

'What?'

'Look after everyone else. Keep everyone else happy.'

'Someone's got to.'

She fished into her bag. 'Let's not lose touch.' She took a business card and scribbled a number on the back. 'My private mobile. Give me a call. Perhaps we can meet for lunch.'

'Thank you. I'd like that.'

'It's hardly the time – or place (she glanced back at the door) – but, well, you'll be thinking about your future at some point soon.'

'I haven't really …'

'I know. I'm sorry. I just wanted to say, I'd be delighted to … work with you. In my business. Think about it.'

She handed me the card, kissed me on the cheek, and walked off down the lane.

In the days that followed, we all tiptoed around each other, saying little, thinking much. But bookings were honoured and guests treated to an experience unsullied by the sadness that, in private, none of us could shake off.

Edmund spent long hours outside Robbie's workshop, polishing every inch of his beloved Bentley. Occupying his mind. Venting his frustration. His anger at the injustice.

I walked out to him with tea. That great British tradition of tea and sympathy seemed impotent. He looked up, surprised, his eyes rheumy.

I tried to be breezy. 'She looks good.'

'She does. For what it's worth.'

I knelt down beside him. 'I'm so terribly sorry.' I didn't know what else to say.

He turned towards me. 'I was immensely proud …' He turned away '… but I didn't …' There was a catch in his throat.

We stared at the gravel for a minute. Then I lifted a cloth. 'I'll do the other wing.' He looked up. Without protest, he handed me the polish.

For the next hour, we buffed the Bentley together in silence, until she shone like a goddess. We stood back and admired her gleaming lines. Edmund smiled. Then he grew thoughtful again.

'Don't wait.'

I looked blank.

'To do the things and say the things that matter. Don't hesitate.'

'No.'

'You'll only regret it.'

He turned away to wipe a smear off the bumper. I gathered the empty cups and made my way back to the kitchen, leaving him to his private grief.

Camilla had become very withdrawn, rarely straying outside her room, eating nothing but the medicinal soup, swathed in her own private darkness. She would occasionally come to the door when I knocked, eyes red-rimmed and swollen, and would allow me in for a few minutes.

But she'd accept tea only from Edmund. There seemed to be an unchallengeable authority in the gift of tea from a father-in-law, and in the instruction, delivered with a solicitousness I wouldn't have thought him capable of, to keep her strength up, for George's sake.

Rosemary couldn't believe it, either.

'He's like a different person.'

'It's hit him hard. I guess it makes you realise what's important.'

'It does.' It was a pointed remark.

'How's things with you?'

She smiled a faint smile and, Mary-Poppins-like, pulled several folded sheets of paper out of her apron pocket. Her son would be over in a couple of weeks but, in advance of the trip, and knowing she might be in a state about seeing him, had put together a long letter explaining his feelings and something of his life. She stood smiling, eyes aglow, while I read.

He'd been brought up well, by kind and loving parents. He had three adoptive siblings and talked of a warm and supportive household. He'd been taught not to judge others until he'd walked in their shoes. He was looking forward to meeting her and hoped they'd be friends.

26

Changes

A sort of normality began to return to Thornhill. Rosemary cooked and baked, and Kate cleaned and arranged. Robbie clipped and mowed and pottered. The big change, of course, was the departure of Veronica. A personal carer needs someone to care for. After serving out the remainder of the month she'd been paid for, largely as a kitchen maid, Veronica packed up the last seven years of her life and took a job in a care home in Didcot, washing strangers, taking them tea, wiping them.

'This'll be my life, I suppose. A maid. A servant.' She loaded the last case into the taxi.

'I think you have more to offer.'

'Do you?'

'Yes.'

'Nobody else seems to think so.' She looked at the gravel. 'You're very kind, Jennifer Brown. I'm going to miss you.' And then she was gone.

Edmund retreated to his apartment and his thoughts, occasionally surfacing to take tea with me in the library, with no trace of the old vindictive bugger he'd been when I'd first met him. Although he never said very much, he did one day expose a mystery. He pointed to the fireplace.

'Where's the painting?'

'Sorry?' I followed his finger and turned to look. Arabella's portrait wasn't there.

'The picture. The woman.'

'I ... don't know.' Oh god. Has Camilla gone berserk with a knife? *'I'll ask among the staff.'*

Camilla began to appear at breakfast, and made an attempt to take an interest in the business of the estate, which I indulged when time permitted. I didn't dare mention the painting. And she didn't seem to register its absence.

One afternoon, she came and joined me in the walled garden. She looked thinner than ever and wore a cardigan, even though it was scorching hot.

'This was George's favourite spot on earth. This garden.' She looked across to the bank of bright red poppies on the south-facing wall. 'And those were his favourite ...' Her face crumpled and she flung her arms round my neck.

'Oh, Jennifer! How will I go on?'

I put an arm round her bony shoulder. 'You will, Camilla. You just will.' It was the first time I'd used her name.

'I'm not like you. I'm not a coper.'

'I'm not much of a coper, either. But we all just get on with it, don't we? Take each day as it comes.'

Her delicate frame trembled and she buried her face in my neck.

'It's such a bloody cliché, but he was my rock.'

'You'll get through it. I promise you. You just ... find the strength. From somewhere.'

She wiped her eyes and looked up at me. 'Have you had to? Have you lost someone?'

'Well, sort of. He didn't die, but he did leave me. At a time when I thought it was all sorted. That he was the one. That we'd be together forever. When it was clear we wouldn't, I thought my life had ended. Thought about ending it myself, actually. Thought I couldn't survive without him.'

'But you're still here.'

'I'm still here. And so are you. You just need to get it back.'

'What?'

'Your inner feisty old bird.'

She laughed. 'Her Ladyship. It's a lie. But you know that.'

'But we all lie. Act, anyway. There are numerous versions of who we are. They're not necessarily all wrong. They're just not completely right. They're not the whole picture.'

'How old are you?'

'Thirty-nine.'

'You're very wise. I'm sixty-eight and I feel like I've not learned a single bloody thing in all those years.'

For the next two hours, we sat and talked about our lives. She opened up. She told me how she'd grown up in a middle-class family. Authoritarian parents. Social climbers. At the age of sixteen, she'd run away to London with dreams of becoming a model.

It was the sixties. It started to be fashionable to be thin. Marilyn was yesterday's beauty. Now it was all Twiggy. The modelling agencies told her she needed to lose weight. That was when the eating disorders started. A professional imperative became a lifestyle choice and eventually an illness.

'Nobody ever suspected I was bulimic. I was so damn good at hiding it. And we didn't have a word for it then. And after years and years of throwing up, it became second nature. It happened naturally. I could even do it in public without people noticing. And it never goes away. And it makes you ashamed.'

Meeting George changed her life. He made her feel special at a time when she felt worthless. He gave her a glimpse of a life in which she didn't need to survive on her looks alone.

'He was basically a very kind man. Impeccably kind, actually. I mistook that kindness for love. And, in his grief, I think he did, too.

For a short while. But I was always second best. I learned to accept it. Well, learned to pretend to accept it, anyway.'

She looked up at me again. 'But I've been happy. Most of the time. That was George's gift.'

Something of the old Camilla returned. She decided on a change of décor and started to clear out the drawing room, earmarking pieces of furniture and other items for auction. Mindful of the library as our place of work, she asked me to handle the task of clearing George's sanctum.

The old bureau by the window had been identified as no longer fit for purpose, so I set about emptying it. In the back of a drawer, I came across an old metal biscuit tin. It was too heavy to contain biscuits, and George had never been one for sweet foods anyway. I opened it.

Inside was a large bundle of letters. Some of them were yellowed with age and brittle to touch. They all carried George's name and the Thornhill address on the envelope. One of the letters was loose. No envelope. The temptation was too much.

Foreign handwriting. Tender sentiments.

My darling
The days come and go and I am miserable without you. I long for …

I thrust it back into the tin and put the lid back on. This was too much of an intrusion.

What would George have wanted me to do? Should I destroy them? What if Camilla were to find them?

'What have you got there?' Camilla was standing at the door, wiping her brow with the back of a hand that held a pair of pink Marigolds.

'A pile of old bills.' *What a proficient liar you've become, Jennifer Brown.*

'Just bin them then, I guess.'

'Yes. How are you getting on?'

'Fine. I've phoned Moore's. They're sending a van this afteroon. Can I tell them to take the bureau as well?'

'Yes. It's empty now.' She turned to go. 'Camilla?'

'Yes?'

'Are you giving them the painting? Moore's?'

'Painting?'

I pointed to the fireplace. 'The one that used to hang there.'

She looked puzzled. 'I assumed you'd taken it down.'

That afternoon, not wanting to trust the post office in the village shop, I took the little blue Peugeot and drove into Cheltenham and found a post office. There I bundled the letters into a jiffy bag, added the note I'd written on Thornhill paper, and wrote out the address on the card Cécile had given me. Job done.

With that awkward task off my plate, I rewarded myself with poshness. A pot of Earl Grey and a slice of apricot and ginger frangipane tart at a pleasant window table in the sumptuous parlour of the Regency Café.

I watched the world go by for an hour. Busy business types, strolling tourists – you can tell tourists by their dress but also by their relaxed pace – and harassed young mums holding it all together.

I was reminded of what Cécile had said to me by the graveyard wall. *You keep everyone else happy.*

And at that moment, I made my decision.

Rosemary was tearful. 'You can't go. Who's going to stop me eating my own cakes?'

Robbie looked thoughtful. 'Her ladyship'll miss you. You've made all the difference. To her, as well as to this place.'

Kate spoke with the optimism of youth. 'Well, I think it's brilliant. You don't want to be stuck in a dusty old morgue like this for the rest of your life.'

Rosemary pretended outrage. 'Hey, you!'

'Well, Jennifer's younger than you. Your life's nearly over.' Rosemary swiped at her with a tea towel and she ducked.

Robbie asked the question I'd been avoiding. 'Have you told her yet?'

'No. But I need to. Now.'

Camilla looked perturbed.

'Leaving?'

'I *am* sorry, Camilla. I've been happy here. Very happy. I really wasn't sure I would be at first. But it's been good. Enjoyable. Fulfilling. More than I could have hoped for. But I only took the job on a temporary basis.'

'I know. Yes.' She sounded forlorn.

'I just feel it's the right time to move on. For me.'

'Where will you go?'

'I have a couple of options.'

'That's good.' She looked out of the library window. 'How will we manage without you? How will Thornhill run efficiently. Without you?'

So I told her my plan. She agreed it might work and she gave me her blessing to pursue it.

'Jen, what a lovely surprise! How did you find me?'

'I spoke to the agency. They gave me the address.'

'Sit down.' Veronica gestured towards one of the brown velour couches the residents used in the afternoons, after lunch.

'Can I get you something? Tea?'

'I'm fine. Thank you. I wanted to talk about something. An idea.'

A tremulous, frail-sounding voice piped up from down an adjacent corridor. 'I'm scared. Please come. Come and play with me.' I must have looked startled.

'That's Audrey. Her dementia's quite advanced. Not much of her memory left. She gets frightened. And very confused. She thinks I'm her sister, Maud.'

'How awful.' I thought of my mum and the postman and Charlton Heston.

'She used to be a lawyer. Travelled all over the world. Now she's a child again.'

I felt my eyes fill with tears and I looked away. 'Don't worry. She's quite happy. And I'm used to it. It's what I do.'

'Well, that's why I'm here.'

'What do you mean?'

'I'm here to see if you'll consider coming back to Thornhill.'

'To look after Camilla? Has she gone downhill?'

'No. Not really.'

'Not Edmund?'

'Goodness, no!'

'Then what?'

'As Estate Manager.' She looked like she'd been hit by a train.

'Estate Manager? Me?'

'Why not?'

'Well, I've got no experience for one thing.'

'I'll show you the ropes. Couple of weeks'll do it. And you know the house and the estate – that's very important. And you ran a hotel.'

'A long time ago. Not a resounding success.'

'But you've got the skills. Anyone can see that. Camilla can see it.'

'You've talked to her?'

'Yes.'

'And what did she say?'

'She's all for it.'

Veronica stood up and walked to the window. She stared out through the smeared glass at the tiny garden where the residents got their fresh air.

'When do I start?'

Driving back to Thornhill, I couldn't get the sound of Audrey's voice out of my head, nor the image of my mum. I remembered us watching Eric and Ernie a couple of Christmases ago. I thanked God for Leon, a very unlikely knight in shining armour. But it was not at all correct that a total stranger was left to hold onto the threads of my mother's unravelling life. I resolved to see more of her, starting with a long visit as soon as I left Thornhill. Time was running out for me to be a better daughter.

Back at the house, Camilla was looking at carpet samples. Even the back staircase was getting a makeover.

But one room was to be inviolate. George's bedroom hadn't been touched since that awful morning. His silk dressing gown still hung behind the door. His reading glasses lay on the beside table, on an open copy of something by PG Wodehouse. If I closed my eyes, I could still hear the slow, steady thump of Benson's tail.

My last supper was a Rosemary classic – roast lamb with mint sauce. The whole household, Edmund included, had gathered to send me off. And we ate, drank and were very merry. Even Camilla managed a smile and a decent plateful.

I looked around. Veronica had never seemed happier – she'd step into my shoes with ease. The shadow had gone from Rosemary's brow now that she'd met her son and had found him to be a charming and understanding man whose company she enjoyed. And, in her son, she now had someone to love. Robbie sat back and took it all in with his customary reserve, seeing everything and saying nothing. A night watchman. Kate was still as daft as a brush. No big romance for her but she was clearly still enjoying the search.

Camilla looked like she was learning to be alone, managing better than she'd imagined. And, while Edmund was never going to win any contests as a charmer, I was confident he'd do a reasonable job as a decent human being.

Rosemary was flushed with wine. 'So, you haven't told us where you're going.'

Camilla joined in. 'She has options. A woman of mystery.'

'Options? You mean you haven't decided?'

'I'm going to stay with my mum for a bit. I've decided that much.'

But I'd grown to hate loose ends. I needed a plan. A goal. A direction.

In the quiet of my bedroom, on the occasion of my last night at Thornhill Hall, I pulled two business cards from my purse and laid them on the bedside table. *What now, my lovely?*

Heart and head.

I looked at David's card. Just the thought of him made me smile. I'd warmed to him from the moment we'd met in the courtyard on that sunny day. On the one hand, if I called him, I'd be stepping firmly back into the corporate world. Did I want that? On the other hand, it seemed there was a chance of romance. Did I want *that*?

And Cécile. Another warm individual whose company I enjoyed. Could I see myself working with her? I was pretty sure I could see myself strolling round vineyards in Bordeaux for half the year.

Heart and head. Was it right to listen to both?

I listened. I looked at my watch. It wasn't too late to call.

I picked up my phone and dialled the number on the card.